The
Stanbroke
Girls

The
Stanbroke
Girls

A Novel of Regency England

Fiona Hill

ST. MARTIN'S PRESS
NEW YORK

For information, write: St. Martin's Press,
175 Fifth Avenue, New York, N.Y. 10010
Manufactured in the United States of America

Design by Sherry Brown
10 9 8 7 6 5 4 3 2 1
First Edition

Library of Congress Cataloging in Publication Data

Hill, Fiona.
   The Stanbroke girls.

   I. Title.
PS3558.I3877S7   813'.54   80-21474
ISBN 0-312-75570-8

To P.C. with love and thanks

1

"But my dear Jemmy," Lady Emilia burst out in exasperation, "if you had no intention of accepting invitations this season you might as well have stayed in Sussex! What was your object in coming to London at all if not to visit with the monde a little? When I think of all the months we have been rusticating at Six Stones, and not a soul to amuse us save John-Coachman—! I protest, Jem, it is the most provoking behaviour I've ever encountered." Lady Emilia had been pacing the room determinedly during this monologue, but she now flung a vexed glance at her tranquil brother and sat down abruptly in a wine-red arm-chair. For a moment it appeared as if she would stay there, but the next minute found her on her feet again, jabbing and slashing at the sunlit air, indefatigable as ever. "It isn't only for your sake I concern myself, you know," she went on, trying another tack; "it looks extremely odd for me, after all, to be out among people all over town without you—when everybody knows perfectly well you are here with me, and might have accompanied me if you'd only cared to bestir yourself. It's awkward for me, to come right to the point. Oh Jemmy, I tell you in all honesty, I can't think why you did not stay at home in Sussex!"

At this point Lady Emilia seated herself again and this time she did remain silent, evidently inspecting the vandyked silk cord on the wrists of her muslin morning-dress (and evidently finding it not satisfactory). Her brother, Lord Marchmont, had been watching her interesting performance with polite attention, and, as he now supposed her to have concluded her soliloquy, he favoured her with a round of light applause. In this he was joined by a second gentleman, a certain Lord Warrington Weld, whose acquaintance Lord Marchmont had made during the recent unpleasantness at Waterloo. Lord Weld had also appreciated Emilia's fine speaking, and considered that her delivery rivalled that of Mrs. Siddons. *"Brava,"* he cried, from the depths of a velvet sofa. *"Brava e bravissima!"*

"Encore, encore," Lord Marchmont seconded, smiling brightly at his sister.

"James, do answer me," she snapped out, striving against nature to keep from smiling herself.

"Answer you? Can such golden rhetoric be answered?"

"It is unanswerable," asserted Weld.

"James, why have you come to London with me? I could have done very well without you."

"Upon my soul, methinks the lady truly does desire reply," Marchmont observed to his friend. "In that case, let me consider. I came to London . . . I came to London—" his handsome brow knitted up in imitation of deep thought. "I have it! I came to London to talk over pistols with Manton, my dear. Now you cannot do that in Sussex; confess it and let us have done. Does the answer not please?" he inquired innocently, as Emilia cast him a look of sheer frustration.

"Myself, I never heard such persuasive logic," said Lord Weld. "The truth is, my friends, if it rested with me to judge between you which was the better speaker—which the more clear and compelling, whether question or answer—I could not choose. A draw, a simple draw! What a delight you are to hear."

"Lord Weld, be quiet," muttered Emilia without looking up. "Jemmy knows what I mean, and why he is being so obtuse is a puzzle no logic can unravel."

"Oh my!" drawled Weld, unruffled.

"Perhaps you are waiting for an apology, Emilia?" Marchmont took up again. "If so, I offer it with profoundest respects. I admit, it never occurred to me that to appear without me among the *ton* might cause you discomfort. But as for my mending the business by attending—out of the question. I am prodigiously sorry, however."

"Oh I protest, Marchmont," Lord Weld broke in, "I can't agree that's a very handsome thing to say. What manner of apology is that, that recognises *should* and *could,* but gives the cut direct to *would?* Lady Emilia, my sympathies are all with you."

"Lord Weld, you may rest assured that is where they belong."

"Heaven save me," murmured Marchmont, "for I see the tide of opinion runs against me. What, both sister and friend in the enemy's camp? How on earth shall I ever hold out? Ho hum," he added, with a pleased smile at the shine of his own top-boots. "I say, Warrington, you ought to start using champagne in your boot polish, as I do. It's the only thing for it. Shall we ring for a glass of something interesting? This argument makes me monstrous thirsty."

He did not wait for the approval of the others but pulled the bell-rope himself and, when Searle appeared, bespoke a bottle of sherry and three glasses. "For Emilia drinks, you know," he observed to Weld when the butler had gone. "It's really too shocking of her."

Lady Emilia, who at the age of thirty had the freshness of twenty and the wisdom of forty, relented sufficiently to laugh at this sally. "It's true," she admitted to Weld, whom she had known only during the week since her arrival in London. "I am practically disreputable."

"Good Lord, Jem! You might have warned a fellow," exclaimed Warrington Weld. "And here am I, a guest in your house—not a friend in London but you, and promised to stay here all season . . . I dareswear worse things can happen to a gentleman, but I'm sure I can't think of a one of them. I only hope you haven't any more terrible secrets between you."

"Only a few," Emilia told him. "Most of them no worse than—oh, a murder, for example."

"Or two, for two examples," Marchmont joined in.

"Or three."

"Or four."

"You're acquainted with the seven deadly sins, no doubt," Lady Emilia remarked to Weld.

"Slightly."

"We're on intimate terms," she announced grandly.

"With every blessed one."

"You can imagine our secrets!"

"They can't be imagined," asserted the earl, breaking off to receive the sherry from Searle and handing the glasses round. The Earl of Marchmont was hospitable, and there was little he liked better than the company of trusted friends. He was proud of his sister, only six years his junior yet still as straight and tall and beautiful as she had been at her come-out. Her clear grey eyes and her dark glossy hair, so like his own, her handsome mouth, strong chin, her pliant neck and supple waist, all—so far as he could tell—went on quite heedless of the years, the eye never losing its bright glitter, the mouth its frank and easy smile. The fact of her never having married mystified him. At first, after the early death of their parents, he had thought she kept single through a dutiful (if needless) devotion to himself—but their frequent discussions on this point convinced him he was wrong. That she might have married if she liked to he knew for certain, but she remained a spinster. He had come to accept it, but in the end he had no notion of why it was, or how it was. That she was happy, he knew, and no more. And indeed there are very many who live in close quarters, year upon year, with no more idea of the shadows in their fellows' hearts than they have of the dark side of the moon.

As for Emilia, her idea of her brother's heart was a little shrewder. In appearance he was more than her equal: tall and slender, with a handsome head proudly carried and her own wide grey eyes, he had broken the hearts of women whose names he never even knew. His manners were as impeccable when out in society as they were careless among his intimates; among match-making mammas he was widely acknowledged both extremely eligible and extremely unattainable. His wealth was considerable; except for his charming (if somewhat eccentric) sister, he had no dependants at all; he *must* marry—they whispered to one another year after year—or permit the estate to pass into the hands of that reprobate de Guere . . . and yet he did not marry! Many were the girlish hearts that wavered cruelly between hope and fear when Marchmont went to the Continent under Wellington, and many the pretty pairs of eyes that scanned the lists of war-wounded during those days, seeking, praying they would not find, his name. Nor did they—but he might have been killed for all the good that came of their concern, for here he was safe back again, *and* in London, *and* a full se'ennight into the season—and not a hostess had seen his face!

The war had done something to her brother, Emilia knew; and even more than that, she divined, the marriage of a certain Miss Charlotte Beaudry during his first campaign abroad had done something to him. Even his mother had died before her time. Women, to Marchmont, were a race of turncoats—one could as well trust them as serpents, and, like serpents, it was scarcely worth the trouble of learning which were poisonous and which were not. But her comprehension of his difficulties did nothing to alter the facts. The match-making mammas were absolutely right: he must marry and produce an heir or forfeit the estates, at his death, to Sir Jeffery de Guere. The very thought of de Guere wandering over Six Stones at his leisure was sufficient to make her feel queasy. A ghost of this image in her mind, she accepted a glass of sherry from her brother and renewed her assault on him simultaneously.

"Jemmy," she began, speaking somewhat more softly though far more directly, "if you do not go out among the world a little, how can you ever hope to find a wife?"

"Aha," said Marchmont, gesturing significantly to Lord Weld. "Take a second glass, dear fellow, for the spectacle is about to become interesting. Did you see that cannon behind my sister? I did not, till now. Her skirts must have hidden it," he added sardonically.

"My dear brother, perhaps we ought to take up this discussion at some other time," Emilia suggested, with a glance at Weld.

"I should not dream of depriving our guest of the pleasure," objected he. "I assure you, he likes nothing better than a scuffle—is that not so, Weld?"

"I must confess it is—though if you do not like to have an audience, perhaps I must leave—"

"Dear me no, I insist on your staying," cried Marchmont. "When Emilia begins on this topic two against one is scarcely equal—I mean, our two can hardly begin to resist her one."

"Jemmy, you make me sound like a battalion."

"A regiment does you more justice."

"But it's true, it's true!" she almost wailed, breaking suddenly from the banter. "You must find a wife, Jemmy, this is impossible. My darling—forgive me, for you know this weighed very little with me at the time, yet it is true all the same—consider that if you had been killed in the wars Sir Jeffery would now be installed at Six Stones and I living on his mercy! Well, my dear, it *is* true," she insisted, when her brother did not answer.

"The way I see it," he brought out slowly, after a moment, "the real blame attaches to Warrington here. If it were not for him, you know, I should indeed have been killed in Europe. So, Weld, how do you plead? You are guilty of saving my life; that is indisputable. But this other charge—how do you answer?"

Lord Weld looked bewildered. "What charge, exactly, am I facing?"

"Why, this business of my having to take a wife, of course! It's all your fault—you can't deny it. In my opinion, the only honourable thing for you to do is to go out and find one for me yourself. If you could marry her for me too—well, that *would* be something! But I set aside that possibility . . . much too difficult, I'm afraid—"

"Now see here, old man, if what your sister says is true, you ought to have found a wife years ago! It's not my fault you were idiot enough to run off to Belgium with Lady Emilia unprovided for, unthought of, it appears. Why, if there's any question of culpability—"

"And there is," Emilia interjected.

"It would seem to belong entirely to you. If I were in your shoes, I'd rush right out and get married tomorrow; today, if it could be arranged. Don't wait another minute, Marchmont. Why, this is monstrous! Lady Emilia, how do you bear his selfishness?"

"Long practice."

"No doubt."

"This is out-and-out treachery," exploded Marchmont suddenly. "If I'd had any idea you would behave so fiendishly, Weld, I'd never have let you stay and watch this battle. The last thing I ever expected—! How would you like to be ordered to go out and marry tomorrow? I should like to see you in my place; I assure you you'd look at things very differently."

But Lord Weld hardly attended him. He had sat up on his sofa at last and was conferring tête-à-tête with Emilia. "Who is this Jeffery de Guere?" he inquired, while Marchmont fulminated unheeded. "Can he really be worse than March-mont?"

"Oh dear, I am afraid so," confided Emilia. "Demon though Jemmy may be, he is preferable to Jeffery. Naturally Jeffery is family—a cousin on my mother's side—and perhaps I ought not to be telling tales," she paused dubiously, "but the fact is, he is an odious rake, quite notorious, and a positively idiotic gamester. He has gambled away nearly all of his fortune; it is common knowledge everywhere that it was he who was responsible for poor Miss Partridge's nervous collapse two seasons ago—well it *is* common knowledge, Jemmy, you know it is!" she broke off, as she noticed her brother glaring at her.

"There's no use in making it more common than ever," he observed.

"My goodness, what a nice sense of privacy we seem to have developed in the past ten minutes!" she returned. "Come now, Lord Weld will not repeat what I tell him. Will you, sir?"

"I should die before that," he asserted blandly.

"There, you see? He should die before that. Such being the case, I may as well tell him about that business at Crock-ford's—"

"You do and I'll—I'll put ground glass in your orgeat," threatened Marchmont at once. "Lord Weld knows quite enough about Jeffery right now. He will agree with us, at all events, that it would be unpleasant for you to be—cast upon his mercy, I think is how you put it?"

"Something like that."

"Very well. It would be unpleasant. But you know, Emilia, there is another alternative besides my marriage."

She sat up a little straighter. "Indeed? And what exactly might that be?"

"Why, naturally, if you were to marry, dear ma'am. That way your husband would provide for you, I should do nicely till I die at some ripe old age, and de Guere can have the title then and the devil with the business. What say you?" he asked, rising and bowing towards her with a look of pointed inquiry.

"I say—it will not answer," she finally replied.

"Because—?"

"Because every tenant in the neighbourhood would be ruined before Jeffery had had the estate five years. There is more at stake than my welfare *or* yours, Jemmy. I do not even mention the disappointment Father would most certainly have felt had he known how readily you contemplate the loss of all he cared for so deeply," she added, stopping at nothing in her ruthless attack.

The blow went home. "You don't even mention it, eh?" said the present earl hollowly, sitting down again with a weary sigh. "That's very odd, because I could swear I heard someone speak of it not thirty seconds ago."

"Well, Jemmy, I'm only telling you what you already know is the case. I am sorry to be obliged to confront you with it, but we are none of us growing any younger, and if you do not choose a wife this season—or at least go out a little!—people will begin to believe you are positively peculiar."

"They are more than welcome to believe that."

"You know what I mean," she answered, with a sensation of having said these words rather too often already.

A silence settled on the young people. In the street below them a rattle of coach wheels was heard, then a burst of shrill laughter, then more silence. Lord Weld grew uncomfortable. He pushed a pale hand through his red hair and remarked with an uncertain laugh, "If I had know it would come to all this I'm not sure but what I wouldn't have let you perish at Waterloo after all, Marchmont. And as for accepting your invitation to stop with you this season—"

"Poor Lord Weld," Emilia broke in ruefully. "We have presented quite a spectacle for you this morning, have we not? Pray believe me, however, when I tell you that Jemmy and I have had precisely this argument—oh, perhaps not precisely, but in any case variations on the same old theme—every season for years. Every spring we go through it! We are half crazed with being shut away in Sussex all winter, we contemplate with mutual delight the change of scene ahead; we pack up the house, alert all the servants, and rush in a gay dash up to London—where bang! We have the same discussion again: won't Jemmy come to this rout, can't we go together to Vauxhall, even once, just to hear Madame Catalani . . . isn't Miss Everett pretty, she seems to have bloomed like a flower since last year . . . But no, nothing will answer, nothing will do. Jem goes to Manton's, takes in Tattersall's, hangs about idly at White's, and before we know it it's time to go home again. Why, three years ago (or was it four?) our dear old Marchmont did not even have the grace to appear at a dinner-party I myself gave! Can you imagine?"

"Difficult," murmured Weld.

"I can tell you, it was damned awkward to explain," she went on, then appended hastily, "I beg your pardon! My language is not what it ought to be. There's scarcely a soul within twenty miles of Six Stones that I can converse with, save Jemmy."

"I've offered to hire her a companion any number of times—" the earl began.

"Hired companions," she spat back at once. "Nonsense! Hired companions are for young girls and old ladies, and I have neither the misfortune to be the former nor the honour to be the latter. What could I want a companion for? I still have wit enough, thank God, to amuse myself."

"But she has never received the idea well," Marchmont continued mildly, as if Emilia had said nothing.

Lord Weld laughed. "What's needed here," said he, "if I understand the circumstances correctly, is a treaty of sorts. A compromise. An Accord in the Matter of Invitations. Shall I continue?"

"Pray do," said Emilia, with a nod of her dark head. "A compromise is a good deal more than I've ever gained before."

Lord Weld looked to Marchmont.

"Oh, do go on," said he. "I am all curiosity."

"Very well then," said Warrington, rising at last from his sofa and sauntering up to where he could stand facing both of them. "The solution is simple. Lord Marchmont wishes to ignore all invitations. Lady Emilia wishes him to avail himself of all. Therefore, Lord Marchmont will attend exactly half of the functions to which he is invited. Simple," he concluded with a pleased wave of his arms, "and fair." He lay down again on the velvet couch.

"Dear God, not a soul in London goes to half the parties he's asked to," objected Marchmont immediately. "A person would go mad. You don't know what you're suggesting, Weld. It's beyond reason."

"I rather liked it," Emilia remarked. "It put me in mind of Solomon."

"Solomon, indeed," snorted his lordship. "A child of six could have managed something better. If you don't mind my saying so, old fellow," he added.

"Of course it is only the initial proposal," Weld answered imperturbably. "There is always bartering over any treaty."

"Very well," Emilia took up, "in that case I am willing to go as low as one third of the invitations we receive."

"An eighth would be more humane," said her brother.

"I'm terribly sorry, but a third is as low as I can contrive."

"What about a fifth?"

"Not even close."

"Then I'll tell you what," said Marchmont, his hands clutching the arms of his chair as if seeking strength in the polished wood, "if you'll let me choose the occasions at my own discretion, I'll go up to a quarter of the total received. But that is my final offer."

"I'm sorry, that would never do. You would go to a series of bachelor breakfasts, and a couple of hopelessly crowded routs—where you'd stay ten minutes and bow to a dozen people. No, my dear, I will settle for a quarter of the total, but you must go at my discretion."

"I'm sorry, Emilia. If that is how you feel, we are at an impasse." The earl settled back in his chair and reminded himself that no one could force him to go anywhere, if worse came to worst.

"I see it is time for me to intervene again," Warrington Weld spoke up in his gentle rasp. "The quarter of engagements to be attended," he pronounced, "will be drawn by lot. Strictly. And by my hand only. To insure impartiality," he closed.

Lord Marchmont said nothing, but Emilia looked satisfied. "I only hope the Stanbroke girls' come-out is among the chosen. Elizabeth Stanbroke would be perfect for you, Jemmy, I know she would. She was in town last year, while you were across the channel, and we spent the most delightful afternoons together. An extraordinary mind, I assure you. Of course she was not out then—so you'll have first crack at her, all the better! I'll ring for Searle immediately, and have him bring the week's cards in here," she went on smoothly, pulling the bell-rope. "I tell you, Jemmy, you ought to go to that come-out whether the card comes up or not. You'll regret it if you don't," she added, while her brother groaned and rubbed discontentedly at his forehead.

"How I got into this . . ." he began, but did not finish.

"I haven't met Lady Isabella—her sister, that is—but she is certain to be beautiful, if nothing else. It's her come-out, too. She was too young last year, I suppose, so they waited . . . In any case, I should think you might know their brother, Lord Halcot. He's a good ten years younger than you, I dare say, but he's spent a little time in the metropolis. Charlie Halcot, don't you know him? High-spirited fellow, with yellow hair."

Lord Marchmont raised his head. "Yes, I think I do remember him. Emilia, do you think you could stop prattling for a moment? It's giving me the headache."

"Stop prattling? Oh dear, I don't know. I'm feeling so enormously braced, you see. What a cheerful prospect! Even if you don't go to the Stanbroke debut, you're sure to meet them somewhere. And then the Lemon girls will be in town again—real *élégantes* they are, every one of them. Not in your style perhaps, but then, one never knows. Lord Weld, you might enjoy meeting Augusta Lemon. She sings like a bird. And then there's Lady Juliana, Lord Grandison's daughter you know . . . and Amabel Pye, she never did marry that Freddie person—what's his name?—portly fellow, with a dreadful lisp. As a matter of fact, I'm pretty sure Miss Partridge is back on the market again—but I suppose after that business with Jeffery you'll do just as well to stay away from her."

"Emilia, in the name of mercy," Lord Marchmont began to plead, meaning to quell this terrifying gush of prospects, but he was cut off by the entrance of Searle. Within moments the invitations had been delivered, and Lord Weld appropriated them.

"Hat, please," he said. "Or basket. I need something to put them in."

"Will this do?" asked Lady Emilia, upending a bowl of fruits which had stood on the Pembroke table behind her and offering it to him.

"Perfect." Lord Weld dropped the cards and envelopes inside.

"I don't even recognise that one," said Emilia peeking in as he stirred them about and spying an unopened missive. "It must have arrived this morning."

"Well, let's have done with it," urged Marchmont, ever more miserable. "How many were there in the first place?"

"Twelve," said Weld, still mixing them. "I counted. Isn't that lucky? Just divisible by four."

"Get on with it, get on with it!"

Lord Weld dramatically covered his eyes with his left hand and plunged his right into the bowl. He drew out the first card. " 'Lady Mufftow requests the pleasure . . . rout at ten o' clock evening of the—' oh my, that's tonight," he read out. "Very good, that's number one."

Lord Marchmont sent a pleased glance over to his sister.

"Lady Mufftow's start-of-the-season rout," he said triumph-antly. "Not my fault if it's a hopeless crush! You see—perfectly blameless. Warrington chose it."

Emilia, looking annoyed, murmured, "We'll go early."

"Second one," Lord Weld announced, reading, " 'Supper, Mr. Henry Luttrell, nine o'clock, Tuesday.' Oh dear, I'm afraid this one doesn't even include you, Lady Emilia."

"I should think not!" cried she, despairing. "Bachelor suppers! And any lady you meet there . . ." She shuddered, feeling suddenly defeated.

"Never mind, I'll escort you wherever you like to go that night," comforted Weld; but she was not consolable.

"My my, this is turning out a good deal better than I'd expected," remarked Marchmont jauntily. "Henry Luttrell! I shall be very happy to see him again."

"Dear Lord," said Emilia faintly.

"Number three," Weld called out. He held in his hands a sheet of cream-coloured vellum, ornately lettered. " 'The Earl of Trevor and Lady Trevor . . . request the presence et cetera . . . their two daughters—!' Oh my goodness, it's the Stanbroke girls after all," he exclaimed, looking excitedly at Emilia. "It's true what Pangloss said, then," he continued. "All *is* for the best in this best of all possible worlds."

"Well, at least," said Emilia, with a relieved, if rather wicked, smile at her brother, "it is something."

But Marchmont, though he knew he had miraculously escaped horrors beyond imagination, nevertheless could not repress a final, hollow groan.

2

THE ORIENTAL saloon in Haddon House, Grosvenor Square, was as a rule a very attractive room, well-proportioned and fitted up in a style of restrained but unmistakable elegance. At the moment of our entering it, however, it showed signs of deep fatigue. If walls could speak, the silk-hung walls of the Oriental saloon would cry (as Macbeth puts it) "Hold, enough!" For they had had sufficient indeed for months to come. "No more fashionably-frizzed, well-pomatumed heads to lean up against us, please!" the walls might say. "We pray you, no more pale, almond-shaped fingernails to drum slowly upon us to the solemn one-two-three of a minuet! If you must drum, let it be a waltz next time. We are not to be annoyed again for such a tedious crush as this has been!"

But of course these were walls that had seen some gay times. One must expect them to be critical. Moreover, they were irritable after their long winter's hibernation. Indeed, I should not be surprised to learn the whole of Haddon House resented the use it was routinely put to; for every spring it was invaded by a noisy, cheerful bunch of visitors, every spring aired out and refurbished here and there—brightened, its windows flung open and its chandeliers shined—only to be cruelly jilted just as routinely each summer. No wonder, then, that the remarks of the walls were a little dry and acid. One cannot blame them.

The three young ladies who sat in (or rather, had draped themselves in various weary attitudes round) the Oriental saloon were by contrast not at all annoyed. They were tired, it is true, but each of them was contented in her own drowsy way. The last of the guests had gone home a few moments before; Lord Trevor had already retired to bed; Lady Trevor had gone down to the kitchens for a moment to survey the evening's aftermath—and the girls, a little to their surprise, found themselves officially and irreversibly "launched." They were two sisters—the Stanbroke girls (the reader will not be astonished to learn) and their lifelong friend, the Honble. Miss Lewis. Conversation among them was desultory but satisfying, for this was the moment (perhaps the best in any evening among society) when the intimates at the core of the party assemble at its finish to praise, review, and—most delicious—dissect the guests. Lady Elizabeth Stanbroke, whose scalpel was much the sharpest among those present, had just laid the good name of Miss Amabel Pye upon her table and was beginning to wield her delicate knife.

"It isn't so much that one dislikes that sort of girl," she was saying calmly, from the depths of a green velvet sofa in which she reclined, "as that one wishes to throttle her. For her own sake, of course! Quite for her own sake. A near brush with a gangrene of the head almost always does such girls a world of good, don't you know. One fondly figures to oneself one's thumbs upon her throat—"

"What was she like, exactly?" interrupted Lady Isabella, Lady Elizabeth's sister. "I did not speak with her, I think."

"Certainly you did," Elizabeth contradicted. "She was the one who told you all about Mamma."

"Mamma? Our Mamma?"

"No dear, indeed not. *Her* Mamma. *Mamma,* don't you know! 'Mamma is so clever, really so terribly clever. Why, hordes of other ladies ask her for her opinion of the Paris fashions. And even Papa—you know Papa,' " she went on, imitating Miss Pye's mincing whine with mortal accuracy, " 'Why, even Papa asks Mamma her opinion about—well, *you* know, political issues and so forth. Parliament, I mean, and . . . oh, legislation, *après tout.* Perhaps some ladies think it is not quite nice to know about such issues—why, Mamma has even been called a blue-stocking! by—well, but I won't tell you by whom; I shouldn't. The point is, and Mamma herself has said so, if a woman does not educate herself about . . . er, about issues and so on, then she is utterly at the mercy of . . .' Oh come, Isabella, surely you remember her," she broke off. "She was wearing a little pink shawl of Norwich silk."

"Oh!" said Isabella suddenly. "And little pink sandals? I think I do remember. A pink gown?"

"With little pink rosebuds round the hem, and little pink puffed sleeves, and a little pink coronet of little pink—"

"Roses in her hair," finished Isabella, laughing. "I do recall her, only I thought she was one of the Lindsey girls."

"Oh no, the Lindsey girls are the ones with the horsey faces. I remember them from last year; we used to have them to tea."

"Indeed?" said her sister, who had been too young last year to be taken to London. Elizabeth was three years older, though her come-out had been delayed till tonight so that the sisters could be presented together.

From a far corner of the room the third voice was now heard. "Lizzie," it said, sweetly but firmly, "I do think you are being a little hard on poor Miss Pye. After all, it may well be that her mother *is* an extraordinary woman. And if she is, it is only natural for her daughter to be a little . . . overwhelmed by her," she finished.

"A little overwhelmed!" exclaimed Elizabeth, briefly peering over the back of the settee. "Why, the girl hasn't got a thought to call her own! A little overwhelmed indeed." She subsided, with an exasperated growl, back into the depths of the sofa.

"Why don't you come and sit with us, Amy?" invited Isabella. "You're so far away."

But they were all too tired to move. "Did you speak to Mr. Stickney at all?" Miss Amy Lewis (for it was she in the corner) inquired at last of her companions. "I thought him extremely agreeable."

"Oh, extremely," agreed Isabella. "He's one of Charlie's friends. We've met him before at the Abbey. Didn't you meet him when he visited us?"

"I don't think so."

"Oh. Well, he is a jolly fellow. If you like jolly fellows," added Isabella, who did not. "Not much for looks, I must say."

"I thought him quite pleasant-appearing," defended Amy.

"He's married, you know," Elizabeth interposed. "Dorothea Frane that was, the tired-looking woman—tall, with auburn hair. Not much of a match on her side, but they seem happy. I daresay Stickney will be happier still when she's borne him an heir. Three daughters already; think of it!"

Miss Lewis had coloured immediately at the thought that she might herself be interested in Mr. Stickney, and though no one could have seen the blush (for Elizabeth had shut her weary eyes and was stroking them gently, while Isabella was staring abstractedly at a chandelier), she hastened to disclaim, "Good heavens, Elizabeth, you don't suppose I could entertain—oh dear, what an imagination you have!"

"Oh yes," said Lizzy languidly, "I'm a perfect Byron. Fancy you taking an interest in—! Oh, what a thought!" she laughed.

"Elizabeth," intoned Miss Lewis, a trifle shocked, "please stop." It was as it always had been for her when she was in the company of the Stanbroke girls: as dearly as she loved and admired them (and she did, very dearly), she could not help but be just a little scandalized by some of the things they said. Elizabeth was so abrupt! And Isabella—well, though Isabella was her own bosom-bow, and always had been—none the less it sometimes seemed to Amy that Isabella was even worse than her sharp-tongued sister. She was so fantastical, so dreamy! To her, everything hinted at secrets and mysteries. A box was not a box: it was a casket. A glass was a goblet, a letter a missive, a shadow a shade. It was exciting! But it was unwise. Amy Lewis would have passed but a drab and quotidian childhood had it not been for her friend Isabella; but Isabella was destined for a disastrous collision with the real things of this world, Amy feared, if she did not learn more sense.

And then both Stanbroke girls were so emphatically beautiful! Not the least of the pleasures of the come-out had been, for Amy, the opportunity of learning that most other girls were no prettier than she—in fact, that some were a good deal less so. She had grown up with Lizzie and Bella. They were the only girls in the neighbourhood to whom she could compare herself (excepting the servants), and she always came off, after these inevitable comparisons, a lamentable third. Naturally she had been pretty sure that the Stanbrokes were extraordinary beauties—but it was a relief to make certain of it at last. If the truth be known, Amy Lewis had a particular reason to hope she was—well, at least attractive, if not stunning. The name of the particular reason was Charles Stanbroke, his title Viscount Halcot at the present moment and someday (if things took their natural course) the Earl of Trevor. Just as Miss Lewis had grown up with no one to compare herself to but the Stanbroke girls, so had she found no object on which to exercise the growing scope of her affections but their brother Charlie. Amy's parents were aware of their daughter's sentiments but did not encourage them. For one thing, it did not seem to them as if Lord Halcot returned Miss Lewis's regard. Moreover, even if he had done so, Lord Lewis was not at all sure the boy's father would smile upon the match. Not only was the Lewis's income moderate, it was also a fact that, for the son and heir of an earl, a marriage with the daughter of a minor baron, (even one of very ancient lineage, as was the case here) was less than brilliant.

Lastly, Lord and Lady Lewis were not entirely persuaded that Amy and Halcot would be happy together. The Lewis's estate adjoined the county seat of the earl in Warwickshire, and as the two families were the only nobility for miles around their children had naturally seen a great deal of one another as they grew up. It concerned Lady Lewis, however, that her daughter had seen very little of anyone else. Outside of a few cousins and men of business, Amy had met no young gentlemen at all save Charlie Halcot; small wonder then that she fastened her hopes to him. Not but what they might be right for one another after all—only before one could know, Amy must have a little more experience of the world. So it was that, when Lady Trevor offered to present Miss Lewis along with her own daughters this season, Lady Lewis had been very grateful indeed. Lady Trevor, despite her spending ten months of each twelve in the country, still had a large and excellent acquaintance among the *ton;* whereas Lady Lewis knew hardly anyone. It was the perfect solution to a difficult problem—especially since it spared the Lewis's the burdensome expense of a season in London. Miss Lewis was consequently equipped with all manner of fashionable clothing, laden with very superior advice, and packed off to London in the company of her dear friends. That the Stanbroke girls might, with their extraordinary talents and beauty, disastrously outshine little Amy had never occurred to her doting Mamma. She did not like to say so, of course, but in her estimation Amy's steady heart and unfailing goodness was worth ten of the Stanbroke girls. Though naturally they were very nice girls as well, in their fashion.

Elizabeth, applied to by Miss Lewis "please to stop," now obligingly did so and instead turned her considerable powers of observation to other objects. "Well, I shall know in the future who to stay away from," she remarked, opening her eyes at last and sitting up a little. "That Lemon man—what was his name?"

"Middleford, I think," supplied Isabella.

"Yes, just so. What a dead bore! Can you imagine? He spoke to me for thirty minutes—really, thirty minutes!—about porcelain. Porcelain, if you will! Evidently he is a collector. But don't you think he is too young to be a collector? Surely there must be some law prohibiting the collecting of porcelain before the age of five-and-thirty. Or if there is not we must ask Papa to introduce one when he is next in Parliament. It's a positive scandal." She was silent a moment, again stroking her eyelids. Then, "Well, whom will you marry, Bella? I'm afraid you've seen the pick of the *ton* tonight, so you might just as well make your decision among them and have done with it."

"Good heavens, Elizabeth, what a thought!"

"Why, what's the matter? Didn't you see anybody who struck your fancy?"

"Unfortunately Mamma kept me so busy being charming and courteous I had no opportunity to notice any gentleman in particular. Why, whom will you marry?" she asked in her turn.

Elizabeth spoke without hesitation. "The Earl of March-mont," she said.

Isabella sat bolt upright. "Elizabeth, what can you mean?" she demanded.

"There is no great mystery, my love," laughed the other. "I am going to marry Lord Marchmont—see if I don't!"

Miss Lewis, upon whom this announcement had also had a galvanic effect, now rose and crossed the room. She seated herself next to Lizzie and brought out haltingly, "You don't mean . . . my dear, is it possible—he cannot have asked you tonight?"

"Goodness, no," cried the other, still smiling. "I dareswear he won't ask for months. But he will ask," she added deliberately.

"Do you really like him so much?" Amy asked wonderingly, while Isabella exclaimed, "Isn't it splendid! You knew at once, didn't you Lizzie? The moment you set eyes on him." She sat up and folded her legs before her, hugging her knees to her chest.

"Oh come now, my pets, this is nothing to fly into the boughs about. It was only a thought. How serious you both are!"

"But Elizabeth, to say you are going to marry a gentleman—! And then, that gentleman in particular," Amy remonstrated.

"Why not 'that gentleman in particular'?" inquired Lizzie. "Is there something about him you object to?"

"Oh gracious, not at all," said Isabella. "He is a little old for you, perhaps . . ."

"A little old! How old do you suppose him to be?"

"Dear me, I should think at least forty," her sister hazarded dubiously.

"Forty! He is hardly that, dear girl. And even if he were, that is not so very old."

"It is more than twice your age," Miss Lewis pointed out mildly.

But Lady Elizabeth suddenly coloured. "Oh pooh, this whole discussion is silly. I merely said, quite idly, that I—Let us drop the subject, shall we? Lady Emilia was very kind to me last year, and she made me feel quite as if I knew her brother, and so I suppose that is why he made such—I mean to say, that is why his name stuck in my head."

"You love him," Isabella pronounced flatly.

"Bella, how could I?" she retorted, her blush deepening. "I have only just met the gentleman tonight."

"That is how it happens. All at once, you just know—"

"Fustian!" insisted the other angrily. "You read too many novels; I have often told Mamma you do. And yet even you must have more sense than to believe—"

"Look at you, you are crimson!" accused Isabella, interrupting. "Oh, my darling, I am so happy for you. I think he's awfully handsome, even if he is a little old, and he is certainly charming. And what a catch—"

"Isabella!" cried her sister, seeking furiously to quell this torrent. "I forbid you to—"

"Where will you live, though? Aren't they a Sussex family? Oh dear, you will be so far away from us—"

"Isabella!" Elizabeth jumped to her feet and rose menacingly over her sister to her full height. "My dear, this is sufficient. I was merely making a little joke. I beg you will forget it."

"I wish I may be so fortunate when I fall in love," Bella continued, undismayed. "Think of it, you will be a countess, like Mamma."

"Isabella, I am warning you. In fifteen seconds I shall—I shall take this cushion," she threatened, snatching up a velvet pillow, "and smother your unstoppable mouth with it!"

"We shall have to call you Lady Marchmont, I suppose. How well that sounds," she went on tranquilly, now introducing a note of grandeur. "My sister, Lady Marchmont, always bespeaks her biscuits from Gunther's. Yes, even when she is at home in Sussex! She has them delivered specially. She says they are much better than any her cook can—"

"That's it!" exclaimed Lizzie, and flew at her, weapon in hand. Isabella dodged her attacker by diving head-foremost into the cushions of her settee, leaving Elizabeth only the back of her blond head to smother—but since Bella's face was consequently squashed against the settee's silk upholstery she did not gain much by the manoeuvre. In fact, she was saved from extinction only by the very timely entrance into the Oriental saloon of her brother. He took in the scene with a single glance, then grabbed Elizabeth by the shoulders and dragged her away from her squealing prey.

"Hello, what's all this? Bit of a dust-up? You girls ought to wait for me, really you should, before you start going at one another like that. I might be able to give you a few pointers. Lizzie, for example," he went on smoothly, "if you are going to smother someone with a pillow, you oughtn't to start with an ornamental one. In general they are much too small for the business . . . and in any case the *really* elegant murderess makes certain she has a goose-down pillow before she makes a move. Why, this pillow is stuffed with horse hair, I should think, at least by the feel of it. Oh, you girls are impossible, 'pon my word; I don't know why I bother with you." He seated himself, grinning, on the green sofa, his fingers still tightly clamped round Elizabeth's wrist.

"You may leave go of me now," she suggested primly.

"Oh my, I don't know if I should just yet. What do you think, Amy?" he asked, with great geniality. "Does she look as if she can be trusted?"

Miss Lewis turned her large, soft eyes on him. To say truth, she had trouble turning them anywhere else when he was in the room. And he was indeed very pleasant to look upon: he had his sisters' butter-coloured hair (just a shade darker than theirs, though, Amy always thought, and a shade glossier) and was every bit as handsome as they were beautiful. They all had intensely blue eyes, as had both their parents. The family resemblance was very strong among them in all respects, in fact. Lady Elizabeth's features were perhaps a trifle more delicate than any of the others, her hair finer and her complexion more subtly tinted. Amy supposed that she was, of the three, the most beautiful, at least in the strictest sense. She had an extremely graceful demeanour as well, and stood a full two inches taller than her sister. Isabella was somehow more dashing than Lizzie. Her movements were quick and sure, her features more clearly defined than Elizabeth's. Altogether she gave the impression that she might at any moment spring up from her chair and leap into the saddle of a waiting stallion, which would then bear her off to a life of noble adventure and daring deeds.

And then there was Charlie, tall and lean and agile, with a full red grin and eyes of a liquid blue that hinted at great tenderness (though it must be admitted his behaviour seldom justified this intimation). Amy had hardly ever seen him in full evening dress before: the tight stockinet suited his legs so well! She was ashamed to admit she had noticed it (even though she admitted it only to herself), but his figure seemed to her far superior to that of any other gentleman who had attended tonight. Lord Marchmont, to take an instance, was all very well in his way. He was broad-shouldered, where her Charlie was narrow, and sleekly muscular where Charlie might be called wiry—but what were broad shoulders and perceptible muscles? Merely so much unnecessary baggage, in her opinion. Miss Lewis's introduction to fashionable gentlemen had left her affections quite unmoved: the notion that there might be some man who would appeal to her more than Charlie did not cross her mind at all.

Just now this paragon was continuing, in his melodious voice, to quiz his sisters on the cause of their recent dispute. Neither would satisfy his curiosity, however. Elizabeth was glad to observe that, whatever else her faults might be, Isabella was not a tell-tale; still, she adroitly turned the conversation as soon as she could. "Well, my dear," she said, "if you will leave go my arm I will tell you all about what Sir John Firebrace told *me* about Cribb's match with Bill Neate last week."

Since Charlie was an avid spectator of pugilistic bouts—and an amateur of some standing himself—this was strong inducement indeed. He released Elizabeth and begged to know the details.

"According to Sir John," she said, "that mill was rigged. He says Mr. Neate was given three hundred pounds to take his fall, and a hundred more to make it look convincing."

"Damme, I *knew* there was something queer about that fight! I lost five pounds on Neate, you know. Who fixed it?"

Elizabeth shrugged, rising strategically as she did so and beginning to cross to the door. "I have no idea."

"You have—you mean, John Firebrace told you it was rigged, but didn't say who by?"

"That's right," she returned, laughing.

"Well what the devil use is that to me?" he demanded. "To be told a fight was crooked, and not told who was responsible! Lizzie, now I'll never sleep, trying to puzzle this out! I'm going to call on John at once—oh damme, no—that won't do. Well, first thing in the morning," he asserted, ever more excited. Elizabeth, who had known how frustrating her limited information would be, had now safely crossed the threshold of the wide double doors.

"Good night, my dears," she called gaily, thoroughly enjoying her brother's discomfiture. Then she retired altogether, shutting the doors behind her.

"What a minx it is!" swore her brother as she disappeared. "It's not the five pounds, of course, it's the idea of being taken in. When a man makes a wager he expects a fair chance at—" Charlie had been planning to continue these fulminations for some time, but was interrupted by the entrance of his mother. "Oh! Good evening ma'am," he broke off, with grudging politeness. All well in the kitchens I hope?"

"Where is Elizabeth?" she inquired, ignoring his question and seating herself on the green sofa her elder daughter had just vacated.

"Gone to bed, the coward," young Halcot informed her. "Wait till you hear what she's done, ma'am! She told me—"

"In the morning please, my love. Dear Lord, I'm tired!" exclaimed Lady Trevor. She reached across to Isabella and took the girl's hand. "You were splendid tonight, my dear. Truly charming. And so were you, Amy," she added, with only a slight diminution of enthusiasm. She was a small woman, fragile and elegant, with the same fine blond hair and large blue eyes she had given to Lizzie.

"Thank you, ma'am."

"In fact you were all wonderful, my chickens. Charlie, I must thank you for coming to my aid with that Lemon man. What an extraordinary trial he is! Porcelain, if you please!"

she went on, unconsciously echoing her daughter. "I thought I would scream."

"Oh, it was nothing, Mother," Halcot said carelessly. "In fact, he rather interested me."

Lady Trevor stared. "I beg your pardon? You must be joking."

"Not at all," said Charles, reddening slightly for no apparent reason. "It isn't just the quality of the porcelain itself, you know. It's the glaze as well—" he commenced.

"I do not believe what I am hearing," cried his progenitrix. "Do you?" she asked of Isabella.

"Not particularly," said she. "What can you mean, Charlie?"

"It is a very interesting topic, that's all," insisted he, colouring ever more deeply. "I mean to call upon him and learn a bit more about it presently."

"Call upon him?"

"Certainly," he continued, with an attempt at dignity. "You know I *do* have some interests other than boxing and horseflesh. The arts have always appealed to me, and fine porcelain is really an art . . ."

"Oh, this is too much," exclaimed his exasperated mother. She was far too intelligent to be taken in by a ruse like this. "What is the meaning of this—this *unnatural* seizure? Are you well, my boy?"

"Dear ma'am, you refine upon it too much! I do not see why I may not take an interest in the more . . . er, recherché pursuits of life without—"

"Mamma, is not Mr. Lemon the brother of all those exquisite sisters?" Isabella suddenly broke in, a little incoherently.

"The brother of—Oh, yes, the Lemon girls. Susannah, I think is the oldest. And Augusta, and . . . is it Amelia? In any case, yes."

"Well then, I think we've solved our mystery. My brother does not wish to further his acquaintance with Mr. Lemon at all—much less increase his knowledge of porcelain, forsooth!" she went on drily. "It is those Lemon girls he wishes to cultivate, depend upon it. Oh, look at him, one can see it at a glance."

Charlie did in fact appear pretty well confused. He was at this time about twenty-six years of age, but he had had very little experience of ladies, and his manner of dealing with the subject was far from polished. "Preposterous," he sputtered awkwardly, adding at once, "and even if it were so, what would be the harm in it?"

"No harm," his mother reassured him, amused, but she cast a curious glance at Amy Lewis. The poor girl's secret was a secret to no one but Charlie himself—though perhaps the depth of her feeling was not guessed at by the others. "I am sure the Lemon girls are very pleasant," she added quietly.

"Pleasant! I should say so," asserted young Lord Halcot. "Why, she's—I mean to say, *they* are diamonds of the first water. What elegance, I mean to say. And as graceful as a . . . er, as swans," he concluded lamely.

Isabella looked to Amy, whose rosy complexion had gone suddenly white. "I found them almost as dull as their brother," Bella remarked, regretting with her whole heart her stupidity in allowing the discussion to take this turn. Poor Amy! Isabella could not see what there was to worship in her brother . . . but since Amy did, it was the least one could do to be discreet in her company. "Did not you, Amy?" she now added, hoping to vote the Lemon girls down before Charlie became really attached to them.

But Amy was not capable of such stratagems. "I only spoke to one of them," she answered softly. "Miss Susannah, I believe it was. She was very civil." Her dimpled chin lifted proudly with these words, while her cheeks (if possible) went a little whiter.

It had obviously been an effort for her to make the speech. Lady Trevor felt it was time to draw the discussion to a close. "Come, my pets," she said, extending a hand to each girl. She rose adding, "It is extremely late. Let us see if we can catch Elizabeth before she goes to sleep. I want to congratulate her," she continued, drawing them towards the door, "for I believe she charmed Lady Jersey quite thoroughly. We shall soon have vouchers for Almack's, I am persuaded."

Isabella dropped her mother's hand and drew Amy's arm through her own instead. It had been an awkward scene and had left her a little sad. Romantic though she was, she saw nothing poetical in Miss Lewis's attachment to her brother. Charlie was a silly, cork-brained boy, scarcely worth mooning over in her opinion—and what was more important, he never gave the least sign of having noticed Amy. When she was present, he behaved to her as he did to his sisters; when absent, he never spoke of her. Whereas he had indeed noticed several other women, to her certain knowledge. Before the Lemon girls, it had been a Miss Hammond; and before her, Miss Stickney, his friend's younger sister. Naturally very little had come of these fits and starts—but it was painful for Lady Isabella to see her friend persevere in her devotion without any reward, or even the promise of a reward. She was angry with Halcot for failing to notice Amy's merits; still, to speak with him on the subject was out of the question. So she limited herself to hoping energetically that Miss Lewis would find some gentleman among London society who would appreciate her more, and whom she could love as well—while in the meantime the whole unspoken weight of Amy's unrequited affection grew daily more perceptible and more burdensome.

3

THE JOLTING report of a pistol split the air, then another, then another. Above the men hung the crisp evil odour of exploded gunpowder, a gathering if invisible cloud. The noise of the shots reverberated and faded. In a moment Warrington Weld rushed up to his friend Marchmont and shook him vigorously by the hand. "Well done, by Jupiter," he exclaimed. "Well done! They'll think twice before they challenge you again."

Lord Marchmont lightly tossed his discharged pistol from hand to hand. "Perhaps they will," he conceded, with a smile that was more than a little weary. He relinquished the weapon to a waiting servant, then received from another attendant a wafer with a single hole through the centre.

"Mr. Manton hopes you will speak to him before you leave, my lord," said the man. "Captain Gronow has been asking for a contest with you, sir."

Marchmont exchanged a glance with his friend. "Think twice, eh?" he asked, amused, then turned to the attendant. "Very well, tell Mr. Manton I shall speak to him tomorrow. Just now I am in something of a hurry."

The man bowed and disappeared. "I hope I am with you tomorrow," said Weld, as they strolled from the shooting-booths back to a private dressing-room. "I am curious to meet this Manton. They say he is quite the gentleman."

"He's a good fellow," said Marchmont, who had known Joe Manton nearly half his life. The shooting-gallery the latter operated was justly famous: it was the best in London, and so attracted London's best marksmen. Lord Marchmont had heard of Gronow, for example, and had known it was only a matter of time before he and the Captain proved their skills against one another. The wager he had won today by shooting his wafer through thrice had been hardly a trial at all; as his challenger strolled up to pay off his debt Lord Marchmont hoped Captain Gronow would provide him with more of a test.

The gentlemen reached their chamber. Marchmont dismissed the waiting valet with a nod, observing quietly to Weld after he had gone, "More gossip is retailed out of these rooms than flowers are sold in Covent Garden, take my word for it. The place is an absolute hive." He knelt softly to peer through the keyhole, then stood and flung open the door. The crouching valet straightened himself, looking sheepish.

"Just coming to fetch your lordship a towel," he sputtered, going red.

"I have a towel, thank you," answered the earl repressively, adding after a moment, "which is more than I can say for you."

Frightened away, the man scurried off with a final bow. Mr. Weld, who had dropped into a leather-covered arm-chair, stretched out his legs luxuriously and observed, "Remarkable, isn't it, how eager people are to know one another's secrets? They're always the same—change the names, I mean, and they would be—but people do go ahead prying, don't they, just as if they might discover something wonderful! Well . . . human nature I suppose."

"Human nature, indeed," the other agreed drily, casting off his shirt and donning a fresh one. "What astonishes me is how blithely people go on committing indiscretion after indiscretion, year upon year, without acknowledging to themselves that *nothing* in London ever remains a secret, and so they are sure to be found out. Someday I must make two lists: all men whose names have been connected with a political or gaming scandal, and all women whose names have been connected with a romantic scandal. I shall then publish them and put Boyle's Court Guide quite out of business. In fact, my listing is likely to be the more complete."

"Oh come, please do not tell me London is so wicked a place as that," begged Weld. "Surely there must be men of conscience, as well as honourable women! You've left a button undone," he added, pointing to it.

Marchmont corrected the smaller oversight but insisted on the large one. "If there is an honourable woman," he asserted, thinking of Charlotte Beaudry, "it is only because she has had no opportunity to disgrace herself. A few are too young, and a few are too ugly. But a very few, I assure you."

"And the men of conscience?"

"I must agree with John Donne that the quest to discover what wind 'serves to advance an honest mind' and the quest for a woman true and fair are both equally doomed to frustration. Temptation is a door. A woman's pretty blushes and demurs are no more than the keys to its three or four locks. She may stammer at the threshold, but cross it she will—feeling all the more virtuous, no doubt, for having made such a fuss. I have never seen it fail."

"Never?" persisted Weld.

"Never." The earl let fall this weighty word, then turned his attention to his cravat. "Damn these things anyhow," he muttered. "They take half an hour to tie, and then they make one's neck ache all the day long. Someone should petition Brummel to work some notion of comfort into our idea of fashion—or at least to give a passing nod to common sense. At present they are utter strangers. Do you know of a case to contradict me?" he demanded suddenly.

"What, about fashion and comfort?"

"About women and virtue."

"Oh! Well, my dear old man, a fellow doesn't like to mention a fellow's sister," Warrington replied slowly, "but I can scarcely believe Lady—"

"Oh, Emilia," Marchmont broke in. "Yes, you are right there. Emilia is pure as snow, no question about it. And she is very handsome, don't you think?"

Weld agreed heartily.

"I can't imagine why she doesn't marry," her brother went on. "Certainly not for lack of suitors. Yes, I must concede her the exception. But only the exception that proves the rule, after all! I suppose you and I must pass for men of conscience, in order to prove that rule correspondingly. Though some of the things I saw on the Continent," he went on, "and some of the things I did . . ." His voice trailed away as an involuntary shudder actually took hold of his body. The war against Napoleon, necessary though it was, had deftly stripped him of illusions concerning his fellow men. He had seen much evidence of courage (his friend Weld being principal among examples), but he had seen even greater evidence of stupidity, of narrow savagery, of men eager to surrender to their basest desires. Perhaps it was the smell of gunpowder at Manton's that brought it out, but he always left that place steeped in deepest cynicism. For besides his discoveries of the nature of other men's souls, he had had to confront in his own young spirit a number of failings he had rather have been permitted to ignore.

Weld saw the shudder and stretched out his hand to grasp Lord Marchmont's briefly. "Never mind, old boy," he said, with some clumsiness. His mind cast about for a diversion.

"That's behind us now. You've got a new battlefield to worry about, after all—the marriage mart, I mean. What did you think of those Lemon girls at Lady Trevor's last night, eh? Fairly prime, I'd say!"

Marchmont smiled gratefully at Weld, then shrugged. "Not much above the ordinary, if I know who you mean."

"The devil a bit they weren't! Those tall gals, with the copper-coloured hair—don't you remember?"

"Oh yes, I remember. Miss Susannah's been hanging out for a husband these past two seasons or more. Augusta, too, I think. Emilia thought I didn't know 'em; she tried to trap me with one at the supper table. Shall we be off? I'm ready."

Warrington rose to accompany him out to the street, where the earl's curricle waited. "*Trap* you with one," he exclaimed as they went. "Those girls are perfectly magnificent, every last one of them. Just what are you looking for, my good man?"

Marchmont gave a second shrug. "A little wit, perhaps. A little honesty, a modicum of talent. A dash of modesty, if it's not too much to ask—and done up as attractively as possible, if I'm lucky. I'll never find her," he laughed despairingly. They passed out of Manton's into the damp afternoon. "I'll drive," he told his tiger, springing up to take the reins.

"Who was that you did take in to supper?" asked Lord Weld. "Not one of the Stanbroke girls, was she?"

"No, a friend of theirs. An Amy Lewis, a neighbour from Warwickshire, from what she said. Pretty little snippet, I thought. Big eyes, sweet expression. Not a brain in her head, God bless her." He started the horses and began to manoeuvre through the muddy, crowded streets.

"Mind that cart!" Weld shouted, as the curricle narrowly avoided the vehicle in question. Country-bred, the hectic London streets unnerved him in a way Napoleon's troops could not. He hid his long lightly-freckled face in his hands and called with a grimace, "I can't look, Marchmont. Tell me when we're home."

The earl tapped the red head next to him lightly. "Take

heart," he smiled, "and tell me what you thought of that mob last night. Speak to anyone worth the trouble?"

"Just Henry Luttrell," he replied, daring to look ahead again. "He *is* a bit of a wag, 'pon honour! One of the serving-girls nearly dropped a tray on his foot, and though she was very apologetic, and though he was very polite in excusing her, he said to me as soon as she'd gone that he thought Lady Trevor ought to *train* her servants better, for the incident struck him as *très outré!* Then Lady Elizabeth heard him, and begged him to re*train* himself! I did laugh."

"Lady Elizabeth?" said Marchmont, catching at the name. "Stanbroke, do you mean?"

"Yes. Elizabeth is the older one. Now those two are beauties, admit it!"

A muscle at the corner of Lord Marchmont's mouth pulled just visibly. "I thought Lady Isabella a trifle hoydenish, if you must know."

"Oh, Marchmont, this is ungenerous!" remonstrated Weld. "What about Elizabeth then, the fair Elizabeth? Surely you don't object to her on those grounds; I never saw anyone so elegant."

"Perhaps."

"Perhaps! Devil fly away with your 'perhaps,' old man! She had half the men in the room clustered round her."

"It was *her* come-out," observed Marchmont drily.

"Nevertheless! And anyway, it wasn't only hers, it was her sister's too . . . and that Miss What's-her-name—"

"Lewis."

"Yes, that Miss Lewis you approve of so highly. I say, Marchmont, you seem almost to take offence if a woman is really beautiful. Now that little Lewis chit can't hold a candle to the Stanbrokes, but you call *her* very pretty. It isn't reasonable!"

"A thousand apologies, my friend," said the other lightly. "You see, in my opinion a woman is not truly attractive unless she is intelligent as well as good-looking. Moreover, a little vanity can ruin her for me, be she never so smart and lovely. So indeed can a shallow spirit, or a too-susceptible heart. Now your Lady Elizabeth, for instance—"

"Not mine," disclaimed Weld.

"This Lady Elizabeth, then, I observed to be rather flirtatious. Extremely flirtatious, indeed, and the observation ended my liking for her."

"Your— Oh, I say, this is doing it a bit brown. You don't mean to say you disliked her? But she was charming!"

"Charming? I don't call it charming to threaten to run someone through with a poker."

"I beg your pardon?"

"Your Lady Elizabeth. She—"

"This Lady Elizabeth, she stood for half an hour encouraging that inhumanly tedious Middleford Lemon, and then, as soon as he'd drifted off, she turned to me and declared her intention of running him through with a poker. I presume that when our conversation was at an end, she dropped a word in someone else's ear on the subject of garrotting me . . . or perhaps smashing my head with a hammer . . . or it may have been—"

"Marchmont, she was certainly jesting!"

"Not the point," he insisted, swerving in the nick of time to avoid a pedestrian. "The point is, she is two-faced. I never saw a woman smile so sweetly as she did at Lemon—but, when she knew him to be out of earshot, she all of the sudden despised him."

"Faugh!" spat out the other. "How do you know she wasn't just doing the pretty to him all that while? You say yourself he's a famous bore. Perhaps she could not get away from him! In that case it was no more than civil to smile at him—and seem to encourage him. Note that word seem, Marchmont."

"If she could not get away from him for full half an hour," his lordship replied unmoved, "I think it speaks very badly for her wit."

"You *are* a study!" exclaimed Lord Weld. "All of this puts

me very much in mind of Lady Emilia's complaints of you, that day when we drew invitations by lot. I begin to see her—"

"I'm glad you brought that up, Weld," the earl broke in quickly. "I've been meaning to speak to you on that head for days now. I never saw such a treacherous—"

"Never mind all that," Warrington persevered. "I'm beginning to get a pretty good idea of your methods, old boy, and very devious some of them are! First of all you find fault with everybody around you. Next, when you can't find fault, you fend them off with interruptions—"

"Tell me how close I am to that carriage, please," the earl interrupted. Traffic had become very dense, and they appeared to come within an inch of the opposing vehicles.

"You're in no danger," Weld assured him. "I was saying, if you can't undo your acquaintances with fault-finding, you inter—"

"I like *you* pretty well," said Marchmont with a smile.

"This is impossible! When you're presented with an unexceptionable gal, you turn the conversation by—"

"What I don't understand is how all this comes to concern you, my good man. Why should you care whether I marry or no? It's nothing to you, I presume."

"Naturally it's nothing to me. I'm thinking of Lady Emilia. So should you be. Listen to me, dear fellow: you've an obligation to your sister, and I like your sister, and I'm not going to sit idly by while you wriggle out of your duties one more time. Now you tell me one real objection to—er, well, to this Lady Elizabeth, for instance. One honest objection!"

"Very well," Marchmont replied, refusing to be cornered. "I happened to see her glance in the pier-glass not once but three times in the space of an hour. And each time she did it—very surreptitiously, I might add—she gave herself an odious little smile of approval. Now, how do you like that?"

Weld was bewildered. "What on earth sort of objection can you make to that?" he asked.

"But she is vain, of course!" said Marchmont. "Fancy looking at oneself again and again, every chance one has. And then smirking at one's reflection—and in a room full of people too! Of course she thought no one was looking—"

"But you were!" Weld interjected triumphantly.

The earl paused. "Well, yes, I was," he confessed. "After all, it is nothing to be ashamed of! You are quite right, she is a very elegant woman. I noticed it, and I did look at her. Very well, I admit it. I have just finished telling you, however, that to me a woman's looks are nothing if they are not complemented by intelligence, and modesty, and—"

"Just because a young girl is anxious to appear to advantage at her come-out," Weld broke in firmly, "does not mean she is vain. Now it just so happens that this Lady Elizabeth—"

"Your Lady Elizabeth—"

"Not mine! This Lady Elizabeth is also a woman of intelligence. I have just told you how easily she capped Luttrell's remarks about the serving-girl's tray. As for modesty, I maintain your pier-glass incident proves absolutely nothing, for any girl might do the same and probably would—"

"She is scarcely a girl, Weld. I should have to call her a woman."

"All the better, then, do call her a woman," invited the other. "Any *woman* would do the same, I dare swear, and—no, don't say it, I know what is coming! As for honesty, I submit that your Middleford Lemon story proves no more than did the pier-glass, for it is certainly more incumbent upon a hostess to be courteous than it is to be honest, and it would have been shocking of her ladyship to do anything else than what she did."

"You mean by listening to Lemon drone on?"

"Precisely."

"And what about telling me she contemplated running him through with a—"

"Perfectly charming! Very amusing!" insisted Lord Weld. "I hope you have no objection to a little humour in a woman!"

"Every objection. They begin by laughing with you, and they end by laughing at you, depend upon it."

"This is outside of enough! You just informed me you insist on wit in a woman—"

"The difference between wit and humour, my dear Weld, is considerable," observed the earl.

"Nonsense, nonsense, nonsense!" came the exasperated response. "I tell you, Marchmont, I have a feeling about that Stanbroke girl. She's the genuine article. You're a fool not to see it."

"So you have a feeling, do you? Then you marry her," suggested Lord Marchmont. He repeated softly, with a faint air of disgust, "Feeling, indeed!"

"Call it what you will, then," Weld continued, ignoring the last suggestion. "Call it intuition. I liked her. She could do you a world of good. And you would deal well together. Even Lady Emilia said—"

"Lady Emilia likes everybody."

"Not half she does," said Weld, who was a close observer. "Quite the contrary, I should say: she's almost as niffy-naffy as you."

"She likes *you* well enough," said her brother.

"Am I to be dragged into the conversation every time one of you is charged with misanthropy?" demanded Weld, but he could not suppress a smile.

"We are home," remarked the earl, handing the tiger his whip. "Why don't you go in and despair over me with Emilia? I'm sure you'll both enjoy it enormously. I would gladly join you myself, but I have some household accounts to review."

Lord Weld shot him a look of mock disapprobation as the two disappeared indoors. "Mind what I say," he murmured obstinately. "I shall not sit idly by while you contrive to stay single."

But the earl only laughed.

4

"DEAR HEAVENS!" burst from Lady Isabella's lips, as she entered the vast domain of Lackington, Allen, and Company. "Dear heavens," she repeated, trying to recover herself, "who could have thought there would be so many books in one place?"

Her mother smiled indulgently, but begged her to compose her countenance. "It *is* quite extraordinary," she agreed. "Don't you think?" she asked, turning to Amy Lewis, who was silent with wonder.

"It is impossible," was all that young lady could bring out.

"Evidently not," said the Lady Elizabeth, then added a bit more kindly, "I had just that same thought, though, when I first came here last year."

Lord Halcot, who was the fifth and last member of their party, laughed a little at the ladies. "What a sight you are," he teased Miss Lewis in particular. "Anyone would think you'd never seen a book before!"

"A book yes," answered Amy. "But there must be—there must be a hundred thousand here!"

"Half a million," Charlie informed her, very pleased to be able to present this figure. "At least, that is what Mr. Lackington claims. Claimed, I should say. I believe he died last year." He went on, enjoying his rôle as teacher. "They say a coach-and-six were driven round this room—before the counters were installed, naturally."

The apartment in which they stood was indeed awesome, and though Charlie enjoyed teasing the girls, it was not difficult to see why they should be overwhelmed. Dozens of clerks flitted in and out from behind a huge circular counter; about the counter rose a series of spiralling galleries lined with books, surmounted high above their heads by a lofty dome. Employees and patrons scurried along the steps. Up a broad staircase to one side of the huge central chamber two lounging rooms were visible, their handsome arm-chairs and settees occupied by *tonnish* ladies and gentlemen leafing through elegant volumes. "The binding-rooms are over there," said Charlie, pointing to a doorway. "And also the accounting-rooms, I think—"

"Do you mean to say they publish books as well?"

"Oh, by the hundreds!" he informed them cheerfully. Acting the part of a seasoned Corinthian put him in very good spirits. "Perhaps I can arrange for you to see the work-rooms, if you like."

"This is sufficient," Isabella answered, smiling. "Mamma, may we wander about a little?" she asked, beginning to do so as she spoke. Permission granted, the girls dispersed, each admiringly seeking out those authors and subjects she most enjoyed. Isabella inspected the shelves of Sir Walter Scott, Elizabeth the volumes of Suckling and Pope.

"Do you think it's true about the coach-and-six?" Amy Lewis asked Halcot shyly, when he joined her before a row of Miss Burney's novels.

A shopman bustled up officiously behind them to obtain a

copy of *Evelina*. "I don't see why not," said Charles. "If they didn't drive it round in fact, they certainly could have. The place is more than large enough. Have you looked at the books in the lounging rooms? Some of them are quite rare and beautiful—Oh Jupiter," he interrupted himself, as he turned to point her out the way. "Speaking of rare and beautiful . . . excuse me." He hurried off very abruptly indeed and hastened up the broad staircase. Miss Lewis, watching him closely, saw him accost a tall, elegant female—with copper-coloured hair.

"Miss Lemon," she breathed to herself, tears starting at once to her eyes. "Oh, Charlie!"

Lady Isabella, who had been looking for Amy, chanced to overhear her friend's soft murmur. " 'Oh, Charlie,' indeed," she said scornfully, unable to stop herself. "Forgive me, dearest—but how can you possibly bear my brother? He is intolerable! First prosing on to show us what a man about town he is— oh, they say this, and Mr. Lackington claimed that! And then—to leave you standing here alone so—it is too bad of him," she asserted loyally, slipping her arm round Amy's. "The monster!" she went on, as she looked more carefully at Miss Lewis. "He has made you weep!"

But, "I am not weeping," contradicted Amy softly (and mendaciously). She went on in her steady, quiet voice. "My dear, I know your brother has his faults. I know he is a little of a bully, and I know he is a little . . . careless. He likes to seem more important than he is, perhaps—so do we all, in our hearts—and it is true I have seen him be selfish more than once. But, oh Isabella, these are human faults—and I cannot help it! I—" she stopped just short of a full confession and fastened her eyes on Charlie once more. "I cannot help it," she amended. She struggled at once to get hold of herself, for Lord Halcot was fast bearing down upon them with Susannah Lemon in tow.

"Lady Isabella, is it not?" breathed Miss Lemon as she approached. She extended her hand gracefully to Bella and gave a slight bow.

Charlie beamed at them both. "Yes, yes, m'sister. You met her at her come-out, I dare say."

"Such a pleasant occasion," said Susannah.

There was a silence, during which Isabella looked purposefully at her brother.

"Miss Lemon was looking for a copy of *Child Howard's Pilgrimage*," Charlie informed her after a moment.

"Childe Harold," Isabella corrected tightly.

"Yes, exactly. Lord Byron, isn't it?"

Swallowing a disagreeable smile at his error, Miss Lemon confirmed that it was. "I simply dote on Byron, do not you, Lady Isabella?"

"Charlie, I think you ought to make Miss Lemon known to Miss Lewis," was Isabella's furious reply. For during all this interchange neither Halcot nor Susannah had given the slightest indication of being aware of Amy's existence. Since she was standing within six inches of Bella, this was rather extraordinary—and extremely rude.

"Dear me, have you not met?" blundered Charlie, surprised. "I thought you should have been presented to one another at the come-out. Well, anyhow, Miss Lemon, this is—"

"We did meet, I think," Amy suddenly brought out, dry-eyed and quite pale. "Miss Lemon," she acknowledged, giving her hand briefly. It was a much more chilly greeting than any she was accustomed to give, and considering her lack of practice, she did it very well. The fact was, she had just realized that her birth gave her precedence over Susannah. She had been waiting for the other girl to recognise her, but after all it was her place to choose or not to choose to recognise Susannah. Moreover, it was for Miss Lemon to be presented to her and not the other way round. Since Charlie had also evidently forgotten this fact, and was about to present them as if Miss Lemon were the more consequential, Amy's abrupt interjection saved him from a social solecism as well as restoring to herself a little dignity.

Her behaviour was correct, but it was not agreeable to Miss

Lemon. She was not in the habit of receiving cold acknowl-edgements from green country girls, and she found the experi-ence displeasing. "I am sorry," she replied very stiffly indeed. "I did not recall our having been acquainted."

"But now you do," returned Amy with emphasis, astonished at her own words. Her voice was quite clear, and she had no trouble at all holding Miss Lemon's eyes steadily. She was even, she realized with amazement, rather enjoying the con-frontation. It gave her a curiously giddy sensation.

This chit behaves as if she were royalty! thought Susannah to herself, but she was obliged to say aloud "Of course."

Amy smiled freezingly. "If you will excuse me," she added in a murmur, and turned away. She walked off only a few steps, drew a book from a shelf at random, and pretended to glance through it with interest. I've done it! she exulted in-wardly—at the same time demanding of herself frantically, What have I done? The book she was looking at, she slowly became aware, was a military history. It was also—as Isabella, presently joining her, pointed out—upside down.

Isabella righted the book for her and whispered delightedly, "You were magnificent! Splendid! Amy, I am so proud of you."

But these words of praise rather upset Amy than reassured her. "I was terribly rude," she replied, abashed. "I've never in my life insisted on taking precedence, till now."

"Well, you were never in your life so rudely ignored, I expect," answered the other sensibly. "Oh, I should have liked to slap her, the—the snake!"

"Oh no, Bella, I am persuaded . . . that is, I fear Miss Lemon simply did not see me. She could not have slighted me on pur—"

"My dear girl, this is no time for charity! I never saw such discourtesy. Indeed, you were much too generous! You ought to have refused to know her at all."

Horrified, Amy said, "I could not have done that! Only think of the awkwardness. No, no Isabella, I am afraid I did very wrong as it is. How cold I was! I shouldn't have thought it possible. Do you know, I believe I ought to apologize to her."

Charlie and Miss Lemon having by now mounted into the spiralled galleries, Isabella allowed her voice to rise a little above a whisper. "My dear Amy, if you ever, ever think of such a thing again, I shall lose all my respect for you. Why should that . . . that spiteful wretch be permitted to make you uncomfortable? I shall simply murder Charlie when we get home. *Childe Howard*, indeed—what an idiot he is! I am sure Miss Lemon is laughing up her sleeve at him, too, for all her superior airs and graces. Who is she, anyhow?"

"Isabella, if you say one word about this to Charlie I shall never forgive you," Amy now said, ignoring the question. "Promise me you won't; swear it."

Indignant though she was, Bella saw the reasonableness of such a demand. Accordingly she promised. "But if I ever have an opportunity to do Miss Susannah a disservice," she threatened vaguely, "and I certainly hope I may—"

"I certainly hope you may not," interrupted Amy, who was perhaps just a little more charitable than even the reader would wish her to be. "If Charlie likes Miss Lemon, I am sure she must have many virtues. Everyone has *some* virtues, in any case," she insisted in response to Bella's skeptical glance.

"Have they? Oh, no doubt you are right. Miss Lemon would make an ideal hassock, I should think," Isabella answered, sounding for a moment more like her sister than herself. "I know I should be very pleased to use her for one."

Lady Trevor, with Elizabeth on her arm, now drew up to the girls and ended their conversation. "Where is Charlie?" she asked. "We must go home."

"He has climbed up into the boughs after a Lemon," answered Isabella, with a gesture at the galleries above them.

Elizabeth raised an eyebrow. "You are getting sharper, Bella," she remarked.

"Run up after him, and tell him we must leave, will you, my dear?" asked Lady Trevor of Amy.

"I'll go," Isabella muttered, "though I should prefer to wait until they fell down. They are rotten enough fruit," she added as she stalked off. Elizabeth gave her a puzzled glance, but Lady Trevor did not even bother to do so much as that. She had been a mother quite long enough to know when to ask no questions.

———————

Lady Emilia Barborough laid down her pen for a moment to rub a cramp out of her fingers. Really, Jemmy was too absurd! It was one thing to be so obstinate about accepting invitations as to force her to the device of a lottery—that was sufficiently silly—but to insist he would not attend his own sister's dinner-party unless Lord Weld happened to draw her card from among the others . . . well, that was outside of enough. He had maintained it was only fair: nothing had been said, when they made their agreement, of exceptions for family. Emilia had argued that such an exception must be understood without any explicit discussion taking place, but she could not sway her brother. Very well, then! If he insisted on being preposterous, she could play that game as well. There was plenty of paper in the world, and plenty of ink. She had just written out her eleventh invitation to him; one more and she would be satisfied. She took up her pen again.

When she'd finished she tossed her cards into a bowl with the others she'd collected during the week and went off in search of Lord Weld and her brother. She found the former in the breakfast-room, engaged in reading a journal of some sort. He was very startled indeed when she called his name, for he had been deeply engrossed in his reading, and then—surprise upon surprise—proceeded to blush till his pale skin almost matched the colour of his hair. "Oh, Lady Emilia—I . . ." He jumped up as if she'd caught him committing some heinous crime, laid his journal on the table, took it up again, set it down again (touching it as if it burned his fingers), and ended by placing it on his chair.

"Lord Weld," Emilia returned with amusement, "I seem to be disturbing you!"

"Oh, no, oh, no, no," said he, evidently in great discomfort. "Not at all. Can I be of service to—"

"What on earth have you been reading, dear sir, that is so excessively absorbing?" she inquired, just as if she hadn't realized this was the very question he hoped to avoid. Innocently she made her way round the table towards him, her blue muslin skirt whispering as she moved.

He stood before the chair. "Nothing, no—that is to say," he sputtered brokenly, "nothing of great interest."

She stood before him and extended her hand in the manner of a schoolmistress who waits to be given an illicit note. She was enjoying his embarrassment.

"Oh dear, you don't—Lady Emilia, how pretty you are looking today!" he exclaimed awkwardly.

"None of that, my good man," said she. "I've asked you a civil question, and I expect a civil—Oh my, the *Ladies' Monthly Museum!*" she read out, for she had darted behind him and snatched the journal in question from his chair.

"Dear madam, this is too bad of you," said poor Weld.

"My goodness me," she crowed, ignoring his plaintive accusation, "if I had known ladies' magazines interested you, I would have offered you my own!" She flitted away from him at just the instant he reached out to recover the disputed pages (a technique she'd perfected through long years of practice with Marchmont) and read aloud gleefully, " *'The Child of the Battle,* by H. Finn.' Is that what you were reading, sir?" She skipped to the end of the story and read, " 'A handkerchief was firmly tied across my eyes, and I prepared myself to resign my spirit beneath the surface of the ocean.' My dear sir, you have been reading tragedies—and so early in the day! Oh no," she went on, resolved to tease him without mercy, "I see it is to be continued! What a relief, Lord Weld, don't you think? I know *I* shall sleep better!"

"Lady Emilia, it is most unkind of you to chaff me so. Anyone could become involved in a story of that kind. They are very—er, compelling."

"Oh, yes, anyone could who was looking through the

Ladies' Monthly Museum. Were you looking for information on the Paris bonnets for summer, my lord? If so the *Repository of the Arts* is a much more complete source, I assure you. Allow me to lend you my copy."

"Lady Emilia," he began, shaking his head vigorously and trying to sound stern.

"Oh, no, I insist! You read my copy; I haven't time anyhow. And then you can tell me all about what we must wear this July."

"My dear ma'am, you must surely be aware the *Museum* includes more than notes on fashion."

"Indeed! It includes novels, in serial form."

"I am sure you must realize," he persisted, his blush receding at last, "there is quite a bit of political commentary to be found there. What I was looking at, before the—er, before *The Child of the Battle* caught my eye, was an account of the vote on the income-tax. You will find it on the previous page," he pointed out stiffly, though with returning dignity.

"You must permit me to share with you my subscription to the *Journal des Dames et des Modes,* Lord Weld," smiled Lady Emilia regardless—but his lordship cut her short.

"My dear ma'am, I am afraid you do your sex a great injustice. You seem to imagine that nothing printed for their benefit could possibly be of interest to a gentleman. I am sure you would not agree to the reverse of such a formula."

She considered. "You mean, that what is printed for the benefit of gentlemen can be of no interest to a lady?"

"Precisely."

Nonplussed, she equivocated: "That is not quite the same, somehow."

"Just how, pray tell?"

"Well, because—gentlemen . . ." She set the *Monthly Museum* down absent-mindedly and thought for a moment. "Well, *everything* is printed for the benefit of gentlemen. Gentlemen own the world, sir. And sometimes one is not even certain of the label 'gentlemen.' Perhaps 'men' would be better."

"I do not see what that has to say to the matter," said Weld, now quite himself again. "And it is certainly not true that everything is printed for men. Mrs. Radcliffe appears to have a largely female audience, for example, and yet one can scarcely turn round without stumbling over one of her—ah, her productions."

"Aha! You see, you do not even like to use the word 'book' with regard to Mrs. Radcliffe. The literature that is created with women in mind is hardly literature at all, and you know it. It is trash."

"What about Miss Austen?" he demanded.

"What about Alicia Mant?" she parried.

"What about Madame d'Arblay?"

"What about Caroline Scott? Or even better, what about our good friend H. Finn, author of the illuminating *Child of the Battle?* Tell me *that* isn't nonsense!"

"I liked it!" he asserted flatly, and so honestly that she forgot even to try to contradict him. She laughed instead, reaching for his arm.

"Come, my dear sir. You are too much for me, I confess. I shan't soon tease you again, depend upon it. Will you come and find my brother with me? It is time for another drawing in our famous lottery."

"Oh good, is it?" he asked, gladly escorting her. "Won't Marchmont be pleased? We were just discussing these little drawings yesterday, and he was saying . . . ah, well, perhaps he will not be pleased exactly, but—Marchmont," he broke off, calling into the library. "Marchmont, come out of there, will you, and join us. Your sister and I have planned an amusement for you."

The earl emerged warily. His shoulders were stiff from sitting hunched at his desk, and he kneaded them a little and rubbed at his neck.

"Do come, old boy. This won't hurt a bit!" Weld assured him as they followed Lady Emilia into the drawing-room. "Now you just sit here" (planting him in the wine-red armchair) "and close your eyes, and if you are a very very well-behaved young man, I think there will be a chocolate for you afterwards. Isn't that true, ma'am?"

"Two chocolates," agreed Emilia pleasantly, stirring the contents of the bowl with a delicate hand. The invitations rustled. She arranged a few of her own on top. "Twenty invitations this time, Jemmy," she remarked brightly. "Only imagine, five lovely events! What fun, eh?"

"Are you two planning to go on with this for a very, *very* long time?" the earl inquired acidly. "If so there are some papers in the library I was going over—"

"No no. We are quite ready now," Emilia broke in hastily. "My lord, will you do the honours?"

Lord Weld covered his eyes with his left hand and plunged his right into the bowl. He drew out a pasteboard card and scanned it expertly. "Dinner, Lord Yarmouth. Wednesday at nine."

"Yarmouth! How do you come to know that reprobate?" demanded Emilia. "He's the wickedest man in London, or so I hear."

Lord Marchmont merely winked at her and gave a smug smile. Warrington had come up with a second card.

"Pic-nic, Lady Hassall. Hampstead Heath, it says. Oh! That's tomorrow."

"That will be agreeable. I hope the weather holds," murmured Emilia. "Miss Pye is sure to come; she is Cynthia Hassall's dearest friend."

"Oh my, what a treat," came from Marchmont.

"Third card, Lord Trevor. Yes, another from Trevor. This one's a ball. Goodness, a ball! They *are* giving those girls a push, aren't they?"

"When is it?" inquired Emilia. She was thinking what a good thing it was the Trevors' ball had come up, but she was also wondering frantically how it could have happened that not one of her own invitations had surfaced yet. It must certainly be the next one, she assured herself.

"Next week, Thursday," Weld informed her, while Marchmont said unkindly, "It takes money to make money, my boy. What's a couple of balls, compared to the chance of a couple of wealthy suitors?"

"Do stop, Jemmy," begged his sister. "You make it sound like some sort of . . . of industry."

"And so it is," said he. "Marriage-making. Small investments, ladies and gents, possible high profits. Very genteel among the trades. Favoured by all the Quality."

"Please, Jemmy, you are about to be invited to my party," said Emilia. But he was not.

"Fourth card, recital by Mr. Braham and supper—oh my, very high style your friends keep," remarked Lord Weld.

"You mean—how can it be? Weld, why haven't you chosen my card yet?" asked Lady Emilia, suddenly suspecting him of cheating somehow (though it was true he covered his eyes pretty thoroughly).

Lord Weld looked at her. "Luck of the draw," he shrugged.

"Well, mind you pick it this time," she warned. "This is the last one!"

"Madam, I hope you do not imagine I could waver an inch from impartiality!" said he, shocked. "I am awfully sorry if things are not going your way, but—"

"Live by the sword, die by the sword," said Marchmont firmly to his sister. "Go ahead, old man—give them a good stir."

Lord Weld stirred vigorously as he finished reading: "Fourth card, recital and supper, Lady Mufftow, Friday week. Fifth card—" he went on, reaching in deeply. "Fifth card . . . is . . ."

"It's got to be mine!"

"Fifth card is . . ." he repeated, hand still in the bowl.

"Weld, pick a card!" ordered Marchmont, catching the suspense. "And it hasn't *got* to be yours at all, Emilia. Remember, there were twenty to begin with."

"Yes, but twelve of them were—"

"Yours!" shouted Lord Weld of a sudden. "It *is* yours, Lady

Emilia. Isn't it simply marvellous how these things come right in the end?"

The suspense had nearly overcome her, but now that it was done Emilia realized things could not have turned out better. "Marvellous," she agreed aloud, with a brilliant smile at her brother. "I just know you are going to enjoy that pic-nic tomorrow. Miss Pye was telling me the other day what a wonderful chat you and she had about her dear Mamma. She said you showed a great deal of insight! I was quite, quite pleased." She stood and walked—strutted would be more accurate—to the door, where she bade the gentlemen adieu.

"What is it called when you kill your sister?" asked Marchmont. "Fratricide? That doesn't sound right."

"Murder," suggested Weld.

"Murder," echoed the earl, standing. "Mmmmurder," he pronounced, savouring it. He made his way to the door rather dreamily. "Murder. Yes. Murrrrderrr. I like the sound of that, Weld. Murder."

5

Sir Jeffery de Guere was feeling in excellent twig. His new
blue frock-coat suited him; the cool April evening suited him;
the note he had just received from a certain Mrs. Butler suited
him. He would dine at his club, he decided, as he climbed into
his phaeton, then pay a visit to that new gaming-hell near Pall
Mall . . . and perhaps, if his pocket was a little plumper when
he left there than it was just now, perhaps Mrs. Butler would
not be averse to seeing him when he left there. He was aware,
as he started the horses, of a distinct sensation of well-being.

His path to the club took him, as luck would have it,
through Cavendish Square. There was a good deal of traffic in
that neighbourhood, he noticed, and could not help but observe further, as he gained the Square itself, that the traffic
was centred at the house of the Earl of Marchmont: his
cousin's house, in fact. This interested Jeffery. In his mood of
bonhomie he could almost think of his kinsman with fondness,

he discovered; and in a flood of cousinly emotion, he determined to stop in at number twenty-one Cavendish Square and give these relatives of his the advantage of his company. The fact of his purse being rather low at the moment, while the prices at his club were rather high, also weighed with him a little, it is true.

Mr. Searle, the butler, received him with surprise. "I was not aware, sir," he began, and stopped. He knew very well that Sir Jeffery had not been invited, and he could guess that he was not welcome either. What ought he to do? He decided to treat the call as if there had been no party in progress. "Shall I send your card up to Lord Marchmont, Sir Jeffery?"

"That will not be necessary," said the young visitor pleasantly. He removed his light cape with something of a flourish and looked about himself. "I daresay with this sort of a crowd one guest more or less will hardly matter." He handed the cape and his hat and stick to the second parlour-maid and made as if to go upstairs. "You might tell the staff to lay an extra place."

"If you don't mind, sir," commenced Searle, but his attention was immediately diverted by the arrival of the Charles Stickneys. Sir Jeffery made use of the momentary diversion.

"But I do mind," he said quietly, and slipped up the staircase. Discovering the manoeuvre an instant afterwards, Searle sent a footman up to Lord Marchmont with the news of his cousin's presence, but he knew it was too late to be of any use.

"Damn him to hell," Lady Emilia muttered from between tight lips as she caught a first glimpse of Jeffery. She had been standing by Marchmont greeting her guests, and her brother heard the malediction with a little ripple of surprise.

"Dearest Emilia, you must not abuse those nasty words," he began, bowing and smiling to Lord Mufftow, but then he too caught sight of de Guere, and revised his opinion. "On the other hand, what are nasty words for if not to be employed judiciously?" he murmured. He went forward hastily and grasped Jeffery rather roughly by the hand. "Well, well, old fellow! What the devil are you doing here?"

"Happy to see me, are you?" said the genial cousin with a grin. "Emmy, you are a picture of springtime. You'd have made Thomas Gainsborough weep, indeed, you would."

"I don't suppose there's any hope of persuading you to leave quietly," she greeted him in return.

"I like a girl whose head can't be turned by flattery," said he equably.

"I don't want you to be here. You are not invited," said she.

"But I *am* here. And I'd hate to leave! Don't make me," begged he charmingly.

"I cannot make you leave," was the sharp reply. "Not without a scene, as you perfectly well know."

"Then it's settled!" he cried, looking about the room as if taking possession of it. His dark hair gleamed beautifully. "I'll stay."

Emilia looked grimly to her brother. "Jemmy, say a few words like a good boy, will you?"

Lord Marchmont obliged. "De Guere, if you cause the least little trouble tonight, if I hear of you vexing a single lady, or embarrassing one, I shall make you regret it, on my word. Do you understand?"

"My dear coz," replied the other, looking him straight in the eyes, "I'm afraid it is you who does not understand. I do not vex the ladies! Oh, no! Quite, quite, quite the contrary. Ladies simply adore me," he explained, adding, "I see you've one or two delicious little bundles here tonight whom I've never seen before. I look forward to making their acquaintance." He bowed briefly to Emilia again and began to move off.

"Sir Jeffery," her ladyship hissed, clutching at his sleeve to prevent his departure, "Lucilla Partridge is coming tonight." She spoke in an intense undertone. "You are not to go near her, do you hear me? I will not have it, scene or no scene."

"My dear, you are asking a gourmet not to go near spoiled meat," said he rather fastidiously. "The request is entirely superfluous."

"A gourmet!" she sputtered to his back as it disappeared into the growing crowd. "A gourmand, he should say. Or rather, a vulture. Spoiled meat is just his dish. And anyhow, what a thing to call a woman! And who spoiled her?" she demanded in conclusion, beside herself with rage.

Lord Marchmont attempted to calm her as Lord and Lady Trevor were announced, followed immediately by Lord Halcot, the Stanbroke girls, and Amy Lewis. The handsome drawing-room at number twenty-one was now alive with the high hum of early-evening conversation. Clusters of guests tied themselves into elegant knots, as if by design, then slowly untangled and trailed away in beautiful, slow, ever-shifting patterns. An hundred candles lit their faces and caused their elegant silks and satins to glisten. As chance would have it—as fate, perhaps, would have it—one particularly high blaze of candlelight in a far corner of the room attracted the attention of Lady Isabella Stanbroke as she swept towards her hostess. That particular blaze revealed below it the gleaming hair and striking features of (has the reader anticipated Fate?) Sir Jeffery de Guere. In that moment poor Isabella's heart was lost.

The ordinary courtesies were passed between arriving guests and hospitable hosts. Lady Elizabeth looked into Lord Marchmont's eyes and let her steady gaze rest there just a trifle longer, it may be, than was strictly necessary—but then, this was only her second opportunity of seeing the handsome earl, so perhaps it was natural she should look a little carefully. Lord Marchmont, for his part, had had no better opportunity of observing Lady Elizabeth than she had had of him, and so his equal return of her briefly arrested glance was, no doubt, only natural as well. It was really nothing out of the common. Bells did not ring, nor flames flare. As a matter of fact, barely two seconds later Lord Marchmont was discussing carriage-springs with the lady's father, while the lady herself exchanged words with Emilia regarding the health of the King. What greater evidence could one desire? Here was no hero, nor any heroine to meet him. I daresay everyone is satisfied on the point.

Lady Isabella on the other hand was fairly atremble. "Who can he be?" she breathed in a low voice to Amy, whose hand she clutched in a damp grasp, while the two of them wandered into the crowd.

"Who can who be?"

"But that . . . man!"

"My dearest, what do you mean?"

"Oh Amy, can it be you have not observed him? The tall, handsome gentleman in the corner, in the blue frock-coat. He is staring at us," she insisted, of course striving mightily as she indicated the person in question to appear to be doing anything else in the world.

"The one with the long chin?" asked the other.

"How can you say it is long?" cried Isabella, though quietly. "Have you no heart at all? Oh, my dear, I am positively faint."

"Shall we go out for some air?" asked the innocent Amy. "Or, I am certain Lady Emilia will let you lie down in her room, since you feel unwell."

"Unwell? I don't remember when I have felt so vigorous. I could not leave the room for a moment. Amy," she repeated, "have you no heart?"

To Isabella's great sorrow and frustration, she was given no opportunity of meeting the marvel she so admired until well after dinner. That repast was announced within minutes of her arrival, and she found with despair that Lady Emilia meant her to sit between Sir John Firebrace and the distressingly jolly Mr. Charles Stickney, quite at the opposite end of the table to where the mysterious gentleman was placed. She could see that he too regretted the distance between them; indeed, she observed him trying to take a seat closer to her

than had been given him, but Lord Marchmont prevented the
move. Isabella did have time as they gathered round the table,
however, to inquire of her hostess in a hasty whisper the iden-
tity of the young man.

"Dear Lord, I hope you don't mean Jeffery," came the
heartfelt reply. "If you mean the fellow next to Lady
Mufftow—"

"Yes!"

"Forget him, I pray. There is a very particular reason why
you must. He is—"

"Is he married?"

"No, but he is—"

"Then it is all right," sighed Bella.

"Scarcely! I shall tell you in the drawing-room. Remind
me," said Lady Emilia, moving off to attend to other duties,
but making a careful mental note to be sure to speak to Isabella after dinner. It would not do to let the poor girl suppose
Jeffery was a suitable object for her affection. Unfortunately,
her brief words of warning had had the contrary effect to the
one she desired: Isabella, assured that the man was single,
spent the greater part of dinner vowing to herself that no
other difficulty could stand between her and this adorable
Jeffery. (And what a sweet, solid sound that name had, now
she thought of it! Jeffery!) Perhaps he is ill, she said to herself,
and this is the reason Emilia warns me against him. Perhaps
he is consumptive and has only a few years to live. No matter!
I shall love him none the less; our love will be a bright, hot fire
till the very last moment—and then I shall expire of a broken
heart.

But perhaps he is poor! she next considered. Well, that is of
no moment. If Emilia thinks I should be stopped by such a
circumstance, she knows me very little indeed (of course Emilia *did* know her very little indeed, having met her only once
before, but this fact did not impede Lady Isabella's indigna-
tion).

Having dispensed with this, the dim thought occurred to her (but only very dimly indeed) that the paragon might be untitled. Perhaps he was even—oh, unspeakable possibility!—illegitimate. Lady Isabella paused in the midst of chewing a salmon croquette and struggled with the idea. After a moment she swallowed. It was no matter: she would stand by him still.

Had she thought of every possible objection? She believed she had. She stole a glance at Jeffery (she had by now stolen quite a packet of them in fact) and felt her determination redouble. She had always known her destiny would find her one day. It had certainly declared itself clearly now: young Jeffery was looking back. When the ladies withdrew from the table, Isabella experienced a positive pang of grief at having to leave the neighbourhood of her beloved. She dragged listlessly into the drawing-room with the others, nor did life recover meaning until Lady Emilia sat down beside her and addressed the subject of Jeffery.

"De Guere is his full name," she said, with her beautiful, generous smile, "Sir Jeffery de Guere, and he is—though I say it myself, and he is a cousin of mine—the greatest beast in nature. I am glad you asked me about him, for I should not like to think of you wasting a minute on him."

A minute! My life! thought the loyal Isabella, but she said aloud only, "How exactly is he a beast? He does not look a beast."

"Oh, my dear!" Lady Emilia took her small hands with her own, strong ivory ones. "He was not even invited here tonight. He simply came. Can you imagine the impudence?"

Destiny! thought Bella.

"And then—well, you are a deal too young for the particulars, but you must take it from me he is a dreadful, odious rake. That may sound dashing to you," Emilia went on, for a vague intimation of the truth was beginning to come to her, "but all it means in fact is that he has caused a very great deal of pain and unhappiness to people who deserved it very little.

And he is a gamester, too," she added in an afterthought. "And not even a good one."

Isabella took this all in in silence. She made no response now save a nod of her pretty head. Lady Elizabeth had seated herself at the pianoforte and was playing a delicate, serious air by Handel: the lovely music made Bella's head feel even lighter than it already did, and she regarded Emilia as through a mist of solemn joy. She felt as if God had been good to her: here she had been prepared for illness and poverty and low rank, when after all Jeffery's only sins (and he *was* Sir Jeffery) were a little carelessness in love and at cards. These were light burdens, indeed. She said over the name to herself: Lady Isabella de Guere. It sounded very well.

"Are you all right?" Emilia asked at length, for the girl beside her looked strange indeed. "Miss Lewis," she called, "come and sit with us, will you not? I think your friend may be ill."

Amy Lewis joined them, pleased at all events to be released from the conversation of Miss Amabel Pye. She had been extremely glad to find the Miss Lemons were not among the company: it had been beginning to seem as if one could not go anywhere without meeting them, for they had been at the Opera the previous evening, and at the Lindsey's the night before that. She sat down now on Bella's other side and looked at her anxiously. "You do not feel faint again, I hope?"

"Was she faint earlier?" asked Emilia, concerned.

"Oh no," said Isabella.

"Yes, a little," said Amy.

Emilia's smile returned. "Which is it?"

"A little of both," Amy said. "I thought she ought to take some air."

"Indeed she ought."

"It is really not—" began Isabella.

But Emilia led her firmly to a long Venetian window, through which the three ladies stepped onto a balcony overlooking a tiny garden.

"How pleasant the night air feels!" exclaimed Isabella, struck with its cool freshness.

"Oh for the days of girlhood!" Emilia said comically. "I am sure at your age I should have said the same, but now all I can think of is the chill, and how likely one is to take a cold from the dampness."

Amy Lewis began, "I can stay with Bella. Please, go in if you are uncomfortable—"

"Not for the world," said the older woman firmly. "Not until you tell me what is in young girls' hearts these days— though I suppose it cannot be too very different from what was once in mine. Tell me, do the gentlemen look very fine to you?"

"Oh, very fine," said Amy indifferently, when Bella did not answer.

"Oh my, this is weakly spoken! Can it be that they have no charms to move your generation? I must warn my brother. He will need some new tricks!"

Miss Lewis laughed a little. "I am afraid I do not look too closely at them, as a rule. At least . . . I mean, I am sure the company here is as splendid as any could be, only—"

"Oh, Amy thinks only of my—" Isabella stopped just short of the whole secret and amended, "thinks only of one gentleman. If gentleman is the word I want," she appended scornfully.

"I gather the fellow in question is not a favourite with you?"

"Hardly."

Amy, much relieved by the comparative quiet of the balcony, found the strength to speak up. "I fear Lady Isabella is in no position to judge fairly. Really I am quite happy with— with my lot."

"The fellow in question could not by any chance be Lord Halcot?" Emilia suggested lightly, and was afraid for a moment that both young ladies might fall off the balcony in surprise.

"How can you know?" demanded Isabella, while Amy gasped. "What a thought!"

Emilia laughed, inwardly thanking heaven for removing her from the dangerous waters of extreme youth. "When one young lady disparages the idol of her best friend," she explained, "it is a good bet that idol is related to the first young lady. There is no magic to it. But is Lord Halcot not—does he not return your esteem, my dear?" she asked as delicately as she could.

"Lord Halcot," pronounced Isabella, "is an idiot."

"I am sure he is fond of me," said Amy bravely, for she was not even really sure of this.

"Only he thinks of her as—"

"As his sister's friend," finished Emilia for her. The girls both nodded agreement. "It is a difficult position," Emilia went on, as if thinking aloud. "I once had a friend who simply adored Marchmont. Naturally he never looked twice at her. Men are so obtuse." She fell into silence.

"What happened to your friend?" Lady Isabella finally inquired, for she could not rest till she knew the whole of a story.

"Oh! She married a duke," said Emmy. "But you would not care to marry a duke, would you, Miss Lewis? No, it is not in your style at all."

Amy agreed, with a sad shake of the head, that a duke would not answer. "I beg you will not exercise your mind upon this—situation," she said, repeating, "I am quite happy."

"Amy could be happy in a dungeon," alleged her friend.

"I fancy she could. However, we must see to it she is kept out of dungeons nevertheless," Emilia said briskly, "and moreover, we may perhaps be able to open Lord High-and-Mighty Halcot's eyes a little. I shall think on it."

"Dear ma'am—" began Miss Lewis.

But, "Not another word, I pray. We have subjected you to what must have been a very painful scrutiny," interrupted

Emilia. "Now you must forget all about it and see if we can't salvage some good from all this curiosity. Lady Isabella, if you are feeling quite well now, I think I ought to return to my guests." With these words Emilia led the way again into the drawing-room where Lady Elizabeth was still playing sweetly upon the pianoforte.

In a few moments the gentlemen began to return to the assembly, not a few of them quite obviously in improved spirits for having drunk a little port. Miss Partridge, who had been looking a little pale ever since catching sight of Jeffery de Guere, now drew up to her hostess on the arm of her mother to murmur an apologetic farewell. "I hate to leave so early," she said earnestly, "only—I can't think why, I feel a little dizzy. Now that Papa is ready, I believe I ought to go home and lie down."

Emilia looked into her large brown eyes sympathetically. "Of course, my dear. I am so awfully sorry. I assure you—I mean I hope when you come again there will be nothing to disturb you." It would have been rude to allude to Jeffery any more directly than this, but Emilia knew the girl understood her. At that moment de Guere himself entered the room. Miss Partridge fairly shrank back to the protection of her mother. Emilia knew without even looking what must have caused this alarm, and she expertly guided the girl and her parent to the door in such a manner as to prevent Jeffery's coming close to her. She bade the family good night with a surge of bitter anger at her cousin. The look of fright and pain on Lucilla Partridge's face had been unmistakable. Really, it was a crime to allow such a man to roam loose in the streets.

Lady Elizabeth still kept her place at the pianoforte; indeed, when she had tried to rise from the instrument a murmur of distress had gone up among the ladies and she had been persuaded to continue. Now that the gentlemen were with them, a few drifted over to listen. Among these few was Lord Marchmont, observed from a little distance (but with no little interest or amusement) by his friend Lord Warrington Weld.

Elizabeth played very well. Music had indeed been always her greatest pleasure, and she excelled at it naturally. Many otherwise empty and tedious hours at Haddon Abbey had been made pleasant and satisfying for her by her sessions at the keyboard in the music room there, and her musical prowess was considered quite remarkable among the neighbourhood. Nor did Elizabeth limit herself to the ordinary airs and ballads young ladies were expected to play. Not without difficulty (for Haddon Abbey was hardly at a centre of culture) she had procured music by the finest composers of her own age, as well as those of preceding eras. Complexity did not daunt her; her small, graceful hands were also strong and supple; in short, the music she produced was hardly less beautiful than what might be heard in a concert hall or theatre. She was playing, when the gentlemen returned, a sweet, grave sonata by Mozart.

"Beautiful," pronounced Lord Marchmont quietly, when she had done. "Quite, and simply, beautiful. I dare say Mrs. Mozart herself did not understand her husband better." The gentle spell the music had cast over him began to break, and he added (a vision of Charlotte Beaudry in his head), "Though I doubt there was a Mrs. Mozart. If there had been he would not have had time to accomplish all he did."

Lady Elizabeth laid her pretty hands in her lap and looked up at his lordship. "There *was* a Mrs. Mozart," she informed him. "In fact, I should not be surprised to learn there still is one. She may yet be living, for he died so young."

"She may yet be living," said Marchmont, "but I should be very surprised indeed to learn she is still Mrs. Mozart. No doubt she has found some nice Viennese confectioner, whose masterpieces come a little easier. I am sure it must have been very vexatious for Mrs. Mozart—Mrs. Mozart that was, I mean—to be obliged to listen to that scratchy old harpsichord all day long . . . and all night too, sometimes, in all probability."

Elizabeth raised her eyebrows. "My dear sir, what a very black picture you paint of marriage!"

"Paint?" he echoed. "It is hardly necessary to paint it: it is visible all round us."

"I beg your pardon?"

"I mean, dear ma'am, that one had only to take a look at any married couple in the room to see what a grim institution marriage is."

"Institution? You make it sound as if it were a prison."

"Here we are again: 'You make it sound.' Make it sound, indeed! It has no need to be made to sound anything. It *is* a prison."

Elizabeth was not without her sharp edges, but she had no such cynicism as this, nor had she ever encountered the like before. For a moment she sat silent, nonplussed. A voice broke into this lapse between them, the voice of Sir John Firebrace complaining because the music had stopped. "It is all very well for you, Marchmont," he said, "for you hear the music of the lady's speech. But the rest of us are suffering." Elizabeth smiled at this sally and began to play a little air—but she had hardly managed two measures before she left off again to address the earl. Those who had been clustered round her to hear the music now began to drift away, soon leaving her *tête-à-tête* with Marchmont.

"If marriage is so dreadful as all that, my lord," she asked him finally, "why do you suppose people continue to enter into it?"

The earl did not hesitate. "Property," said he.

"Property?"

"Property and propriety. The two great *pros* of marriage."

Again she knew not how to answer, but only looked at him.

"On the *con* side," he went on after a moment, "we have conviviality, contentedness, constancy—all of these go on a great deal more easily outside of marriage than within it. But we must satisfy society, oh, indeed we must, and so we invent this appalling ritual."

Elizabeth began to feel amused. "Allow me to mention *progeny,* my lord—and to suggest it is your *convenience* more than anything else which is disturbed by marriage. But you interest me greatly," she went on. "Would you be so kind as to let me know exactly who, in your opinion, suffers more in the jaws of this odious machine? Is it the wife or the husband, do you suppose?"

"Oh, the husband by all means," he answered at once. "Sometimes I think the wife positively enjoys the business!"

"Though of course such an idea is ridiculous."

"Yes, of course. In my more lucid moments I see that."

"Though there is no doubt in your mind it is the husband who fares worse?"

"*Can* there be any doubt?"

She searched the drawing-room briefly, looking for one party in particular. She noticed as she did so her sister deep in conversation with Sir Jeffery de Guere. How different if Marchmont had made this observation, for he would certainly have removed Isabella from so perilous a place! But his back was to them. Lady Elizabeth searched on, presently finding her target. "Look," she said to the earl in a low tone, indicating by her glance whom she meant. "Look at Mrs. Charles Stickney, if you will. Do you remember her when she was Miss Frane? I do."

Lord Marchmont acknowledged that he did, but continued to appear unmoved.

"Was she not a pretty girl then?"

"Yes."

"A happy girl?"

"To all appearances."

"Full of fond dreams?"

"We may presume."

"And high hopes?"

"If you like."

"How does she seem to you now, my lord?"

He quizzed her briefly through his glass. "A pleasant-enough woman," was the verdict. "A trifle worn, perhaps."

"Worn indeed," she murmured. "Now do me the kindness to look at your sister, my lord."

"My sister? It is not necessary, I think. I remember her pretty well," he smiled.

"Very good. Would you call her a pleasant-appearing woman?"

"I would do a great deal better than that! I would call her very handsome," he replied indignantly, placing one foot neatly in the trap. "Wouldn't you?"

"Indeed I should. And would you characterize your sister as—a trifle worn, I think you said?"

The earl obligingly lifted his other foot and set it alongside its mate. "Certainly not," he maintained energetically. "There is not another woman half so fresh as she within five miles of here. Saving yourself, naturally," he added with lame courtesy.

"My dear sir, you have proved my point entirely. The great difference between Mrs. Stickney and Lady Emilia is, you will confess, that one is married while the other is not. Had Dorothea Frane shown the sense your sister has, she would not have married either, and instead of calling her 'pleasant-appearing' (oh abominable faint praise!) and 'worn,' you'd be panting to impress her with your wit and charm, and hoping against hope for a smile from her. Just as," she continued resolutely when he tried to interrupt her with a protest, "just as my Lord Weld is even now attempting to wrest a smile from Emilia."

Lord Marchmont turned in surprise to find that, indeed, Weld was leaning down to whisper to Emilia with, to all appearances, the intent of making her smile. (The reader might imagine he would also, on turning, have seen Isabella and de Guere—but these two had disáppeared by now, of which more later.) Marchmont returned his attention to Elizabeth and spoke rather too emphatically. "First of all," he told her, "if Weld is trying to make Emmy smile, it is only to be agreeable for my sake. She is my sister and he is my friend, and I assure you there is no intrigue there."

Elizabeth neither looked nor felt convinced, but she kept silent.

"Secondly, with all due respect for Mrs. Stickney, I must maintain that she never was Emilia's match, and that if she had not married she would now be seated in a corner with a cap atop her head, looking rather grey and exchanging last month's gossip with some elderly matron or other."

"Instead of looking practically dead with fatigue," Elizabeth supplied, "and being squashed to the end of the sofa by Sir John Firebrace, whose back is to her, and who is so absorbed with the perfections of Miss Pye (whatever these elusive items may be) that he does not even realize she is there."

This description was too accurate to be denied, but, "Perhaps she has only exchanged one middling fate for another," said Marchmont in reply. "You have proven nothing, in any case."

"Fustian!" cried she. "I have proven everything. And if there were need of more evidence—which there is not—a look at her husband would suffice. Do look at him, I pray you," she urged. "He is standing by the mantelpiece. Observe the pinkness of his cheeks, his sleek skin, his well-fed belly. Why, I dareswear he's put on two stone since they were married—but is he loved any the less for that? No. Has he thrice been confined, thrice suffered unspeakably, in the struggle to bring forth an heir? No. No!" she repeated. "All he has had to do is sit back and try not to show his disappointment in his wife too very much—for she has failed to give him a son. She! Failed to give him a son! I ask you, what sort of a failure is that? But if you don't think she herself is miserable over her inadequacy, I assure you you are very much mistaken. Easier on the wife, you are sure. You have a very interesting idea of logic, dear sir," she finished rather wildly. To say truth she had had no intention of revealing so much emotion, but there was something smug about his attitude that provoked her intolerably. Now that she had finished, she felt embarrassed by her passionate display, and she sat staring quietly at her hands.

Lord Marchmont regarded her with a new curiosity. She was very lovely: her cheeks had gone pink with excitement as she spoke, and a few tendrils of her fine blond hair had worked themselves loose from their plaits and coils. He saw her raise her hands unthinkingly to the keyboard, but she merely held them there as if frozen, then dropped them again. The thought of the music she might have made, had been making when he came into the drawing-room, affected him suddenly, and he said, with an oddly tender tremble in his voice, "Will you never marry then, Lady Elizabeth?"

She looked up as if startled, and her blue eyes met his grey ones with a full, momentarily unguarded glance. For an instant she did not know what to answer, then, "I suppose I must do as my father says in that regard," she murmured. "It is not an idea on which I exercise my thoughts a great deal."

This was not the answer he had expected. He leaned forward so abruptly that she involuntarily withdrew a little. "Will you indeed do as your father says?" he asked gently. "Does it not frighten you to place your future in his hands?"

She reflected briefly. "My future has been in his hands so often before," she brought out at last, with a smile, "that I expect I have got accustomed to it. To be frank, it is a little frightening; but then, nothing good is easily gained. And in any case, my alternatives are few."

"If your father desired you to marry a man you did not respect, would you do so?" he pursued.

"I do not believe my father would desire such a thing. No, I am sure he could not entrust me to anyone unworthy of respect."

"Granting that, then, suppose he were to desire you to marry a man you could respect, but for whom you felt no affection. Would you still serve your father in that case?"

"I do not think of it as service," she said a trifle stiffly. "My father loves me, and so do I love him."

"But if he gave you to a man you could not love. Would you go?" the earl persisted. His face was only a few inches now from her own, and she felt almost dizzy.

"If I felt I could not be a good wife to him," she said slowly, "I imagine I would be obliged to refuse to marry altogether."

"You would remain always a spinster rather than marry a man you did not care for?" he clarified, still watching her closely.

She felt like an animal brought to bay. Striving to hold her own, she gave an emphatic nod.

"Though it meant you would be alone all your life?"

"The terrors of solitude are not so great if one enjoys his own company," she returned.

"And that no one would love you?" he persisted inexorably, as if she had not spoken.

"I am already loved."

"But that no *man* would love you," he insisted.

"My dear sir, this interrogation has taken a rather eccentric turn," she finally exclaimed, feeling cowardly for breaking the emotional intensity between them but fearing she might faint if it went on much longer. "In fact, one would have to call it quite exotic. Can it mean anything to you, my lord?" she inquired.

He was looking at her hard; then, as if he had satisfied himself of something important, he broke his long scrutiny and gave an odd, short laugh. "You would not refuse to marry," he declared. "Not if you knew eternal spinsterhood lay the other way."

Lady Elizabeth jumped to her feet. "Do you suggest, sir,

that I would marry and prove a bad wife before I would brave a single life?" she demanded.

"To be blunt, I do."

Fury was visible in her every feature as she stood before him. The idea of knocking him down was uppermost in her mind, but as this was impossible she only locked eyes with him and hoped he could guess her emotions. "Lord Marchmont," she said tensely, "you have a very low idea of women. Where you acquired it I do not know. I am certain it was not from your sister. I can only be glad to reflect, however, that neither the responsibility of causing it nor the desire of changing it belongs to me. Good evening, my lord."

She started to move past him, though with no very clear idea of where she was going. Out of the room, was all she could think, before she lost her temper altogether. The insufferable Marchmont jumped into her way, however, before she had gone three steps. The expression of his countenance suggested both horror at his own behaviour and abject apology towards her—which was indeed what he wished to express. "I cannot imagine—Lady Elizabeth, please, I pray you will believe—I have no notion what could have made me speak in such a—" he sputtered, "such a beastly . . . My dear ma'am, I beg you will tell me what I may do to repair . . . It is quite unpardonable, quite—Lady Elizabeth, I am so sorry! Give me another moment, I will not abuse it," he pleaded, as she continued to try to get past him.

"My lord?" she said. She bit her lip in anger, but she held still.

He looked wildly about the room. He seemed surprised and annoyed to find it still full of guests. "Please, come with me where it is quiet. I must do something to—please." He took her arm with too much urgency for her to resist and led her out the drawing-room doors and into his own study. There was no one there; a few candles had been lit, but no fire. Mechanically he started to close the door.

"I beg you will leave that ajar," she said quickly.

The earl withdrew his hand from the knob as if it had been a live coal. He looked at his hand, appearing to examine it as one would an object of unknown origin and purpose. "I cannot fathom what has made me so odd tonight," he presently began, though in fact he knew it was the memory of Charlotte Beaudry's faithlessness. He faced her. She was standing in the middle of the room looking out into the corridor.

"There is no need to explain," she brought out primly.

"There is every need, and to apologize too. I am so—"

"I beg you will not apologize," she broke in with the same prim demeanour. "Nothing so out of the common has occurred as to occasion an apology."

"But it has," he replied, with great simplicity, then almost pleaded, "admit that it has, dear ma'am."

She looked down at her feet. "Very well, then. It has."

"Something out of the common has happened," he repeated.

"My lord, I should like to rejoin the others," she said.

He looked at her carefully. "Something out of the common. Lady Elizabeth, I cannot say why, but your company elicits some extraordinary response from me."

Elizabeth was really very uncomfortable about being alone with him, even with the door open. She feared she would be missed. Marchmont's behaviour was so very erratic. She said, with more than ordinary candour, "You are frightening me, sir."

He continued to stare at her, then once again broke away as if he had satisfied himself of something. "Yes. Indeed," he said. "Oh! Am I frightening you?" he burst out, as if he had just then heard her. "Small wonder." He offered his arm and began to escort her from the room. "Lady Elizabeth, I give you thanks for this interview. Will you let me have another?"

"I beg your pardon, sir?"

"Will you let me call upon you, ma'am? I should be most honoured."

Her anger now subsiding into bafflement, Lady Elizabeth said diffidently that he might if he cared to.

"I thank you, ma'am," answered he, with what she could only view as fervour. Of all the conversations she could remember, this was surely the oddest. She was just making this observation to herself as they entered the hallway. She must have been distracted by the thought, for she nearly walked straight into Isabella, pink-cheeked and with her blond hair streaming, flying from a darkened doorway further down the corridor.

6

WHILE IT is not so alarming, perhaps, as the sight of a star shooting madly from its sphere, the spectacle of a young lady with flushed cheeks and tousled hair running from a dark room during a dinner party is none the less unusual, and deserves investigation. How then did Lady Isabella come to be hastening down that corridor in Cavendish Square? A brief return in time is needed to discover the answer.

When dinner (itself worthy of description and a place in the annals of culinary history—but not here) had been concluded, and the ladies had taken themselves off to the drawing-room, Charlie, Lord Halcot, found himself sitting next to a man who identified himself as Sir Jeffery de Guere. Charlie, genial young chap, struck up a conversation with him at once and soon learned that this de Guere knew more of the current state of pugilism than either himself or John Firebrace. He even knew (he said) who had rigged the fight on which Charlie had lately lost five pounds, but the gentleman in question was, unfortunately, now out of England. From pugilism the talk drifted on to faro, and thence to horseflesh. Charlie drank off a glass or two of Madeira and considered his new friend a very fine fellow. Another glass and a short dissertation on the finenesses of blind-hookey persuaded him de Guere possessed a keen intelligence, and a fourth bumper left him with the conviction that he had stumbled upon a virtual prince among men. The excellent fortune of happening to make such an acquaintance very naturally put him in a good humour, and by the time the gentlemen rejoined the ladies Lord Halcot would have highly recommended de Guere to anyone who asked.

Nothing could have suited Isabella better, of course. Having first abandoned the timid Amy Lewis to the garrulous Lady Mufftow, Isabella quite naturally wandered over to her brother's side. Here she was at last made known to the gentleman (she felt) she had known all her life. Here, palms damp and cold with excitement, she heard in his compliments the first confirmation of what she had read in his eyes. Her pretty denials of his high praise were suitably feeble; Sir Jeffery escalated the assault; Isabella grew even meeker in her contradictions—and Lord Halcot was soon bored half off his head. With a quick bow he retired from this battle of flowers and went off alone to wonder why his ears were ringing.

Isabella's heart beat ever higher. Observed thus nearly, Sir Jeffery was even more handsome than she'd imagined. The bright intensity of his dark liquid eye seemed to pierce her very spirit, and the mobile beauty of his smile was fascinating. Lady Emilia had talked of him so harshly. Was it possible, Bella began to wonder, that Emilia herself was in love with him and so spoke from a desire to eliminating rivals? Was it possible to see him and *not* be in love with him? Lady Emilia, by the by, was too busy speculating with Lord Weld on the possibility of a match between her brother and Lady Elizabeth Stanbroke (for these two were now engaged in their highly animated discussion) to notice that de Guere had taken Elizabeth's sister for his prey. Lord Weld was being excessively amusing, and Emilia had decided to enjoy the evening a little, even if it was her party.

Sir Jeffery was not the intellectual luminary Lord Halcot imagined him to be, but he was as shrewd a man as ever lived when he wanted a thing. What he wanted right now was Isabella, and an evil angel prompted him to mention Sir Walter Scott. Isabella's whole frame seemed to vibrate at the very name, for it was just such a heroine as Scott's that she longed to be herself, and she responded with great warmth. "Do you read Scott, sir?" she inquired somewhat incredulously, for she had had no experience of romantic men.

"But certainly, mademoiselle," said he. "One would be a fool not to do so, don't you agree?"

Her joy was boundless. "Have you read *Guy Mannering?*" she demanded breathlessly.

"It is my favourite of his."

"Is it? But it is mine as well!" she exclaimed, never for an instant imagining that he had easily guessed as much from her mentioning it first, and had for that reason proclaimed it as his own. As luck would have it, he had in fact read a little piece of it, and so he was enabled to turn the topic to his very good advantage.

"The fact is," he said carefully, smiling down upon her, "I have named my matched greys Salt and Pepper after Dandie Dinmont's terriers."

"But they are not called Salt and Pepper," she objected, prepared to cite chapter and verse if necessary. "They are called Mustard and Pepper!"

"No!"

"But yes, I assure you."

The sight of her earnest blue eyes roused no sense of shame in this consummate rogue, who in fact owned no horses whatever, and consequently was in no position to name them either rightly or wrongly. "Mademoiselle, you alarm me greatly," said he, succeeding pretty well in looking alarmed. "What shall I do? You say I have named my horses in error. Can you be right?"

"But I am right," she persisted, wide-eyed. "I am terribly sorry to be the one to tell you, but . . . I can scarcely conceive how you made the mistake, Sir Jeffery, for since it is your favourite book—!" She left the sentence there and looked up at him almost apologetically.

"Dearest girl, if this is true, it is a blow. Yet I cannot believe—Oh, yes! I know what we must do," he cried suddenly, as if just taken with a shining solution. "Come with me," he commanded, moving swiftly towards the door.

"Where are we going?"

"I have just realized my cousin Emilia is certain to have a copy of *Guy Mannering* in her library," he explained. "We will go and settle this once for all."

"But Sir Jeffery—" she hesitated, not liking to leave the room alone with him. She glanced about for her parents and discovered they had joined Lady Mufftow and Amy. The four were apparently much absorbed in their talk—and Elizabeth was clearly lost in conversation with Lord Marchmont—and Charlie was not to be seen (he was out on the balcony trying to make his head stop spinning), and so . . . Isabella concluded it would be all right to slip out, just this once, with Jeffery— especially since the circumstances were so particularly urgent. She fell into step beside him and followed him down the corridor. "I daresay I could be mistaken," she murmured dubiously as they went, then, "My goodness but it is dark here!"

"Chilly, too," he agreed. "But anything in the name of knowledge, after all! Keep close by me, my dear Lady Isabella; I should not like anything to happen to you in the dark."

"But how shall we find the book?" asked the innocent.

Sir Jeffery took a taper from a sconce in the hallway and used it to light a candle dimly perceived on a table in the tiny, book-lined library. He replaced the taper and took a quick glance at the footman in the corridor. The man did not appear to know or care if anything were amiss. Sir Jeffery rejoined Isabella.

"I have been trying to see the titles," said she, turning to him from the far wall, "but I'm afraid the light is too low even for me. I have rather good eyesight," she confided, suddenly nervous at finding herself in the shadows with him.

"My dear!" he burst out, then was silent.

Lady Isabella hastened towards him. There had been something poignant in his tone—or at least it seemed so to her. "Sir Jeffery?" she barely breathed.

He said nothing.

"Sir Jeffery?" she repeated, trying to peer into his face. She took up the candle from the table behind her and held it up near him. He turned his head away from her. "Dear sir, what is it?"

He emitted a choking sound.

"Sir, are you well?" she demanded breathlessly. Never had her blood raced at such a fever-pitch; she had scarcely dared to dream of such an intrigue as this.

De Guere turned his face towards her again. By the light of the candle she could see it was suffused with emotion. Then she observed a detail she could but with difficulty credit.

"Dear sir," she exclaimed in a hushed tone, "are you crying?"

The tears shone in his eyes; at her words, one spilled onto his finely-coloured cheek. Isabella stared in thrilled astonishment. "My dear!" he finally repeated, just when she thought she would die waiting.

Involuntarily she reached for his hand. It rose to meet hers, and they touched. What a strong, warm hand his was! "Pray, tell me what can have happened to make you—" She could not bring herself to finish the sentence.

"Yes, I am crying," said de Guere at last. "But it is nothing—"

"What is it, what can have happened?" she insisted.

He dropped her hand. She regretted it and moved an inch

and a half closer to him. "Lady Isabella, may I tell you the truth?" he asked gently.

"Of course!"

"Lady Isabella—"

She moved another half-inch towards him.

"Lady Isabella, it is only that you are . . . so beautiful," he concluded on a broken note. His hands flew up as if by instinct to frame her glowing face. Her cheeks were hot. She met his gaze fully. "Dear girl, you will hate me."

"Never! What for?"

"What affair is it of mine, how beautiful you are? Were you thrice as beautiful—as if such a thing could ever be!—you could still never care for me." He allowed his hands to fall again, to Bella's great disappointment.

An inspiration came to her. She set the candle down uncertainly and grasped both his hands, carrying them again to her cheeks. "Now do you think I could never care for you?" She looked anxiously into his dark eyes.

"You do not mean—" His eyes gleamed intently into her own. "Can it be you felt it too?"

Her heart knocking against her chest, she nodded ever so slightly.

"From the first moment?" he demanded.

Another nod.

"Can such happiness be mine?" A second tear fell on his cheek as Sir Jeffery de Guere pronounced these words. He gathered her to him with hands that trembled violently. In a moment his mouth was upon hers and his long fingers had pushed deep into her shining hair. From Lady Isabella's throat issued a sound like something fragile breaking.

Now the reader will be growing impatient with Lady Isabella perhaps—and not without some reason. "What manner of heroine is this?" the reader may quite justifiably demand. "Has she no eyes in her head? Has she no ears? This man is a rake. Has she no sense?" Well, the reader will kindly remember, in the first place, that Isabella is not *our* heroine—Isabella is her *own* heroine. It is she, and not I, who believes something momentous is afoot here in the Earl of Marchmont's tiny library. It is she, and not I, who insists on seeing Sir Jeffery de Guere as a hero. *Our* heroine, I should like to take the opportunity of pointing out, is her sister Elizabeth—who, I must further observe, at the moment Isabella was carrying on so foolishly was easily holding her own against a peer of the realm. Now I don't care for Lady Isabella's way of doing business any more than does the reader: but if the reader supposes a romantic girl of sixteen will take the advice of a fusty old authoress when she has come to have her first interview ever alone with her True Love—then the reader has not spent much time in the company of sixteen-year-old girls. Not that I recommend such a course, by the way; far from it. Sixteen-year-old girls are preferable only to sixteen-year-old boys, in the general run of things—unless of course we are speaking of sixteen-year-old girls with the elegance and refinement to be reading such a book as this one.

For better or for worse, and whatever we may think of it, Isabella was now in Jeffery de Guere's arms, and the fact is she was extremely pleased and proud of herself for contriving to get into this situation. For such was the subtlety and fineness of de Guere's methods that he had managed to make her believe she had seduced him as much as he had seduced her. This was a specialty of his. He particularly liked it, since the girl's feeling of responsibility for her own predicament increased her desire of keeping the liaison a secret from her parents. It sometimes took a little longer, it was true—but there was no use rushing these things, he had found. Far better to give it time, to let the fruit ripen till it dropped from the tree of its own accord. Sir Jeffery, as he has already amply demonstrated, was a master of timing.

Accordingly he drew back from her as abruptly as he had reached out. "I have done wrong," he whispered hoarsely, to her infinite delight.

"Nothing is wrong which is done for—which is done in affection," she amended. Even Isabella did not presume to say the word *love* at such an early juncture.

He shook his head and seemed to withdraw into himself a little. "I am sorry. Lady Isabella, you must accept my apology. This scene will never be repeated, I assure you."

"But I want—"

"Never, never," he continued roughly. He looked away from her to stare into the candle. "I can never possess you in the eyes of the law. I can never possess you in the eyes of the world. So I must never . . . never . . ." He stopped.

"But why?" was surprised out of her.

He laughed with a sardonic edge he had perfected through years of practice. Good God it was exhilarating! he suddenly thought. There wasn't another game like it in the world. "My poor lamb," he answered, still looking away from her. "You have no idea who I am. I am a bad man."

"No!"

He laughed again, this time on a distinctly rueful note. "Well, in any case, I have a bad reputation. It amounts to the same thing. Your father will never let me near you."

"You wrong him! Father will understand. He does not judge men by rumour—"

"No, he will never allow it, and he will be right. Yes, quite right. No matter who he thought I was, nor how well he might think of me, your reputation would inevitably suffer by the connection, and I—I could not bear to bruise such a delicate flower."

"He would be a beast not to allow it!" asserted Isabella.

De Guere turned to her again, his eyes shining with fresh tears. He straightened himself and held out both hands to her. "So we must harden ourselves to it, my poor girl! This is as much happiness as we have been allowed. It was more than ever we knew before! We must be content."

But she refused to take the hands offered in friendship. "No. I do not accept that. I will not resign myself to that. Dear sir—"

"Say 'Jeffery,' just once, please!"

"Jeffery," she breathed, and he found himself of a sudden so deeply overcome that he simply had to gather her up again and kiss her with a frightful ardour. This time he opened her lips a little with the tip of his warm tongue. Isabella pulled back in surprise, then yielded when he did not let go. Delicious, delicious game! thought Jeffery, and he dropped her again from his embrace.

"Now it is over," he said dully.

"Please, do not say so!" She put an anxious hand up to his hair and touched it shyly. "Promise me you will meet me again."

He shrugged and smiled. "If we meet again, as we may do, in some drawing-room or other . . . well—"

"No no, I mean that you will come to see me. Meet me in public, if you do not care to come to my father's home. Meet me—meet me in the topmost gallery at Lackington Allen's," she burst out on a second inspiration, for the image of that quiet, retired spot had come to her in a flash. "Say you will. Meet me tomorrow. No," she corrected, realizing that the following day was Sunday, "come on Monday. Be there, at three o'clock. Oh, say you will not fail me. I must think this out and speak to you again. Jeffery!"

This plea is the one that resulted in the kiss that, in turn, resulted in Isabella's appearing in the corridor with cheeks aflame and hair streaming. This time when his mouth met hers she had already opened her lips to him, and now he thrust his hands so deeply into her curls that a number of pins dropped out. Satisfied that she would see him again and painfully aware that she had been absent from the others much too long, Isabella ended the interview herself by dancing from his arms and rushing headlong out the door. If de Guere could have stopped her he would have, for she was much in need of tidying up, but she had gone too swiftly. He still stood in the shadowy room a moment later when Lord Marchmont strode in with an oath upon his lips. Lady Elizabeth had caught Isabella in her flight, and the girl had blushed so deeply that

Lord Marchmont knew she must have left some gentleman in the library behind her. The truth occurred to him in an instant, and as he left the older sister to care for the younger he bitterly cursed his cousin.

"Damn you!" ran the spoken imprecation; the silent one was stronger. "What the devil have you done to that girl?"

"Girl?" echoed de Guere innocently.

Lord Marchmont snatched up the candle and employed it to light two lamps over the mantelshelf. Thinking of the footman in the hall a few feet away, he kept his voice low, but he nevertheless achieved a certain intensity. "The girl," he hissed, "is Lady Isabella Stanbroke. You will stay away from her in the future, or I swear to you I will call you out. Do you understand me? I will act for her as if she were Emilia herself."

"You have an interest in her?" Jeffery asked as if mildly intrigued.

"That is nothing to you."

"Oh!" said the other, suddenly recalling the tableau of Marchmont and Elizabeth at the pianoforte as he had left the drawing-room. He had been careful to look out for Marchmont before quitting that place in Isabella's company. "You have an interest in the family," he divined.

"I tell you, it is nothing to you."

"Nice family," remarked de Guere lightly, but his casual manner hid the beginning of a very interesting train of thought.

"You are warned, and warned again," answered Marchmont powerfully. "If I hear one word of this anywhere—or if it comes to my ears that you have so much as spoken to Lady Isabella again—I will meet you on Putney Heath at dawn the next morning."

Sir Jeffery raised an eyebrow. "Always happy to meet you anywhere, old man," he said, and smiled.

Lord Marchmont turned and left.

Lady Elizabeth meanwhile had taken Isabella firmly by the

arm and was shepherding her to an upstairs bedroom. "My dear sister," she had begun, then stopped as she realized servants were everywhere. When they had reached the quiet safety of Emilia's sitting-room, she took up again where she had left off. "My dear sister," she said, on a note in which severity sounded like a gong, "what on earth can have possessed you to wander off like that? Who led you from the drawing-room? With whom have you been—talking?" she demanded, snatching up one of Emilia's brushes and beginning to straighten Bella's coiffure. "Please tell me you did not leave the drawing-room in his company! I had much rather believe you merely wandered into his clutches."

"My dear Elizabeth, I cannot think why you suppose I was with anyone else at all. I simply felt a little faint—ask Amy or Emilia if I did not," she suggested, gaining momentum, "and slipped from the drawing-room for a little air."

"You must have slipped, indeed," said the other dryly, "for by the look of your hair you have been rolling on the floor for some time. Come, my pet, and make a clean breast of it. Who was it?"

But Isabella had not studied how to be a heroine for so many years only to melt under so paltry an interrogation as this. "You seem to have men on the brain just lately, Lizzie," she said. "You have certainly imagined this one."

Lady Elizabeth set down the brush and stared at her. "Are you actually going to lie to me? Well, you little beast! What you want, in my opinion, is to be eviscerated, stuffed and placed on display. What a spectacle you make of yourself! You understand, of course, that if you do not confide in me I shall be obliged to tell Mother."

Isabella was on the point of forbidding such a course when her heroinely instincts reawoke and substituted, "But Elizabeth, there is nothing to tell. I assure you, you refine upon it too much."

"Refine upon it too much! I know the marks of clutches when I see them, and I am looking at them right now. If you won't tell me whose clutches, and how you came to fall into them, I shall—I shall—" she faltered.

"Yes?"

"Well, at the least I shall tell Charlie."

Isabella shrugged.

"Yes, I daresay you don't care if I tell him or not. Charlie wouldn't notice a gorilla in Kensington Gardens if it came up and asked him the way to Lancaster Gate. Very well then, I shall have to tell Papa."

With rather more difficulty, Bella shrugged again.

Lizzie eyed her suspiciously. "Well, at least your cheeks are now near their normal colour," she observed, "and I must say I have done quite well with your hair. Promise me if I permit you to return to the drawing-room you will not jump into anyone's arms and beg him to tousle your golden curls. Do you think you can manage that?"

"Elizabeth, sometimes you are really insufferable," Isabella replied with a sneer. "You talk as if you owned me. Allow me to remind you that I was not the one who sat sniveling up at Lord Marchmont while the rest of the company waited for more music."

Elizabeth decided this would be a good time to quit the room.

"I thought that would strike a chord," murmured Isabella as the two girls made for the doorway. "Is Marchmont really so fascinating? You looked as if you could see no one but him."

"Bella, you are beginning to annoy me," said Lizzie in a low tone. They descended the stairs together.

"Oh, my heart! You break it with your crushing words."

"Keep still, can't you?"

"Goodness me, and just a few minutes ago you were so eager to talk!"

Elizabeth glared at her. "You had better pray I keep my mouth shut on the way home," she said.

"As far as I am concerned the world would be a better place if you kept your mouth shut everywhere," her fond sister returned, tacking a dazzling smile on to the end of this retort since they had now reached the drawing-room and were in full view of the others. The rest of the evening passed without incident (in fact it was all Isabella could do to stay awake, since Sir Jeffery had inexplicably left the party), but it is worth noting that for all her threats and acid grumblings Lady Elizabeth did not say anything at all in the carriage on the way home. There is a special honour among thieves, they say, and no matter how much these sisters might privately abuse each other, before the rest of the family they pretty much kept their peace.

The following Monday Lord Marchmont was again holding the reins in his well-sprung curricle. His companion this time was not Lord Warrington Weld but rather his sister Emilia. As if to make up for the gentleman's absence, however, they were speaking of him as they went—at least, Lord Marchmont was speaking of him, while Lady Emilia for her part did a great deal of nodding. "He's a capital fellow, don't you think?" the earl had been saying over the noise of the traffic and the horses' hooves. "Not an unkind bone in his body, and three times as honest as the ordinary man. Don't you agree?"

Emilia, thus prodded, said "Yes." At the same time she wondered what was up. She was pleased as could be that Jemmy had suggested this excursion to the Earl of Trevor's house—for it was there they were going, and only two days after her own dinner party—and she did not mind at all being solicited to accompany him, but this Warrington Weld line of questioning confused her. When Jemmy tried to be devious he was as transparent as glass: he simply hadn't the knack. It was clear to Emilia that something was on his mind, but what it was she could not yet be sure. The suggestions continued:

"Do you know, when I first saw him—up in Hull, it was, when the regiment was assembling—I did not care for him at all. No, to be truthful, I thought him a rather shallow, foolish sort of fellow. It was only as I came to know him better, don't you see, that I learned his real value. Of course, he saved my life in Belgium . . . a thing like that is bound to prejudice a man. But he is a fine fellow, don't you think?"

He was looking at her, and Emilia (who feared for her life if Marchmont would not pay a little attention to the road) was again obliged to say "Yes."

"His people are all dead, you know," Jemmy went on, deigning at the last moment to yield the right of way to a large brick edifice, while Emilia gasped. "It's a rotten shame. A man like that ought to have some family, don't you think?"

This time Emmy said "Yes" before he began to stare at her for an answer. Really, this conversation was most mysterious!

"He comes of good stock, too. An old Yorkshire family, I believe. The barony was created in the seventeenth century, if I remember correctly. Their motto is *Foy*, just *Foy*. 'Faith,' don't you know. I like that. Simple and succinct."

"Splendid," said her ladyship rather weakly; then, her curiosity getting the better of her, she broke forth, "Dearest Jemmy, will you not tell me why we are having this most enthralling conversation? I have said I like your friend—I should like anyone who had saved your life, come to that—but are we to talk of him all the way to Grosvenor Square?"

"I merely wished to point out," said Marchmont not very convincingly, "that despite Warrington's not having very much money, he would make a pretty good—er, he is a very good fellow."

"James," Emilia suddenly exclaimed, seeing light, "I am ashamed of you. Look at me," she commanded, then instantly revised, "No, don't look at me, I pray you. You are already doing that entirely too often. But James! You are trying to make a match, aren't you? Oh, I don't know when I've been so surprised."

"I am not trying to—"

"Oh yes you are. Don't deny it, you only make it worse. You are hoping I shall marry your Lord Weld so *you* won't have to marry yourself, aren't you? You are planning to give him lots of money so we can set up housekeeping together and you'll let Jeffery take Six Stones, and—Jemmy, I am so ashamed of you I could jump right out of this carriage."

"I never even thought—"

"You did, you did, you coward! Caitiff! I never dreamed you could stoop so low. Let Six Stones pass out of the family after four centuries, just so you won't be obliged— And the title to lapse! James, I am embarrassed to know you."

"My dear girl, you are well off target, believe me," Lord Marchmont finally managed to say, while his driving grew ever more erratic. "One thing I am not is a coward, and if I must marry, then so be it, I marry. I have already promised you that."

"You have not!" she interrupted.

"I have."

"Have not. Promise now," she cried, even in her emotion taking care to press this interesting advantage home.

"Very well, then, I promise now. I will marry."

"When?"

"When? Soon!"

"But when, when? I want to know when. Jemmy, you're thirty-eight years old. In two years you will be forty—"

"Brilliant! Tell me, how did you deduce that?"

"And forty is old," she continued, ignoring him. "Old! Your children will never know you—"

"What, will you kill me off so soon? My God, women are violent!"

"And you will leave your wife to care for them all alone . . . When will you marry, Jemmy? Tell me you will do it within the year."

"How can I promise such a thing?"

"Just do, and you will find a way."

"I cannot."

"Then before you are forty. That is reasonable! Say you will do so before you are forty, and I shall be content."

Lord Marchmont looked surly. "How we get into these wrangles," he remarked, "I have no idea. One moment we are making our way calmly through the town—"

"Calmly!"

"And the next you are practically wrestling me to the ground. Very well, if you insist, I promise to marry before I am forty if I can possibly, possibly do so. Are you satisfied?"

"Yes. Thank you, Jemmy," said she, as charmingly and meekly as can be imagined.

"If you want to know why I was talking about Weld," he muttered a minute later, "it was nothing to do with saving myself from marriage."

"It wasn't?"

"No, it wasn't. Quite the contrary, in fact, I was thinking of saving *you* from spinsterhood."

"Were you?" She considered this. "But I like spinsterhood!"

The earl said "Faugh" in such a way as to make it very plain there were still a few things in this world about which you could not fool an Earl of Marchmont.

"But I do like it," she said earnestly as they drew up to the door of Haddon House. "It suits me very well. You know that."

The earl said "Hmmm" in much the same tone as he had said "Faugh."

"You can Faugh and Hmmm me all you like," Emmy said, as he helped her from the curricle, "but you won't be able to fob me off on your poor innocent Weld. Who commissioned you to play Cupid anyhow? It certainly becomes you ill."

"No one commissioned me," he said, while they waited for the front doors to be opened. "Only I do not like to see the most excellent woman I know spend her entire life alone."

"I am this most excellent woman, I suppose?" she inquired, still sharp but beginning to soften a little.

"You are."

"Well, I thank you for your concern, my dear, but I assure you it is not appropriate. As for Weld I see no reason to go to the length of marrying him merely to secure the advantage of his company. I like him just as he is, and just where he is."

Lord Marchmont was denied the opportunity to answer as they were just then ushered into the hall of Haddon House. "Lord and Lady Trevor," said Emilia, in answer to the butler's inquiring glance, but Lord Marchmont, handing the man his card, had said at the same moment, "Lady Elizabeth, if you please," and the butler hesitated, confused.

"I am sure we would like to see all of them," said Emilia after a moment, with a wide, amused glance at her suddenly ardent brother.

"Yes, of course," said he to the servant. "Halcot, too, if he is here. And Lady Isabella."

"And Miss Lewis," added Emilia for good measure.

"Yes, indeed, why not make it a rout party while we are about it?" grumbled Marchmont to her privately, while the butler showed them into the Oriental Saloon and asked them to wait.

"I believe Lady Isabella and Miss Lewis have gone out," said he, neither he nor the callers dreaming of why this was, "but I shall see about the others, your lordship. Your la'ship," he added, bowing and disappearing.

"My dear, I feel suddenly *de trop*," Emilia remarked gaily, when they were alone. "I shall make myself useful by distracting the others, if I can, while you sit tête-à-tête with Lizzie."

She was spared the retort she deserved by the sudden entrance into the saloon of Lord Halcot. "Heydey, what's this?" he cried pleasantly as he came in. "Just saw Bolton in the hall, and he said you'd called. I'm sure m'mother will be down in a moment. Sherry? Negus, Lady Emilia?"

Refreshments were arranged.

"Glad I caught you. I've just been out myself," went on the genial Charles. Visiting with someone I met at your house, in fact—your cousin, I think. Sir Jeffery de Guere. Clever chap, don't you think?"

Lady Emilia, who felt as though someone had thrown something at her, attempted to control herself. "To be honest, we do not see much of Jeffery. He is a little . . . wild."

"Halcot," said Marchmont in a fatherly way his ten years seniority perhaps entitled him to, "I'm sure you're aware that Sir Jeffery . . . well, he's not . . . in short, he's not a person you'd like your sisters to know too awfully well." His concern had made him blunt, and he continued even more plainly. "The fact is, he was only present at Emilia's party the other night because of—because of a coincidence."

"Is that so? Well, it was a lucky coincidence for me. I've found out who was responsible for the five pounds I lost in that fight between Neate and Cribb a couple of weeks ago. Did you bet on that, Marchmont? Did you know it was—"

"Halcot, this is important. Since you met him in my house, I feel responsible. I want you to know that Sir Jeffery is not the sort of man you can trust. Not at all."

"Well, I must say you take a very odd view of your own kin!" said Charlie, his wide red smile fading.

"It hasn't anything to do with his being our kin," Emilia said gently. Lord Marchmont had said nothing to her of the scene in the corridor that night, but she objected to Jeffery strongly enough on general principles to back up her brother with a whole heart. "He is simply a dreadful rake."

Halcot looked surprised. "Is he? Upon honour! Well, nothing to be done about it now. I've already invited him to the ball we're giving on Thursday. You're coming, aren't you?"

Lord Marchmont sank into an armchair and covered his head with his hands.

"Oh dear, he's not that bad now, is he?" asked Charlie, then added wistfully, "I wish you'd told me before. I wouldn't have mentioned it to him. But Bella and Lizzie are pretty sensible girls," he comforted himself, while Marchmont groaned quietly, "and—Oh dear, maybe Bella isn't so sensible after all," he amended. "But Miss Lewis will keep an eye on her. She's as reliable as they come. And after all, they'll be in my father's house! It isn't as if one couldn't keep an eye on the fellow.

Anyhow, I have a feeling hè doesn't like me above half. He rushed off pretty quickly this morning. Said he had an errand, but I got the feeling he was just doing the pretty, and only wanted to get away from me. Maybe he won't even come on Thursday. I dareswear a ball like ours is not much in his line."

He had finished on a hopeful note, but the look he gave his auditors was full of doubt.

"Perhaps I can drop a word in his ear and encourage him to stay away," said Marchmont. "In any case I shall try."

"Oh, I say, old fellow, it isn't an emergency after all!" protested Halcot, whose idea of a rake's methods was pretty fuzzy.

Lord Marchmont did not trouble to correct him, but he disagreed. Since the doors again opened at that moment to admit Lady Elizabeth Stanbroke, the subject was allowed to drop. Lady Elizabeth was followed presently by her parents, both of whom liked the earl and his sister very much and reckoned them well worth cultivating. Miss Lewis, it developed, had gone out with Lady Isabella to visit some shops, but had come home alone fifteen minutes ago with a sudden sick-headache. She was upstairs nursing it, the visitors were told, but she sent her compliments down to them.

7

For a while conversation in the Oriental Saloon was general. Lady Trevor addressed the other ladies on the subject of the huge drawing-room Queen Charlotte was to hold a week later; and when that topic had been exhausted the rumours of Beau Brummel's being about to flee his creditors were once again dusted off and exchanged. Lord Trevor asked Lord Marchmont his opinion on the Lavalette affair, then proceeded to a rather smug examination of the income-tax question. At this point the butler arrived and whispered into Lady Trevor's ear of some obscure domestic crisis which required her attention, and since a few moments later Lord Trevor in his turn excused himself and vanished, Lady Emilia had but to draw Lord Halcot aside in order to leave her brother on his own with Elizabeth. Emilia had a reason for wishing to speak to Charlie apart in any case, and she easily contrived that he should follow her over to one of the long narrow windows, where she could address him quietly.

It was Amy Lewis's situation that concerned her. An unmarried woman of thirty is frequently suspected by the world of being an enemy to romance: with Lady Emilia this would have been an unjust accusation. She had been touched by Miss Lewis's self-effacing devotion and was determined to awaken Lord Halcot if she could to the gentle warmth that sunny disposition had for so long directed at him. Sly intimation was not in Emilia's style. Had she been allowed a free hand she would have told Charlie straight out that Miss Lewis loved him, but she was obliged to be subtle for Amy's sake, and so she tried to strike a middle ground between tactfulness and candour. "I am glad Miss Lewis did not come down," was what she said by way of an opening, "though naturally I am not glad that a headache prevented her."

Lord Halcot was surprised and confused. "Do you mean, ma'am, that you do not care for Miss Lewis's company?" he inquired.

"Oh no, hardly that! Only . . . I am happy to have this opportunity to speak to you uninterrupted."

"Were you afraid Miss Lewis would interrupt us if she were here? You have a very odd idea of her, Lady Emilia. She is the quietest thing imaginable."

"But that's just it," said Emilia. "Her very quietness is doubtless the heart of the problem."

"Problem?"

"Well, it is not a problem *per se,* I suppose. Except perhaps to—in any event, what I wished to point out was—oh, this is difficult. Lord Halcot, have you ever been in love?"

"I believe so," said he, thinking of Susannah Lemon.

"Then you know how difficult it is to make your feelings known. It can be—frightening," she brought out carefully, "even for a man, who is by custom the one to take such risks at first."

"Yes?" he prompted.

"Well, imagine how much more frightening it might be," she went on, "for a woman. She might well never find the courage to make a declaration. Particularly if she were a timid sort of woman."

Lord Halcot was slightly bewildered. "I am sure that is true, ma'am," said he, "but—with all due apologies—I do not quite see what that is to do with me. Perhaps I am being obtuse," he suggested gallantly.

Lady Emilia, feeling frustrated, looked frankly into his blue eyes. "My dear sir," she said, "it may be I am not making my meaning sufficiently plain. My point is, sometimes one does not see what is taking place under one's very nose—perhaps *because* it is under one's nose. Sometimes a solution is so simple that one fails to arrive at it on account of the simplicity itself. Do you understand?" she asked, fearing that she had not reached him at all yet.

Lord Halcot, silly young man, had begun to have a faint notion of her drift—but he had got it all wrong. Was it possible, he was asking himself, that Lady Emilia had somehow fallen in love with him? He looked under his nose, as she suggested—and there indeed she stood. The poor woman was getting on in years . . . perhaps she was so desperate as to fancy her esteem might be returned. He glanced at her with a critical eye. She wore her age pretty well, it was true (thought he), but she couldn't hold a candle to, for example, Susannah Lemon. Anyway, he didn't really care for that brainy sort of woman. A little too much like Lizzie, as a matter of fact: a good sort underneath, but all too likely to lash out at one in moments of pique. In truth he was a little surprised Lady Emilia should take to him in such a fashion; ordinarily these witty types did not. But then Love was ever a mystery. And Lady Emilia was not, as he had observed, growing younger. He determined to let her down gently. "Dear ma'am," said he presently, "I think perhaps I do. I know it cannot have been easy—I mean, I imagine it would indeed be frightening—for a woman to, er, declare herself, as it were. But perhaps—after all, certain people are not suited to certain people, don't you know. While perhaps we may feel, temporarily at all events, that our happiness lies in some particular direction . . . nevertheless, reflection will doubtless inform us that it was but a momentary illusion which . . . er, which made us feel, um—" His voice trailed lamely into silence.

"Lord Halcot, am I to understand you do not care for—the lady in question? If so, please tell me, and I will let the matter drop at once. I had had the impression the possibility had never occurred to you. That was why I mentioned A—I mean her quietness."

"Oh! Indeed? Well, I should not say I did not care for her," he replied with what he supposed was a kind, chivalrous smile, "but the kind of esteem we are discussing is, if I follow you correctly, so very special that, er . . . it is not enough simply to care for the person in question. One must feel a particular kind of ardour—"

"Please, it is not necessary to say anything more," she broke in. She felt badly for Miss Lewis and gave a sad little smile. "Of course such a thing as this must be wholly mutual."

"I am very flattered," Charlie remarked sweetly, distressed at what he supposed to be her crestfallen smile. "After all, it is not every day a man—"

"Dear, dear!" sighed Emilia lightly, while he floundered. "Why is it life is always setting us at odds with one another? Naturally there is nothing for it but to push ahead regardless . . . But one could wish it otherwise. Now tell me, Lord Halcot, if you think the frock-coat will stay in fashion long. It is a little extreme, don't you agree?"

Moved by her brave attempt, as he supposed it, to turn the conversation, Charlie pursued the trivial topic she suggested and stood speaking to her upon it for several minutes longer. The only thing he could not understand, when all was said and done, was what any of it had had to do with Amy Lewis. For Emilia had begun her remarks by mentioning Amy; in fact, by saying she was glad Miss Lewis was not with them. Was it possible she supposed little Amy a rival? What a remarkable idea! It was the first time he had ever so much as thought of Amy in such a light—and despite the fact that he immediately disposed of the notion as absurd, it may be that Emilia accomplished more by her discussion with Charlie than the sound of it might lead one to conclude.

Lord Marchmont and Lady Elizabeth had, all this while, also been tête-à-tête—just as Emmy had promised. They sat on a confidante, green and gilt and ornately carved, with clawed feet meant to suggest those of a Chinese dragon. Lady Elizabeth sat at a far end, Lord Marchmont only a few inches from her. Lizzie, though she had given permission for the earl to call upon her, had later regretted the decision. It was true that his lordship was very handsome; and a little gossip she had chanced to overhear apprised her that he was, and had been for years, extremely sought after. Nevertheless, she could not get away from a sense that his lordship was continually, in some way not altogether clear to her, judging her. The fact that she was for her part most certainly judging him did not prevent her from disapproving of him on this count. Quite the contrary, in fact: it made him all the easier to dislike. It was a shame, too, for she had been greatly drawn to him at their first encounter. She had come down to sit with him chiefly because she'd given her word he might call, but her mother's departure from the saloon had seemed a betrayal to her, and her father's disappearance minutes later had discomfitted her greatly. Lady Emilia so adroitly engaging Charlie's attention, there was nothing Lizzie could do but sit with the gentleman and hope he would leave soon. To say truth, the frankness she herself had shown him at the dinner-party two days before was as much a factor in her new prejudice against him as anything he himself had said or done: she just did not like the company of someone to whom she'd revealed herself in that way. Perhaps Lord Marchmont guessed this, for it is certain he did not mention their interchange on that night, nor in any way allude to the topic they had then discussed. He began, indeed, by discussing the ball the Trevors were to give that week, and led afterwards to what he expected would be the safe, only mildly stimulating topic of Lord Byron's latest writings. But it seemed as if Providence meant them to debate important issues whenever they met, for this seemingly innocuous subject led, as night to day, to the much more flammable question of Lord Byron's latest romantic escapades. All London was in fact chattering of his separation from his wife of only a year—and so soon after her accouchement. What could it mean?

"I fear the bonds of matrimony, as they are called, are being manufactured of gossamer these days," the earl observed, adding with a smile, "These are wicked times."

"Do you think so, sir?"

He had come determined to like her, for her forthright speech a few nights before had left a deep impression on him, but he could not help feeling she was being a great deal more reticent with him now than he had believed was her nature. "I do," he forged ahead, inquiring, "Do you disagree?"

"Can one time really be more wicked than another?" she asked. "It seems to me the opportunities of good and evil stay pretty equal through the years."

"Perhaps you are right," said Marchmont, "but when I think of such a man as Napoleon, I am persuaded that the ordinary course of history can be changed—that placid times can be made wretched and grim—by the actions of a single person."

"You fought against Bonaparte, my lord?"

He nodded.

"What is it like to be in battle?" she asked, her dark-blue eyes widening with interest. "Are you sorry the war is over?"

Lord Marchmont waited a moment before speaking. Then, "Dear ma'am, while the war continued not an evening passed when I did not pray most fervently for its end. When peace seemed sure I cried for very joy; I do not hesitate to admit it.

My only prayer now is that you and your sister and the thousands like you continue as ignorant of war and its effects as you are today."

Elizabeth regarded him with surprise. "That was feelingly spoke, my lord. Did you find it so very arduous, then?"

He smiled. "Were it only a question of arduousness I should make very little of the ills of war. But there is more than discomfort involved, more even than courage, or pain. Lady Elizabeth, people do not speak of war honestly, not in the general way. There is a deal of horror involved, of anger and disgust, and great waste through the actions of petty minds. It is a subject on which I have strong ideas. Though perhaps idea is not the correct word," he amended. "It is a subject that pursues me, of which my impressions are strong, I ought to say."

Elizabeth had not expected anything like so detailed a response to her question. Hers was a skeptical mind, yet she entirely believed his emotions ran as deep in this area as they seemed to do. It was impossible to hear his tone and not believe it. She did not like to press him, but her curiosity was piqued. "I beg you will not discuss the question further," she began in answer, "if it pains you, but I cannot help wondering just what you saw in Europe that left you with such strong convictions. Were you at Waterloo?"

Marchmont nodded again. "But this is not proper drawing-room conversation," he said. "You must encourage me to speak of something more agreeable."

"But I wish to know what has made you feel so strongly." She was starting to like him again and was suddenly glad after all that he had come.

"Have you ever seen a cat kill a mouse?" he asked at length. Elizabeth said she had.

"Then you know how slowly it is done—with what an appearance, at least, of deliberate cruelty?"

"Yes."

"Very well, then, a war is like that—only it is men who torment one another so miserably, and the scope is millions of times larger. Do you understand?"

Lady Elizabeth was so much struck by his look and voice that involuntarily her hand reached out and for a moment covered his, as it were in compassion. The moment passed. "I hope I have not occasioned you any unhappy memories," Lizzie murmured presently, her hand withdrawn.

He smiled again. "Unfortunately, those memories are always present to me. I cannot seem to rid myself of them. But this is really monstrous; I must not bore you any longer with such melancholy accounts." He shook his handsome head as if to chase the thoughts away and continued resolutely, "How does your first season among society suit you? Are you sorry to be away from home, or charmed with the gay whirl?"

"May I be somewhere in between?"

"Certainly."

"Then I should have to say that while London is continually new and interesting—to me, at least—I shall be very happy to see my home again." She gave a winning grin and went on, "You know, last year Lady Emilia assured me that when I was finally out, as the saying is, I should want nothing so much as to be allowed to stay in. At the time I was incredulous, but I am almost ready to believe her now."

"Emilia is a wonder," said her brother.

"Goodness, I should like to hear Charlie say such a thing of me! What a very fond brother you are, my lord."

"I dareswear Lord Halcot is just as fond of you," he answered. "He simply isn't old enough yet to realize it."

Elizabeth remained unconvinced. "Perhaps there is more to admire in Emilia than in me," she suggested, continuing before he could protest, "for I must agree she is a marvel." Lizzie was in fact very partial to the lady under discussion, though perhaps she was not quite in the habit of calling her a wonder or a marvel.

"I have been trying to persuade her to marry," the earl

went on a little distractedly, "for I am certain Lord Weld would like to marry her—"

"Then I was right!" Elizabeth exclaimed before she could stop herself.

"I beg your pardon?"

"At your dinner-party—do you not recall it? We saw him speaking to her, and I said he was trying to win a smile from her. And you said—"

"Oh yes," he interrupted, "pray do not remind me any more. I was an idiot not to realize it then." He looked chagrined and added, "It will seem very strange to you, no doubt, but I find it is still difficult for me to see Emilia as anything other than my younger sister. I mean, I do not think of her as quite a woman, with a life of her own. Yet I am very eager for her to marry. Perhaps if she married I could realize better that she has grown up."

"Oh dear," said Elizabeth, smelling trouble but plunging in nevertheless, "Here we are again. You see how deviously the institution of marriage threads itself through a woman's life? If she does not marry she is perpetually a child—until she is suddenly an old woman, that is. Whereas if she does marry . . . but we have already had that discussion."

"Yes, pray let us stay away from that!" he laughed, not altogether light-heartedly.

"Is that why you wish Emilia to marry? So that you may perceive her as a woman grown?"

"Oh, hardly! I only wish her to marry—as I have just been telling her, indeed—so that she will not be lonely."

"Is she lonely?"

"She says she is not. But you have no idea how quiet Six Stones can be, with only me for company, and not even that some of the time. She aches to come to London each spring, and she blooms every Season like a flower . . ." He feel silent.

"But—? Does she collapse on her return to . . . Six Stones, did you say?"

He nodded. "It is not so much that she collapses as that . . .

some part of her seems to become dormant. I continually offer to engage a companion for her, but she will not hear of it."

"Do you feel she is unhappy?"

"Oh, not at all!"

"Then why are you so eager to change her state? If she says she is not lonely, and you believe she is not unhappy, I am at a loss to understand you." She waited, genuinely puzzled.

"Good heavens, I don't know!" he finally ejaculated. "What has happened to women? Don't they want to marry any longer? First Emilia, now you . . . I thought it was simply a natural part of every woman's desires for herself, to have a husband and a home and a family and so on. Now I discover myself surrounded by women who speak of marriage as if it were some extraordinary and alien concept, as if it were invented by another race, or another—"

"Sex," she broke in, unable to restrain herself.

"You consider that marriage was invented by men?" he demanded, amazed.

"I do. Dear sir, I have already pointed out to you the effect of marriage upon women. Do you suppose they would have invented such a thing?"

"I certainly—Oh, but Lady Elizabeth! We have fallen into it again, listen to us!" Lord Marchmont looked at her with a grin, and suddenly the two of them burst out laughing together. The ridiculousness of their having arrived, though each had fought against it with a whole heart, at exactly the same juncture that had proven so disastrous two days before seemed more and more obvious, and their laughter fed on itself until they were both near tears. Inevitably Emilia's attention was attracted, and when she could no longer pretend not to notice them she came over, still with Charlie, and asked what on earth was the joke?

But neither lord nor lady could be persuaded to give an explanation. Lord Marchmont said it was not a joke at all, and Lady Elizabeth said it was a joke, but was not really funny, and by the time they had choked out these lame responses

Lady Emilia had decided she did not care to know. A few moments later she and Jemmy took their leave. Marchmont murmured, as he bent over Elizabeth's hand, that he would look forward very much to Thursday, when he would have the honour of seeing her again. Lord Halcot shook Emilia's hand rather than kissing it and alluded to Thursday in a much more general way. He did not want to hurt the girl, naturally; but sometimes one had to be a little cold to be kind.

The reader may be a little surprised to observe that our hero and heroine have not only clearly shown their enjoyment of one another, but have actually left each other's company (and at such an early juncture!) on excellent and harmonious terms. This is a trifle shocking, I admit, and I hasten to assure all and sundry that I for one had no notion, when first I made their acquaintance, that they would conduct themselves so peculiarly. This pair does not seem to spar; they do not appear to joust. So far from flinging barbs at one another when they meet, one would almost say they positively listen to each other, while their conversations show an uncanny tendency to deepen their relationship. In order for sparks to fly in the traditional fashion it is necessary that one partner either refuse to reveal himself honestly or decline to see the other as he actually is. It is even better if both partners can be persuaded to follow such a course. But while it is true that Marchmont and Lizzie each take one step backwards for every two forward, they cannot honestly be said actively to grate on one another. This is very curious! How can a love story proceed when the principals persist in liking each other? It is perplexing; but if the reader is prepared to follow me into this unknown territory, I shall not fail in leading.

I may point out on a more cheerful note that, if the course of true love is running uncommon smooth in the case of James and Elizabeth, it is on the other hand a veritable churning rapid when it comes to Isabella. Today was the day appointed by her for her tryst with Sir Jeffery de Guere. She had announced her intention of visiting Lackington Allen's that morning at breakfast, and to her great annoyance found that Amy Lewis was also eager to revisit that place, and had joyfully volunteered to accompany her. Any attempt to dissuade her would have had a suspicious look, so Bella had been obliged to accept the offer with as good a grace as could be mustered and trust Providence for an opportunity of losing her later. It is not the least of a clandestine affair's disadvantages that it does lead inevitably to this kind of deception and division among friends. Here was Amy Lewis, for fifteen years (since she could speak, forsooth) a good and honest ally to Isabella, now suddenly become the adversary, a mere obstacle to the fulfillment of her desires. If Elizabeth's behaviour is shocking, what is Isabella's? A perfect embarrassment, I am sorry to say. The silly girl has utterly taken leave of her senses.

The same evil angel that had whispered to de Guere the name of Sir Walter Scott murmured to Isabella, once she and Miss Lewis had reached Lackington Allen's, on the subject of sick-headaches. She began her campaign by asking Amy if she felt quite well, for she looked (said Bella) very strangely indeed. This was followed (after Amy's expected reply that she felt fine) by a worried glance and, presently, an offer to accompany her outside for a breath of air, "For you really are awfully pale, my dear."

Miss Lewis repeated her opinion that she was fine.

"I should be so sorry if you were to fall ill before Thursday, my pet. Fancy not being able to attend our very own ball! I only hope—you say your head does not ache?"

"Not at all," Amy smiled, moving towards the lounging rooms. "Do I really look so dreadful?"

"Not dreadful," said the traitor, "you could never look that, for you are too pretty. But so terribly fatigued! I only ask because . . . well, I hesitate to tell you, since perhaps it is better if you do not know, but Miss Pye told me on Saturday that Cynthia Hassall has the most abominable fever. It's lasted nearly a week already, and it came on her so suddenly! One morning she woke feeling quite fit—then all at once she realized she was a little pale, and felt a bit faint, and then, before she knew what was upon her, her head began to ache intolerably, and her fever rose, and—"

"Bella, please, you terrify me!" pleaded Amy only half jokingly. "The only symptom I have had so far is the one about waking up feeling quite fit. You paint this picture so vividly I'm afraid you will evoke the others—"

"Well, I only mention it, my dear, because you look so odd! I do not mean to alarm you, of course, but with Thursday coming up I thought perhaps you ought to go home at once and rest. Are you afraid of spoiling my day?" she asked with a great appearance of innocence. "Do not think of me, I beg. I shall gladly go home with you since your health is at stake."

Miss Lewis sat down on a leather couch. "But we've only just arrived," she objected.

"Well, that is nothing. I can go home and then come here again tomorrow. Oh dear, no, not tomorrow, I promised Mamma I would sit with her at home. But perhaps the next day—well, not then either come to think of it, since—"

"Oh my, you will never have time to come back!" said Amy, who was by now beginning to feel anxious and consequently a little unwell indeed. "I'll tell you what: send me home in the coach alone. I'll draw the shades so no one will see—and you keep Betty" (naming the maidservant who had accompanied them to the book-shop) "with you. Then when I am home I'll send the carriage back to you, and you can return with her at your leisure. Will that do?"

It was necessary that Lady Isabella protest for a while at the cruel idea of allowing her dearest friend to travel alone while in a state of ill health, but these objections were at length overcome, and Miss Lewis (who still did not really feel sick but was quite distressed enough at the idea of missing the ball—where she might dance with Charlie—to want to go home for safety's sake) went off alone in the stately carriage. Isabella easily dispensed with Betty by pointing out to her a knot of young persons like herself who had gathered round the doorman at the entrance of the shop, and then (looking anxiously for de Guere, since it was nearly the chosen hour) mounted the spiralling staircase to the very topmost gallery.

She had known she was early but was disappointed none the less to find she had preceded Sir Jeffery. Ought not an ardent lover to arrive well in advance of the great moment? Isabella nearly expired of impatience waiting for him, but at last his handsome head showed on the staircase and her trial was ended. He came to her a bit out of breath from the exertion of running up the steps, but otherwise he was everything a forbidden correspondent should be. "My angel!" were his first words. He took her hands and kissed them. The large central chandelier was far below them now and the gallery dim and (blessedly, thought Isabella) deserted. She leaned her back against the row of books and smiled up at him tremulously.

"Was it very difficult for you to come away alone?" he asked her, in a whisper not altogether necessary since the nearest person was two levels below them.

"A little. Jeffery, I have been thinking about Papa. I do not believe he will judge you before he even comes to know you. Jeffery, one moment!" she interrupted herself in a very unheroic fashion, for her beloved was covering her hands with kisses and apparently did not hear her at all. She was thrilled, in a sense, with the romance of this secret rendezvous; but in equal measure she found it unsettling and was desirous of avoiding such shadowy meetings in the future. Unlike the average heroine, she had not at all enjoyed lying to Lizzie and Amy.

"My adorable girl," said Jeffery between kisses. "Is it too dreadful of me? I cannot seem to let go of you."

She smiled in spite of herself and allowed him to kiss first her forehead, then her mouth. "But Jeffery, we must speak. I do not believe my father will forbid you to pay your addresses to me. He is a very reasonable man. Promise me you will speak to him—or shall I speak to him first?"

This talk of fathers made Sir Jeffery nervous. "My dear, I am afraid you have no notion what kind of wickedness I am generally held to be responsible for," he said, looking sharply into her eyes.

"But listen to me," she pleaded. "This is just what I am saying: my father will not judge you on the strength of rumours and gossip. He is a magistrate at home, you know. Everybody says he is uncommonly fair—even some of the prisoners."

De Guere was silent for a moment; then he grasped her shoulders rather tightly and demanded, in a low voice, "Suppose some of the stories were true, my angel? Would you love me the less? I do not say they are . . . but *if* they were—?"

She looked back at him, mildly puzzled. "Do you mean—can you be capable of wickedness? I cannot believe it."

"Not wickedness, my angel, but—foolishness. Before I met you, my dear, I had but little reason to be good, remember. If I had erred—could you be divinely merciful, and forgive me? Say you could, I beg you!"

Lady Isabella, feeling unaccountably limp, said she could.

"Darling!" came the reply, and another shower of kisses.

"But will you not speak to my fath—"

"No more talk of fathers. Let us not speak of anyone at all, except ourselves. That is the prerogative of lovers. We *are* lovers, did you know?"

"But Jeffery—"

"Shall I see you on Thursday? You are so lovely! Your brother came to see me today; he asked me to your ball. Did you send him? He nearly made me late."

"No—I mean, yes. That is, of course I shall see you on Thursday, if you come. But Jeffery, could you not speak—"

"Adorable! Adorable!"

"Jeffery—"

"Kiss me. Quickly, love, for I hear a clerk coming up the stairs. There, that is all," he added a moment later, when she had embraced him as he asked. He arranged her arm on his very properly, smoothing her hair with a deft gesture that ought to have informed her he had had a lot of practice in the art, and began to lead her sedately down the steps. "Say you will dance with me Thursday," he murmured as they passed the clerk. "Say you will hold me in front of everyone."

"Of course I shall. You'll see, on Thursday I'll introduce you to Papa—"

"Not now, my darling," said Sir Jeffery de Guere. They were reaching the bottom of the staircase. "I must leave you here or your abigail will see me. Good-bye. Life will be nothing till we meet again."

With these words he left her, a little frustrated it is true at not having been able to speak as she'd intended, but with her pulses and her emotions in a delightful state of tumult.

8

WHY—IT MAY well be asked—why was Sir Jeffery de Guere
so especially loth to meet with Lady Isabella's father? Granted,
rakes and loving papas are not in the nature of things what
one could call allies; indeed, their relationship is more along
the lines of diametric opposites. Still, this particular rake has
been so very averse to the notion of winning the trust of Lord
Trevor that the question may bear particular examination.

The fact was that de Guere had made a few shrewd observations about his cousin Marchmont at their last meeting, and
had done a little thinking since then. His conclusion: that
Lord Marchmont was considering taking Lady Elizabeth
Stanbroke to wife. He was not surprised therefore when, on
the Tuesday following the tryst at Lackington Allen's, Marchmont paid him a call. His object was to dissuade Sir Jeffery
from attending the Trevor's ball. Not mincing matters, he offered de Guere one hundred pounds to be absent.

"Thank you, thank you, dear coz," said Jeffery, who was still at his dressing-table tying his cravat when Lord Marchmont arrived. "It is good of you to think of me, really good of you. But what is there in the world to equal an evening in the company of fine and much-loved persons? A hundred pounds? I am afraid not. Still, it was good of you to think of it."

"I want you to keep away from Isabella," pronounced the earl grimly. "I've already told you."

"So you have, old man, come to think of it. But I dare say I shan't listen to you very closely until you can prove to me there is some law—or at least an ordinance—against my seeking out the society of that young lady. Anyhow, I don't know why you worry about my spending time with her; really I fancy I shall be so much occupied with the company of her fascinating brother, I shall have no time for ladies at all. Do you feel better, old fellow? Can I get you a cup of chocolate? My house may be poor, but I am not without my little hospitalities."

"You will be without your little teeth if you don't shut up," remarked Marchmont, who was losing his temper. "Do you not recollect my promising to call you out if you went near Lady Isabella again?"

"I do," said the other generously. "Are you worried about breaking your promise to me? I beg you will forget it, if so. I have. Anyhow, my good fellow, a man may be called out and not accept, you know. Frankly I don't think my—going near Lady Isabella, I think you called it?—is adequate provocation at all. If I accepted every duel that was offered to me," he added airily, "I'd never have time for breakfast in bed at all, would I? No, I'd be out at Wormwood Scrubs, or wherever it was you said you wanted to see me—"

"Putney Heath."

"Yes, exactly, Putney Heath. I'd be out there on Putney Heath brushing bullets off my waistcoat every morning, instead of here where I can be cosy. Now I dare say the Heath is very beautiful this time of year—very beautiful! But I had rather not go every day, thank you." Having at last succeeded in arranging his cravat to his satisfaction, Sir Jeffery sat down and studied his cousin. "Was there anything else?" he asked at length.

"Five hundred pounds," said the earl. "No more."

"My dear man, some things are past purchase, don't you know! I could not dream of accepting your very generous offer. Surely you'll take some chocolate? Coffee? Tea—?"

"A thousand," offered Lord Marchmont.

"My good fellow, I tell you some things cannot be bought! No doubt you will be surprised to find I am one of them, but I am, and that is that. Life is full of mysteries."

"I swear I will make you regret this."

"My dear coz, pardon me if I say you are beginning to bore me."

"Damn your hide, I don't care about your boredom! I don't care about your feelings or your finances. I don't care about anything except—" He broke off suddenly. "A thousand pounds," he said more quietly after a moment. "Think it over. A thousand pounds to stay away. I'll be going now."

Sir Jeffery jumped up and followed him to the door of his dressing-room. "Oh I say, I hope I haven't driven you off with that little remark about being bored! I didn't mean a thing by it, 'pon honour."

Lord Marchmont did not answer. A moment later Sir Jeffery heard the front door shut behind him.

"Humour is lost on him," he remarked to himself with a shrug. "He always was a sober old chap." He returned complacently to his toilette, making mental notes as he did so on the subject of what to wear Thursday night.

What was the value of his invitation to the ball, that one thousand pounds could not induce him to part with it? Briefly, this: de Guere stood to inherit the entire estate of the Earl of Marchmont if his lordship died childless. It was his aim, therefore, to prevent the earl from marrying. Till now, history and fate had conspired with him; but his instincts had told him on Saturday night that the moment was not far off when Lord Marchmont would ask Elizabeth Stanbroke for her hand. Very well then, if Sir Jeffery succeeded in embroiling the Trevor family in a scandal, would the proposal still be made? Jeffery thought not. He was determined, therefore, to precipitate a scandal as soon as possible, before Lord Marchmont could make up his mind to offer for Elizabeth. Ruining Isabella was the natural and pleasant way of bringing about a scandal, of course; in fact, he was rather looking forward to it.

It will be thought, perhaps, that Sir Jeffery was foolish for supposing that merely because he prevented the earl from marrying one woman he would gain materially. But Sir Jeffery knew his man: very few indeed were the women Marchmont admired. Nor did de Guere believe his cousin would marry merely for the sake of securing an heir. If he could contrive to eliminate Lady Elizabeth from the earl's life, it would be years before his lordship thought of marriage again. And during those years—who knew? Perhaps this rash passion of Marchmont's for a duel would result in an untimely death. Life was, as he had just pointed out to his cousin, full of mysteries. The same circumstances that made Lady Emilia desire her brother's marriage so urgently made Sir Jeffery hope to gain from preventing it. It was not an altogether unreasonable point of view.

Lord Weld and Lady Emilia sat in the drawing-room at number 21 Cavendish Square waiting for the Earl of Marchmont to come downstairs. It was Thursday. Evening had claimed London for her own: the long shadows cast by the setting sun had stretched themselves to exhaustion and expired, leaving the drawing-room washed in weak moonlight. Lady Emilia wished it were not too late in the year for a fire:

the room could do with some cheering up. "What an age he takes," she remarked, for the second time, to Weld. "I feel as if we've been waiting for him this hour."

"Perhaps we ought to play a hand at cards," suggested Weld. "If he is dressing, as we suppose, to please Lady Elizabeth Stanbroke, then he may keep us waiting here till midnight."

"If we wait till midnight Lady Elizabeth will have no dances free to give him," she replied moodily, then added with more animation, "Do you really think he is looking forward to seeing her? I have waited so long for him to take a fancy to someone, it almost seems too wonderful to be true."

"Naturally your judgement is superior to mine, for you have known him longer, but in my humble opinion we have lately had the pleasure of knowing an earl head over ears in love."

"Truly? You think it is love?" Lady Emilia sat up straighter in the wine-red arm-chair she occupied and addressed him earnestly. "He has not taken you into his confidence, by any chance?"

Sorrowfully, Warrington shook his head No.

"He has not confided in me either," said she, leaning back again. "But I am pretty sure of it anyhow. The trouble is, now that I seem finally to be getting what I wanted, I am not so certain I want it."

"You do not care for Lady Elizabeth after all? But she is so particularly likeable. You know, I had an intuition about her weeks ago, as soon as we'd met her. I thought she was the girl for Marchmont. Told him so, too."

"You did? And he listened?"

"No. Wouldn't hear of it, in fact. Insisted she was *my* Lady Elizabeth. But I thought you approved of her!"

"Oh, I do," she assured him. "I think she is charming. It's only that . . . I feel as if I have twisted Jemmy's arm."

"Well, you have certainly done that," he observed cheerfully.

"Do you think so? I am so troubled by it. Suppose he is really pursuing her only to please me? I should feel so odious and low."

"In my inexpert opinion," said Weld, standing and crossing the room to her, "that is the very last thing you need to worry about." He stood by her arm-chair and looked down upon her. She was wearing a gown of French gauze, *bleu celeste* over white satin, and her thick dark hair was arranged in dozens of curls. "You know," Weld said, his hands thrust into his pockets, "in the last few days Marchmont has said—well a number of things regarding . . . I don't know how to put this. Perhaps I ought not to say anything at all."

Emilia looked up. "I beg you will be frank," she answered simply.

"Very well, then." He sat down on a sofa only a few inches from her and watched her face intently as he spoke. "Lord Marchmont has intimated a number of times that you might . . . well, in short, that as my esteem for you is profound, and since the affection I feel for you has grown daily more—"

"Oh dear," said Emmy abruptly. "Marchmont's been playing at Cupid with you too. Excuse me. I don't think you ought to go on."

Lord Weld expelled a breath that sounded curiously like a sigh of relief. "My lady, I take you at your word—"

"Since we have agreed to be frank, you may safely do that. I don't know why Jemmy insists on match-making! It is so vexatious."

Warrington sat back on the sofa. "I am sure he only does it out of love for you. He is very much afraid that your . . . ah, your singlehood weighs heavily on you."

"And so he solicits offers for my hand from among his friends?" she answered. "Very pretty."

"Oh no, you must not think— Your brother knows how much I admire you. Without labouring the point, what he suggested was . . . was not far from my mind in any case. Only, if I understand you correctly, I did not expect you would welcome my suit. Please, it is not a painful issue to me," he rushed on, as she seemed about to speak. "To say truth, in spite of my real satisfaction in your company, I did not think we ought to . . . I mean, that we belonged . . . oh dear. If my impression of your feelings towards me has been accurate, then we are not of very different minds on the matter at all," he finally concluded. "I do not take it as a slight."

"Nor should you," she said gratefully. She had refused offers before, but never had she felt so comfortable doing so. Through the moonlight she looked curiously at Warrington Weld's pale, freckled face. "You know, I have often wished to thank you for your being so good a friend to my brother. Of your saving his life, I say nothing; it is too large a debt. But you must understand, my brother does not fall into intimacies easily. You are a remarkable person to have gained his trust so completely."

The poor man turned bright pink under this stream of praise. He was obviously much more discomfitted by this than by her gentle rebuff and was on the point of asking her to turn the conversation when Lord Marchmont at last came in. Marchmont, naturally thinking he had interrupted a tender scene, very nearly offered to go out again, but he felt this would be too awkward (a few things were still beyond him, despite the romantic fog in which he passed most of his days of late) and instead suggested they depart for the Trevors' if they were ready. Emilia bit back a rejoinder to this intimation that he might be ready though they were not and preceded the gentlemen out the door. Half an hour later (the crush of traffic was abominable) they arrived at the doors of Haddon House.

The evening had begun, in that elegant abode, with an argument. At least among the children it had begun with an argument; the servants were too much occupied preparing for the arrival of more than a hundred guests to have time for any highly developed quarrels, while Lord and Lady Trevor made it a point never to become embroiled in debates unless it was absolutely necessary. Not that ›their children were really at liberty either to indulge in controversy, for each had a special reason for wishing to appear well at the ball—but they made time to argue, as busy people all over the world have done before them and continue to do.

Elizabeth, Isabella, and Amy shared a large, pleasant sitting-room on the third floor of the house, and it was in this apartment that the quarrel took place. Lizzie and Bella had finished dressing first, and had come into the room to consult with one another on some small matters of fashion. Preparations were going forward downstairs with such accompaniment of noise and confusion that both girls chose to take advantage of the quiet afforded them by the sitting-room, and curled up (in so far as gowns and slippers would allow) in its luxurious sofas for a comfortable cose.

"Do you think that ghastly Middleford Lemon will come?" Elizabeth asked, when certain questions regarding Alençon lace had been dispensed with. "I was hoping he might be struck with—oh, say a crippling disease or some such, that would prevent him."

"Oh, he is sure to be here, since he knows you will be. He admires you very much, Lizzie. I noticed it at Lady Hassall's pic-nic."

"If he admires me, you would think he would take care not to talk me to death, with his porcelain boxes and figures. I just loathe the way he says the word figures, don't you? 'Figaws,' is what he says, is it not? Pawcelain figaws! What odious lisps these town bucks affect. Did you notice Charlie has begun to adopt one, too? He is really too repulsive."

Lady Isabella nodded vigorously. "I can't imagine how he got through school," she said. "Not that he did so very well, of course, but it surprises me that he did it at all. He is certainly the slowest man living, don't you think?"

"If not the very slowest, then distinctly among the top competitors. What really astonishes me," Elizabeth went on, "is that he expects us to be just as cork-brained as he is. He is so perfectly transparent, with his idiotish airs and fooleries, and yet we are supposed to pretend we have no idea what he is about. 'I am not entirely dead to the finer things in life,' he says. 'Porcelain-work is extremely artful.' That is just what he told me, if you can believe it, not three days ago. Then he went off to visit those numbing Lemon girls."

"Did he say that to you?" asked Bella. "Those are exactly the words he used the first night he met them—or so near as makes no difference. I was simply furious. Amy was right there in the room. I believe you'd gone to sleep."

"He really is a clunch."

"I was so angry when Mamma insisted on inviting all those Lemon people tonight. What are Sir Arthur and Lady Lemon to us? Nobody. But Mamma maintained they must be asked, and their whole crop with them. I know it is for Charlie's sake," she added with a frown. "Mamma always thinks of Charlie. And it isn't even as if Susannah Lemon likes him. Have you seen them together? She positively laughs in his face. Naturally he is too shatter-brained to notice."

"I wonder where he gets it," Elizabeth agreed, marvelling. "I mean, neither Papa nor Mamma is dull-witted, and no more are you or I. Charlie must study it," she pronounced finally. "It's an achievement."

"And when I think of Amy squandering all her attention on him, I could just scream."

"Well, that's Amy's own fault," Elizabeth observed, with a glance at the door that separated them from the chamber where Miss Lewis was still being dressed. She lowered her voice and continued, "She doesn't show any more sense than he does, if you want my opinion."

"I suppose you think she could simply stop caring about him, if she chose to?"

"Certainly."

Isabella, who had nevertheless supposed the very same thing any number of times, now hotly refused to hear it. "It is just like you to say such a thing, Elizabeth."

Lizzie remained unruffled. "Hardly surprising when we consider that I *am* myself."

"You know what I mean. You think everybody can regulate his mind the way you do. Well, it isn't so. Some people's feelings run deeper than others. They can't turn away at will. Amy's feelings run very deep."

"And mine do not?"

"Certainly not, or you would realize love is not a matter of directing ones attention toward a correct object. You and your Marchmont! 'I will marry Lord Marchmont,' you said. On the first night, too! I expect you will do it, just to show us your affections are all orderly and biddable."

"You misunderstood me that night," said Lizzie, tight-lipped.

"Did I? Then you would not accept him, if he were to ask?"

"That is neither here nor there."

"It is. You suggest that Amy could—"

"Amy's feelings and mine are very different matters," Elizabeth broke in. "I am older. I have more experience. I have seen more of the world. Amy is too young; she knows no one but Charlie—so naturally she imagines he is wonderful. She ought to have sense enough to realize a judgement like that should not be made in ignorance. She ought to acknowledge her youth and open up her heart to other possibilities. Sometimes I think I shall tell her so, in fact, but I keep hoping she will come to it herself."

"She would not listen to you in any case. Life is not all sense, Elizabeth," exclaimed her sister, hissing the word sense as if it were something particularly odious.

"Well, it is certainly not all nonsense," cried Lizzie, finally firing up. "Isabella, I hope you are not intending to repeat that ridiculous scene you enacted at Lady Emilia's the other night! Whoever your mystery gentleman is, for God's sake, keep away from the empty rooms with him."

"There was no gentleman!"

"Don't lie to me!"

Charlie strolled into the room, elegant in superfine and silk. "You girls having a bit of a wrangle?" he inquired. "What fun!"

"Keep out of this, Charles," Isabella warned him.

"No, I think he ought to be here," countered Lizzie. "He's just as idiotish as you are. This family simply staggers me. Halcot, what on earth do you mean by running after those Lemon girls? You're six-and-twenty years old now. You're not a child!"

"I'm obliged to you for noticing. What the devil is your point?"

"My point is, you ought to know when someone is laughing at you."

"Oh, and Susan—er, the Lemon girls are laughing at me?"

"Certainly. Everybody is laughing at you."

"Oh, indeed? I daresay you must think yourself very clever to have observed it."

"It's nothing to do with clever," muttered Lizzie, while at the same moment Isabella interjected, "Oh, indeed, she does! Lizzie thinks she is terribly clever—*staggeringly* clever. She knows how to run everybody's life. You should hear her on the subject of Amy."

"Bella—" cautioned Lady Elizabeth.

"Oh, and what has she to say about Amy?" asked Halcot. "Is everybody laughing at her, too, or is that only me?"

"Oh, she says Amy can turn off her feelings if she likes. She says everybody can regulate his feelings. Elizabeth knows these things, Charlie," she added with heavy sarcasm. "She hasn't got any feelings, you see, so she can be objective about them."

"What an advantage! And what feelings, pray tell," he went on, addressing Lizzie now, "should Miss Lewis forget?"

"I don't wish to discuss it," Elizabeth answered, suddenly subdued.

"That's fine! You make me feel a prime fool, and then you don't choose to discuss it."

"It's only a feeling, Charlie," Isabella put in. "Just forget it, why don't you?"

"Tell me, Lizzie—what should Miss Lewis forget? Is she running after someone, someone who laughs at her?"

"Worse than that," Bella said, turning on him abruptly. "Someone who doesn't even notice."

Halcot raised an eyebrow. "And who might that be?"

"Well, it might be—"

"Isabella!" hissed Lizzie.

"Yes, it might be someone in this room—"

"Isabella!"

"What the devil—?"

"Charlie, you *are* such a dolt!"

"Isabella, think of what you are doing," begged Elizabeth, jumping to her feet. "For the love of—"

The door opened suddenly behind her. In the threshold stood Amy, a smile rapidly fading from her lips. The room fell silent at once, while Miss Lewis advanced a step. No one else moved. "Whatever is the matter?" she finally asked, for she was confronted with the spectacle of three siblings, all standing, and all apparently ready to strangle one another. "I thought I heard shouting."

"Oh, my dear, it was nothing," cried Lady Isabella, moving to her side. She took her friend's hand and drew her further into the sitting-room.

"I really think we had better go downstairs," Amy protested. "I have been forever dressing, I thought. Isn't it late?"

"I am sure it must be," Lizzie said, relieved.

As she reached the door she heard Amy ask mildly, "Lord Halcot, are you quite well? You look very odd, indeed."

Lizzie turned to see what prompted this question and saw her brother, still as he was when Amy had entered, staring at the girl. As she watched, Isabella put an arm protectively round her friend and led her again to the door. "It is nothing," said Bella to her. "Charlie and I have been bickering again. That is all." With these words she swept out the door after Elizabeth and followed that lady down the great front staircase. Lord Halcot remained where he was for quite some moments after the girls had gone, however. It was not something he was in the habit of doing, and it took him some little while: but he was putting two and two together, and making four.

9

Is THERE anything so pleasant as a ball? What stirs up the imagination so agreeably in anticipation, and what hours, in retrospect, shine so endearingly as those passed dancing on a parqueted floor? If the joys of looking forward and the charms of looking back upon a ball are (as I think they may be) perhaps a little greater than the pleasures of the ball itself—well, then, there are many occasions of which that same complaint may be made, are there not? If the crush of bodies grows sometimes a little tedious; if the six partners one does not care to dance with wear one out before the sweetness of that seventh can be tasted; if the heat and noise and confusion make one's temples throb ever so slightly—well, after all, is not such a rare satisfaction purchased cheaply at the cost of a little chagrin? For Miss Pye, Miss Hassall (now thankfully recovered), for Sir John Firebrace and Lord Weld, the ball at the Earl of Trevor's that warm May evening was well worth any little inconvenience it occasioned.

Lord Marchmont enjoyed the evening heartily for as much as half an hour. De Guere had not yet come. His lordship danced with Lady Emilia and reserved the hand of Elizabeth for the two fourth. He began to hope his cousin had changed his mind. Of course this same half hour was misery to Isabella: one man's joy was ever another man's sorrow.

When Sir Jeffery did arrive, he did it with élan. He swept into the ball-room, extravagant cravat flowing, white and dashing as a frothy river, and he never paused till he had found his quarry. Isabella became radiant at the sight of him. Eagerly she demanded what had made him so late. Adroitly he turned the subject to her glowing cheeks and eyes. In fact it had been a creditor who delayed him, a timely reminder (if he needed one) of how handy it would be to inherit the estate of the Earl of Marchmont. That gentleman, meantime, had marked his arrival at the ball with almost as much excitement as Isabella herself. He presented himself at Sir Jeffery's side with all haste, and so broke up the tête-à-tête just begun between him and Bella. With the lady listening, Lord Marchmont did not think it wise to speak his mind, so he merely greeted his cousin with as much civility as he could muster.

"Didn't think you'd be so happy to see me, somehow, old fellow," Sir Jeffery replied, in response to these courtesies. He was well aware the earl would hold his tongue when Isabella was near, and so spoke on easily, "I'd been getting the idea you didn't like me much above half. And the way you rushed off from my house the other day—but I dareswear you had some business you'd forgot, that suddenly came back to you."

"Just so," said the earl, from between tight lips.

"It's a pity, isn't it, the way families drift apart," Sir Jeffery went on, his eyes following the turning couples. "Why, it must be years since you and Emmy and I took tea together. But here we are united again, and thick as thieves after all. Ah, family feeling! Something you never forget, I daresay. Like swimming."

"Exactly."

"I'm sure her ladyship," de Guere went on, addressing Isabella, "does not lose touch with her cousins. I can't help but observe how close she is to her sister and brother."

Isabella, still furious at Lizzie in particular and Charlie (as ever) in general, merely looked at him.

"Well, mind you don't lose that intimacy, my dear," he continued cheerfully, then turned again to Marchmont and observed, "Friendship and kinship: two vessels that always sail smooth on the stormy seas of life!"

Lord Marchmont, equally divided between anger and revulsion, had little choice but to nod and smile agreement.

"I say, old fellow," de Guere continued jovially, "you wouldn't feel slighted if the lady and I drifted on to the dance floor together, would you? She's done me the honour to give me the two next, you see."

Lord Marchmont bowed slightly. "Not at all," he brought out.

"You are sure you will not be offended?" Jeffery added. "I promise you, it is nothing to do with your conversation, which is scintillating as always."

"I understand entirely."

"It's only that . . . well, when I hear such music as this, and find such a lovely and graceful lady at my side—" the other continued, savouring his moment. By this time even Lady Isabella had noticed something was rather odd about this discourse, and she looked at her beloved curiously.

"Dear coz," Marchmont finally broke out, deciding to fight fire with fire, "if you do not take her ladyship onto the floor this moment, I shall do so myself. With her permission, of course—"

He turned to her and Isabella, colouring a little, said, "Oh!"

"We're off then," Sir Jeffery declared, suddenly drawing her away. "Perhaps we'll see you at supper, old chap?"

"Oh, you'll see me everywhere, I trust," said the earl grimly. He watched through narrowed eyes as Sir Jeffery, his gleaming head bent to whisper something into Isabella's ear, vanished with his prey into the midst of the dance.

"I see Jeffery's done us the honour," said a quiet female voice behind him. His lordship turned to find Emilia at his elbow.

"Yes, blast him. Do you know, I never did care for Jeffery—but lately I find I actually detest him."

"Despise is a better word. Detestation is too good for him," said Emilia, nodding agreement.

Lord Weld, who had wandered up alongside Lady Emilia now contributed, "Contemn, is good. We contemn him."

"Loathe him," suggested Marchmont.

"Abominate."

"Abhor."

"He's despicable," opined Emilia, after a moment's silence.

"Odious."

"Repellant."

"Revolting."

"Disgusting."

"Execrable!"

"Venomous!"

"Horrid!"

"Oh damn, I've lost him!" exclaimed Lord Marchmont suddenly, for in the pleasure of abusing Sir Jeffery he had failed to preserve his vigilance.

"There he is, under that chandelier," said Emilia. "He's got Lady Isabella on his arm: they're about to go down the line. Do you think he's—ugh! 'making love to her,' I was about to ask, but the very idea is foul!"

Lord Marchmont, who had preferred to take no one into his confidence, now hesitated on the point of telling his sister his fears. He decided not to do so, however, and instead kept silent. After all, it might be an embarrassment to the Trevors as well as to him—for he was sure Lord Trevor, a man of the world, could not countenance any intimacy between his daughter and de Guere—and Lord Marchmont did not like to risk causing Elizabeth or her family discomfort.

"Where was he during the wars, I wonder?" mused Lord Weld.

"In Scotland, the villain."

"On military assignment," explained Marchmont, to be fair.

"Yes, but still!" Lady Emilia had not taken her eyes off the gentleman in question since she had first discovered him, and now she murmured uneasily to her brother, "Do you know, he really *is* making love to Isabella! Look at them together. He is practically kissing her neck. Jemmy, oughtn't we to do something?"

"At the moment, my dear, there is nothing we can do. I can scarcely rush over and tear them from the dance floor."

"Well, where is her mother? Or where is Lady Elizabeth? I trust they would not care to see that poor little romp flirt herself into serious trouble!"

"Emilia," said Marchmont uncomfortably, still unwilling to share his particular apprehension with the others, "I think you refine upon the point too much. Look at them now. They are merely dancing, like the rest."

"Because they have had to part to opposite sides of the lines. I warn you, when the steps bring them together again—you watch them! He really is doing it a bit brown!"

Lord Weld attempted to soothe her. "The dance is certain to be over soon," said he, "and then Sir Jeffery will be obliged to relinquish her."

Marchmont, who knew they were engaged for the following number as well, said nothing.

"I wish that careless Halcot hadn't invited him," Emilia went on feelingly. "Jemmy, did you go and speak to Jeffery after all, as you said you would? It really is too bad if you did not. I feel quite responsible—"

Her words were cut short by the arrival of Lady Elizabeth who, noticing the music was about to stop and being engaged to dance with Marchmont when it began again, and had come to claim her partner. "Responsible for what?" she inquired innocently, catching the last words only. She curtsied cheerfully to Weld, put her arm round Emilia's waist, and confided, "You know your brother is really much too attractive. It's simply criminal, the sight of such a handsome man not dancing at a ball!"

Lady Emilia returned the sisterly embrace and said softly, "I am so glad you think so. But in fact, my dear," she went on more volubly, "what I feel responsible about is our cousin Jeffery. Do you realize he has been dancing with your sister in the most—"

"Ah, the music has stopped!" Marchmont suddenly interrupted. "Come, my dear Lady Elizabeth, for you know you are promised to me." He virtually tore the startled Lizzie from Emilia's side and, with sketchy bows to their erstwhile companions, dragged her hastily onto the floor. "It's de Guere," he finally told her, when they had taken their position in the newly forming line. "I'm afraid he is going to annoy your sister again."

"De Guere? Do you mean, Sir Jeffery—your cousin? Was he—?"

"Did Lady Isabella not tell you?"

"No, she has been most obstinate." The music began again, and over its strains he continued, "He was the gentleman at your house, then? I mean, the one—" she stopped in confusion, looking for a delicate phrase. While she hesitated Sir Fielding Porter presented himself across from her: the dance had begun. Lord Marchmont had only time to nod confirmation at her before she was off; it was some minutes before the steps of the dance brought them together again.

"You have no notion what Isabella has been like," Elizabeth confided as soon as she had opportunity. "Most mysterious!"

"I am terribly sorry Sir Jeffery has come, more than I can say," the earl returned. "I attempted to dissuade him, in fact, but—"

"To be quite frank, I am not entirely sure why he was invited," said she, while her foot kept time to the music. She was wearing a new pair of satin slippers, ivory, with seed-pearls embroidered onto them. They were amazingly comfortable, and she did like dancing very much. She even found, as ever a little to her surprise, that she was liking the earl very much; but Bella's safety concerned her more than these very pleasant distractions, and if it had been possible she would have removed herself from the line altogether in order to carry on a more connected conversation with his lordship. However, it was not possible to do such a thing without causing quite a bit of speculation; so she resolved to move through the dance as best she could and then seek a quiet corner with Lord Marchmont afterwards. She now added hurriedly, "I don't actually recall having discussed him when Mamma and I made up the list of guests."

"I believe it was your brother—" began her partner.

Lady Elizabeth broke in, immediately exasperated. "Of course; who else? Oh, sometimes I should like to gut Charlie!"

Marchmont, taken aback somewhat by this piece of verbal violence, was now obliged to watch her move away from him and down the line. Truly, it was most frustrating, trying to hold a conversation in this fashion. Lady Elizabeth was perfectly fetching tonight, her golden hair caught up in a shining net of worked silken cords, beaded with seed-pearls, her subtly-tinted cheeks rosy from the motions of the dance. It was a shame not to be able to enjoy her more. Lord Marchmont's anger at his cousin redoubled as he made this reflection; then he realized with a start that he had lost track of Sir Jeffery altogether. With a growing suspicion he cast his eyes anxiously about the room: nowhere to be found. The set in which he and Isabella had figured was nearby, but the couple in question was missing. His apprehension mounted. Distracted, he forgot to cross to partner the waiting Miss Pye. The leader had to remind him to do so, and as he scurried across he saw the embarrassment in the poor girl's eyes and cursed Sir Jeffery inwardly. It was damned awkward, that was all. Where was the scoundrel? As soon as he possibly could, he set up his search again, but not a trace of either of the two was to be found. Oughtn't he to break from the dance, regardless of the consequences? Something much more serious was at stake. But he could not abandon Elizabeth; it would look excessively odd. It was a full three minutes before the figures brought them together again; the moment they did Lord Marchmont leaned down and whispered through the golden hair, "They've gone, Lady Elizabeth! I can't see them anywhere."

"What, Isabella and Sir Jeffery?"

"Yes. They were to dance together and now—perhaps it is coincidental," he continued doubtfully, "but I can't see either of them."

Lady Elizabeth, a sudden sense of urgency overwhelming her, grabbed his hand and pulled him abruptly from the line. "Never mind all this. I have the most dreadful feeling," she murmured, instinctively drawing him with her as she made her way through the crowd. Their departure from the dance, rash as it was, could not have suited the earl better. If Lady Elizabeth was willing to let people talk, it was certainly not for him to hang back! Anyhow, they could hardly gossip after he and Lizzie were married.

Married! It was the first time he had thought out the sentence fully—but when he did, hurrying across the parqueted floor in the wake of this abrupt, strong-willed girl, it made sense at once. Of course, they would marry—if she would have him, that was. But she would, would she not? Her hand, the palm now a little damp from excitement, gripped his so completely, so trustingly. The feeling of it fascinated him for a moment. He quite forgot why they were rushing or where they were. Of course! He must ask her to marry him at the first possible opportunity. No, he must ask Lord Trevor for permission first, mustn't he? Was it possible the Trevors had other plans for her? Would they deny him? He would fight them to the last if they tried to—

"Where do you think we ought to look first?" Elizabeth demanded, breaking into his thoughts confusingly. "Shall I go upstairs and see if Bella is in her room? It is just possible. Sometimes she and Miss Lewis go off to giggle together . . . But no, we'd better check the library first, and the breakfast-room, and— Are you quite well, my lord?" she asked, observing for the first time Lord Marchmont's disoriented aspect.

The earl strove mightily to pull himself together. "Quite well, indeed. Yes, by all means let us look in the library. If they are *not* together after all we have plenty of time to discover it, but if they are . . ."

"Yes, just my thinking exactly. Shall we split up for the search?"

"No," he shot back automatically, for though the suggestion was practical he simply did not wish to part from her. "I should not like you to have to deal with them on your own," he explained a trifle unconvincingly.

"You have the most extraordinary idea of me, really," said Elizabeth; but she held onto his hand and led him rapidly down a corridor. "I assure you I feel quite equal to such a meeting, whether alone or with an army. When I find Isabella, I shall break her neck. Imagine her taking such a chance with her reputation!"

They had reached the library and glanced inside, but there was not a sign of the lovers. Lady Elizabeth, oblivious of everything save her sister's plight, did not even notice Lady Mufftow as she passed them (on her way to fetch her smelling-salts, for the ball-room was so very overheated!) in the hall as they hastened to the breakfast-room. Lord Marchmont saw her, however, and saw moreover the pointed look she gave to their clasped hands. Very well, let the old ladies talk! said he to himself. He was not about to give up the pleasure of holding that unconscious, trusting little paw.

"Oh, my father's study!" cried Elizabeth, as they passed a closed door. "Would she dare?" She stopped short and laid a careful hand on the knob, turning it almost unwillingly. She pressed against it: the door yielded. There was no one inside.

Lady Elizabeth sighed her relief. "But perhaps they are out on a balcony somewhere," she suddenly suggested, all her anxiety returning. "How shall we ever find them?"

"Breakfast-room first," said Marchmont, "then the balconies. We'll simply look everywhere—"

"Yes, just so." Lizzie, gripping his hand ever more tightly, once more led the way swiftly down the hall. A number of people saw them as they descended the great staircase, but still Lizzie thought only of her goal. The breakfast-room was at the end of a long passage-way. As they rounded the corner into it they saw that the door was shut. "You open it, please," she asked the earl, for she felt suddenly faint at the thought of what they might discover.

Lord Marchmont laid his free hand on the knob. He turned it. The door remained closed.

"Won't it open?" hissed Lizzie, the faint feeling taking hold of her.

"I'm afraid not." Lord Marchmont looked down at her for a moment. "Are you quite well? Perhaps you had best go back to the others," he suggested gently.

She shook her head, more from stubbornness than courage. "Whatever it is, let us find out. Will you knock?"

The earl said, a little grimly, "With pleasure, ma'am." He raised his fist and hammered several sounding blows against the door. There was at first no answer.

"Did you hear something drop?" asked Lizzie.

Lord Marchmont motioned her to be silent and knocked again. Again nothing happened. "You had better ask who is inside," he told her presently. "It will sound more natural in your voice."

Elizabeth felt an unusual tightness in her throat. She willed it away and called, as steadily as possible, "I beg your pardon, but could I ask you to open the door please?" An unbidden laugh rose in her as she finished this request, and she looked up at her companion a little dizzily. "What if it isn't Isabella at all? What if it's—oh, I don't know, Sir John Firebrace and one of the Lemon girls? Oh Lord, I should die of embarrassment!"

Lord Marchmont began an answering smile, but a noise from within suddenly interrupted him. "They are unlocking," he whispered.

"I'm excessively sorry to trouble you," Lizzie called through the door in spite of herself. Just then the handle turned and the door swung open. Sir Jeffery de Guere, looking very unpleasant indeed (menacing, was the word that came to Lizzie), but not at all surprised, appeared. Behind him flickered a few candles; and beyond them—Isabella.

10

FOR A LONG, unpleasant moment no one moved. Strains of music could be heard drifting down from the ball-room: a gavotte. Lady Elizabeth thought she heard her brother's voice, and the sound of it jolted her from her momentary paralysis. "Isabella," was all she said, in a tone of extraordinary intensity. At once her younger sister broke from her pose behind Sir Jeffery and rushed headlong into Lizzie's arms.

"Thank heavens, you've saved me!" she exclaimed, burying her handsome head against Elizabeth's neck.

As this was the very last thing she had expected to hear, Lizzie could only stammer for a moment, "But—but, my dear—!"

"He was . . . oh, you have no idea! Pray, take me from him, dearest Lizzie! Oh, I beg you will," she went on, clinging ever more tightly to her astonished sister.

Elizabeth met Marchmont's eyes over Bella's shoulder. "I suppose I ought—"

"Yes, of course, take her away," said Marchmont, his face already dark with anger. "It is apparent my cousin has grossly insulted her ladyship. I wish I could say I am surprised."

Elizabeth looked from the earl's face to that of Sir Jeffery; the latter, though evidently strained, was nevertheless curiously still. Eager though she was to remove the distraught Isabella from a scene which had clearly gone far beyond her ability to control it, she was loath to leave Lord Marchmont to deal with the aftermath alone. That a bitter fury had sprung up between the two men was obvious: it was nearly palpable in the quiet air of the breakfast-room. The sense of it alarmed Elizabeth. Not knowing quite what she intended to say she began, "My lord, you will not . . . that is, I think it would be best if I—"

"Lady Elizabeth, you will not take offence, I trust, if I suggest your best course now is to concern yourself solely with Lady Isabella. I assure you I am quite equal to the rest."

"Perhaps I shall put her to bed then," murmured Lizzie, still holding the younger girl, who was now sobbing loudly against her breast. "If your lordship would be so kind as to wait till I come down—"

"I will not leave till we have talked again," said Marchmont, anticipating her. He kept a wary eye on de Guere as he spoke, as if suspecting the other man might bolt.

"Thank you, sir. Then I shall report she has taken a sudden headache, and rejoin you as soon as I may." With these words, received with a nod by the earl, Elizabeth departed. Lady Isabella, who cried noisily at every step and held tightly to her arm, did not so much as look up before they went.

"De Guere," said Lord Marchmont, shutting the door carefully before he spoke, "cousin or no cousin, you will hear from me in the morning."

"Oh, well," Jeffery replied lightly, "if you insist. Though if you've anything to say to me, I don't see why you don't just go ahead tonight. After all—here we are, old boy."

"You are trying my patience, Jeffery. I haven't much of it. My second will call upon you tomorrow. In the meanwhile, I shall show you to the door."

"No need, dear chap," said the other lightly, though even he could not maintain intact his wonted bantering tone. Tension was clearly visible in his features as he continued, "I saw it on the way in. Anyhow, I don't expect to be leaving for quite some time."

"You will leave at once or I shall call the servants and have you thrown out. Don't imagine I won't do it," added the earl, as Sir Jeffery seemed to hesitate.

"Very well, then, if you are absolutely adamant . . . I dare say supper won't be much to speak of anyhow, and I rather expect Mrs. Butler has been wondering where I am. I say, awful shame you and I can't seem to exchange two words lately without one or the other of us having to rush off, eh?"

Lord Marchmont easily ignored this cheerful monologue, which continued all the same till they had reached the front door. He broke his silence only to mention quietly, while a footman helped de Guere with his cape, "If you return, I will certainly have you thrown out on your ear. Remember that." He then turned on his heel and ascended the central staircase, stopping at the top to be sure his cousin had gone. Satisfied on this point he went back to the ball-room, scanning the crowd for Elizabeth.

Before he had spotted her, however, Lady Emilia had seen him. She floated up beside him with a teasing smile and demanded, "How now, young man, where have you been? I could have sworn I saw you leave this room with a lady in tow!"

Lord Marchmont roused himself to some semblance of good humour: there was no point involving Emilia, if he could help it. "Yes," he admitted, "and now the little minx has gone and vanished. Have you seen her?"

"Oh, my poor brother! I knew you would one day regret your ignorance of matters romantic. Why the very first lesson every schoolboy learns in love is: do not allow the lady to disappear. Even if it means holding on to her hand continually, it is absolutely imperative that you keep her at all times in sight. I see I shall be obliged to educate you," she sighed.

"But have you seen her?" insisted Jemmy, his pose of good temper ever harder to maintain.

Emilia noted the sharpness in his voice, but she ascribed it to some contretemps with Elizabeth. Hoping it would prove insignificant, she answered, "I am sorry to say I have not. Would you like me to go and look for her? Perhaps she has ripped her hem, or—"

"No, no, pray do not," he interrupted, all the while searching through the sea of faces.

"Well, I only meant to be helpful," said Emilia, a little stung.

"Yes, my dear; I am sorry. I know you did, but it's rather—" The earl heard the distraction in his own words and pulled himself together again. "I don't seem to be myself just now. It's nothing you need trouble about," he said more kindly, at last fixing his attention on her. Emilia returned his gaze with a careful, steady look.

"Of course," she said quietly. "Suppose I go off and find someone to dance with me then, shall I?"

Her brother nodded gratefully and kissed her cheek. "Let me know when you are tired and wish to leave."

"Oh, you can depend on me for that," said she, still perplexed. It had become clear to her her presence was only vexing him, however, and she was just as glad to quit his company. She was wondering if some quarrel had arisen between her brother and Lady Elizabeth, to cause him to behave so oddly; but just moments after she left him she saw the lady in question come flying up to his side, whisper a few words to him, and proceed in great haste into the thick of the crowd. Far from looking as if they'd quarreled, they appeared to be almost conspiring together. Emilia decided to apply herself diligently to enjoying the rest of the ball.

Lady Elizabeth meantime had gone to inform her mother of

Isabella's sudden ill health. "Is it serious, do you think?" asked Lady Trevor. "It is so unlike her!"

"To be sure, madam, but I do not think it serious," was her reply. She was impatient to get back to Marchmont and worried lest one of the gentlemen to whom she had promised a dance come to claim her hand. Moreover, she did not care to lie to her mother. Isabella, however, had implored her to say nothing to her parents—at least not that night. Indeed, Lizzie had been obliged to promise she would keep silent in order to get the frantic Isabella to stay in bed. A half-truth came to her, and she went on, "It seemed to me less a question of headache and more one of nerves, Mamma. I'm afraid she was so very excited about tonight that the evening has quite overwhelmed her. She seemed to be asleep when I left her, however, so I don't think you need go up."

Lady Trevor, who had enough on her mind with a hundred guests, five musicians, and thirty or forty servants to manage, allowed herself to be persuaded pretty easily, and Lizzie left her a moment later.

"Come to the library, my lord," she said in a low voice to Marchmont, as she regained his side at last. Heedless of appearances, the earl acquiesced at once. The couple hastened again down the long corridors.

"Can you imagine!" Elizabeth burst out the instant they were alone. Lord Marchmont had left the door half open, but Lizzie closed it, for she was more frightened of the servants' eavesdropping than of being closeted with the gentleman. "I can't think who I'm more furious with, my sister or Sir Jeffery. For though I am sure he must have forced himself upon her—"

"I am quite sure," broke in Marchmont grimly.

"—I am equally certain it was her own fault for allowing herself to be drawn into such a position in the first place. The silly chit! I specifically pleaded with her this evening not to go off alone—"

"But there is no excuse for his behaviour. Nothing can mitigate what has happened in the slightest. Taking advantage is taking advantage . . . and I blush to say that that is what my cousin has done. I must speak to your father, I suppose, since he is my—"

"Oh no, I hope you will not do that," interrupted Lizzie.

"But surely he must be told—"

"I had rather . . . wait a bit. The fact is, Bella has begged me to keep silent on this head, at least until she and I have discussed it together. I suppose this must sound silly," she went on, her colour rising just perceptibly, "but I should feel rather like a snitch if I were to carry the tale to my father. It's a kind of understanding Isabella and I have had since we were children . . ." Her words trailed off lamely as her embarrassment grew. She was certain the earl must think her an utter fool—a schoolgirl, and a giddy one at that.

But his lordship looked more concerned than scornful. "My dear girl," he began, then corrected at once, in some confusion, "my dear ma'am! This is too serious a matter, don't you agree, for such secrecy to be maintained around it?"

"But it is that very seriousness which compels me. Oh, you must understand that my father will take just as dim a view of Isabella's behaviour in this matter as I have. He is a very just man, no matter what the issue, and she is sure to catch—oh dear me, how can I explain it? No real harm was done, it appears, and unless some injury comes to light—"

"I fear I must disagree with you, Lady Elizabeth. Some very real harm was done—"

"But—"

"No matter how far things proceeded, or did not proceed," he continued over her protestation, "and whether or not your father is to be informed, whether or not anyone knows of it save the four of us, it is a situation that demands redress. If you are unwilling to tell your father—"

"At least till tomorrow!"

"I shall be happy to take the whole affair into my own hands. In fact, I should much prefer it. At all events you can rest assured your sister's innocence will not go undefended."

Lady Elizabeth stared at him as the significance of these words slowly came to her. "My lord, you do not intend—"

"I think we ought perhaps to terminate this discussion."

"But I want to know," she insisted, ever more alarmed. Impulsively she reached out for his hand, holding it in both of hers. "Dear sir, are you planning to call him out?"

The earl said nothing; then quietly, "Certainly not."

"But you are!"

"Dear ma'am, I beg you will not press this matter."

"Oh no, I cannot allow it. Oh dear, no! That you should risk your life merely because my sister has been an idiotish—good heavens, it's absolutely unacceptable. I could not think of it."

"Excellent," said Marchmont, smiling a little for the first time during this exchange. "Don't."

"No, I mean it is outside the realm . . . that is, if Bella knew, I feel sure— No, come to think of it, she would simply thrive on a piece of gallantry like this. The silly chit! She does make me furious. But my point is—"

"Dear Elizabeth, I know what your point is," interrupted Lord Marchmont. He spoke softly but with much feeling. It was the first time he had ever used her name without her title. The sound of it pleased both of them at the same time as it made them a little self-conscious. "I should like you to put the entire matter out of your head. I shall not fight my cousin."

"You are saying this to protect me."

"Dear ma'am!" he countered, smiling. She still held his hand, and now he grasped both of hers and carried them to his lips. "Your concern touches me, but I wish you will believe there is nothing about which to be concerned."

"So I should like to believe, but I am persuaded otherwise. Give me your word you will not call him out. I promise you nothing has passed to justify it in any case," she concluded earnestly.

"But Lady Elizabeth," he said, "I cannot give you my word."

"Oh, this is wretched!" Lizzie suddenly exclaimed. She had

at this moment a dreadfully poignant sense of what a loss it would be to her if the man now holding her hands so gently should be wounded—or worse. His insistence on imperilling himself for Isabella's sake was beginning to drive her wild, she felt, yet he would not listen to reason. She looked fully into his large grey eyes and demanded without much hope, "Is there anything I can say to dissuade you? If I told my father, would you—"

"Lady Elizabeth, there is nothing. I know when you have had time to reflect a bit, you will understand I can take only one course at this point, regardless of who knows or who would prefer it otherwise. That is what it means to be a gentleman, after all. Do you see?"

She took a step closer to him, feeling suddenly small and still. "I see," she murmured. They exchanged a long, mute glance.

"But I should like to speak to your father about another matter . . . concerning you, in fact, and me—"

"Oh dear!"

"If I might. If you would prefer that I wait, or desist altogether . . ." Marchmont could not find an end for this sentence. He had begun it on an impulse: the girl before him was so very lovely!

"No, oh no," she stammered, her colour rising again.

"No, I ought not to ask, or no, I ought not to wait?" he inquired.

"No, you ought not to . . . oh please, are you quite, quite sure of this, sir?"

"Not if it distresses you so!"

"But it does not distress . . . oh Lord, what has come over me?" For Elizabeth felt all at once very shaky and unwell indeed. Though she did not wish to lose the feel of his hands on hers, she wrested them away from him and went suddenly to sit down upon a sofa. A kind of vertigo had crept up on her. Her ears were ringing with the words she had spoken to Isabella on the night of her first meeting with the earl: "I am going to marry Lord Marchmont—see if I don't!" What insufferable assurance! What smugness! She heard her own voice say the words, heard the conceit in her tone, and her cheeks burned as if Lord Marchmont could now hear them too. Was it possible, she asked herself feverishly, that she had set her mind on having this prize and then manoeuvred the poor man till she got him? Was it conceivable the gentleman was susceptible to such manipulation? Lady Elizabeth had been accustomed since earliest childhood to get her own way in most things: there were not many things she wanted, but what she did desire she made it her business to obtain. Though Charlie was older than she, she easily outwitted him; and though Isabella was her superior in energy and imagination, she could not defend herself against Elizabeth's greater sophistication and diligence. Even her parents she had found the means of swaying, when their demands had annoyed or frustrated her. In short she had come to think of herself as—secretly—headstrong, willful, almost spider-like in her determination to control other people. Was it not possible then that she had, almost without thinking, brought the earl to such a pass that he believed himself in love with her? And did he deserve a wife so ruthless, so selfish, so—Machiavellian? She felt in this instant entirely ashamed of herself. Here was Lord Marchmont ready to die to defend the honour of her madcap younger sister, while she herself—was she worthy of anyone's regard, let alone his? Poor Lizzie was badly shaken indeed, and even her voice trembled as she finally brought forth, "I pray you will forgive me, my lord. I cannot think what has—perhaps the excitement of discovering my sister with . . ." Her voice faded.

"Naturally, quite so," said Marchmont, a trifle dubiously. "The events of this evening have overwhelmed you. I ought to have realized. I ought not to have spoke of this—this other matter tonight. Stupid of me." He bent over her solicitously for a moment, then moved away again.

"No, not at all. It's only—dear me, can you forgive me?"

"No, indeed, the apologies are all on my side. It was oafish—"

"Hardly!"

"Yes, I am not myself, that's all. Please, may I address you on this question some other time? Or oughtn't I even to ask that, perhaps?"

"No! I mean, yes, please! Oh good heavens, I seem hardly able to say two words as I intend them. I should be very honoured if . . . that is, I *believe* I should be happy if you would renew . . . Oh dear God I can't remember ever in my life being so awkward!" she finally finished, not daring even to meet his eyes. She felt her cheeks must be crimson and heartily wished herself any place but where she was. Lord Marchmont seemed to sympathize.

"I shall go then, shall I? Would you like me to call your maid for you?" he went on, edging toward the door. "Perhaps Lady Trevor—?"

"No, please!" Elizabeth remained seated on her sofa, staring disconsolately at her toes. She risked a single glance at him, then averted her face at once. "I only need a moment to compose myself," she mumbled.

"Certainly. Shall I stay with you?"

"Oh no—"

"Then I shall go," said the poor man, thoroughly ill at ease. It was abundantly clear that something in his proposal had upset the girl no end, and he had a strong suspicion she would be glad to see the back of him just now. What had he said? He had been quite confident ten minutes before that she would not discourage his suit. An old resentment flared in him suddenly, and he reminded himself that women were women, after all. The very best of them was bound to be impossible some time or other. He had said so himself to Lord Weld, not two weeks before. It was Charlotte Beaudry all over again, gaining his trust, then marrying someone else. Confused and uncomfortable, he made a final bow to Lady Elizabeth and took himself out of the room. He had a profound sense of relief as he strode down the corridor away from the painful scene. Compared to this a duel with de Guere would be positively enjoyable. At least if he wounded Sir Jeffery he would know how and why.

The thought of his cousin recalled him to the necessity of arranging a meeting. Naturally the cartel must not be delivered till the morning, but he ought to go home and write it and discuss the affair with Weld. He entered the ball-room and found that gentleman in company with Emilia, the two of them being engaged in a lively debate with Charles Stickney and old Lord Frane. The controversy was something to do with the morality of waltzing. Lord Marchmont managed to break it up and disengage his party from the others. "Emilia my dear, will you say I have failed in my duty if I ask to leave now?"

"Your duty—"

"I mean, this is one of the social engagements to which I was bound by lot. Have I fulfilled my obligation?"

"Oh, the poor man!" exclaimed Emilia to Lord Weld. "He is really very good, don't you think? I daresay we can show a little clemency at this point, or do you feel I am too lenient?"

"I am sure the poor fellow has suffered enough," agreed Weld. "Shall we carry him home then, you and I?"

"Oh do let's," said Emilia feelingly, taking her brother by the arm. "There is still such a crush, it hardly seems necessary to take our leave of Lady Trevor. Suppose we call on them soon instead?"

"Yes, very well, my dear," said Marchmont, rather sharply, for he had been through such a great deal that evening that it was difficult for him to maintain the façade of gaiety he considered necessary for Emilia's sake.

"Gruff, isn't he?" she murmured, smiling, to Warrington Weld as the three of them made their way down to the front door. "Turns into a regular bear after midnight, it seems. We're missing supper for your sake, Jemmy, you know. You might at least be civil."

"I expect we'll find something to feed upon at home," said he, essaying a smile.

"Oh, listen to him! Feed upon, he says. You see, he is a bear after all. Next he'll be wanting a nice cave and a six-month's nap."

"Perhaps we can chain him up and teach him to dance," suggested Weld lightly, though it was clear to him something was troubling his friend. It was clear, for that matter, to Emilia as well, but she divined that her brother would prefer her not to notice. She therefore continued to tease and chaff him all the way home and only manifested her concern in the especially tender kiss with which she bade him good night. Then she made her way upstairs, leaving the gentlemen (she hoped) to open their hearts to one another. In order to give them their privacy the sooner she pretended not to be hungry. In fact, however, she was ravenous and secretly sent her maid down to the kitchen to fetch her (under the cover of her apron) a little bread and cheese.

The facts of the matter were soon made known to Weld by Emilia's brother. The two men sat in Marchmont's library, talking over a bottle of claret and some cold ham. Lord Weld took the news with appropriate grimness. "No, you're right, old man, you can't let it go by," he said when the earl had finished speaking.

"Hardly. You will stand me second, won't you?"

"My dear fellow—!" exclaimed the other rather huskily, for he would gladly have died twice over for this friend. "You need not ask."

Lord Marchmont looked his gratitude in silence.

"I'm curious to see what sort of a second de Guere drags up, mind you," Lord Weld continued. "Doubtless some twopenny criminal or other. Should be a joy trying to work out an apology with him."

"But I don't want an apology," Jemmy interrupted.

"I beg your pardon?"

"I say, I want to fight him. The time for anything else has gone by."

"But if he offers an apology, you must accept it," remonstrated the other mildly.

"Then you must prevent him from offering it."

"What, and insure your danger! I jolly well won't."

"Then I must find another second."

"Any second with a conscience would do the same, March-mont! What are you thinking of? Why it's part of the code. Every possible effort must be made to reconcile the parties before the duel." Lord Weld thrust both his long pale hands into his carroty hair. "When did you become so bellicose? I seem to remember you rather peaceful than otherwise."

The earl replied rather brusquely, "I cannot sit idly by while this cousin of mine ruins yet another girl. Especially when the girl in question is the sister of my—well, I simply cannot. I am sorry. If you want to know the whole truth, I mean to shoot to kill."

"You can't! Why, you'd be obliged to leave England, old man! The affair would certainly come to light, and then—"

"I think I had best ask someone else to second me, the more I consider it," Marchmont broke in soberly. "You are going to regret your hand in it, if my aim is true, and there's no point in your involving yourself. I can find someone else easily enough. Perhaps even Halcot would be more suitable. Not that I wouldn't rather have you, but—well, I think you're rather too much a friend to render me this particular service with a whole heart."

Lord Weld stood up. He had not a commanding presence as a rule, but some emotion now transformed his air in such a way as to make him quite formidable. "Marchmont," said he, "enough nonsense. If you are determined, then you are deter-mined. It is well to discuss these matters, but I hope you will not insult me by supposing I am not as capable of acting in deadly earnest as you yourself."

Marchmont paused. "You are certain?" he asked.

"Yes."

"Then I thank you, Weld," said the other, impulsively reaching out to shake Weld's hand. They were silent again, for a moment, then, "My only real fear now is that the coward won't accept. He said he wouldn't."

Lord Weld was shocked. "How can a man hold his head up—?" he broke out in surprise.

"I am sure Sir Jeffery would tell you he uses his neck to hold up his head, and finds it does the job very nicely. Well, I must write the wretch a challenge, I suppose. Will you help me?"

Lord Weld, still musing over the idea of a gentleman who could refuse a duel, shook his head as if to rid it of cobwebs and willingly agreed. The two friends then turned to the literary task at hand.

11

LORD HALCOT found his sisters in their sitting-room, in company with Amy Lewis. Lizzie and Isabella had had a private wrangle earlier, during which a severe set-down by the elder girl had been exchanged for a promise from the younger never to repeat her folly, if only Elizabeth would keep this instance a secret between them. This duly agreed upon, Lizzie thought it best to play mum on the subject of Marchmont's probable involvement. Isabella seemed truly chastened, and there was no point in feeding any stray romantic notions she might still be holding by informing her of a duel. Anyhow it was a good policy to keep such an affair as much as possible under wraps. It was a dangerous business to all concerned. So Lady Elizabeth reasoned, in any case, and therefore held her tongue.

Miss Lewis had naturally been made privy to the events of the previous evening, having first been sworn to secrecy, of course. She was deeply troubled by her old friend's reckless

behaviour—and more than a little hurt when she discovered
how and why she had been sent home from Lackington Allen's that day (for this too came out)—but her sympathy for
Bella, who now seemed so shaken and so miserable, easily
outweighed these other sentiments. The poor girl was piteous!
She had been persuaded to rise and dress only with difficulty;
and even then she took breakfast in the sitting-room, where
she still sat now, shrouded in a quilt, huddled into a corner of
the couch. She was pale and whimpered more or less continually; when she spoke it was mostly of the treacherous
falseness of the opposite sex. It was not what one could call
amusing conversation, and on the whole Elizabeth was as
happy to see her brother as she had ever been.

He entered with his usual enthusiasm, bounding across the
threshold after a cursory knock, and tossed a bouquet at Isabella, while he bowed his salutations to the others.

"Who is it from?" Amy could not help asking, as Isabella
bent her blond head over the handful of flowers. There were
only five or six of them, knotted with a velvet riband, but they
were a fresh, handsome sight.

"Yes, who, Charlie?" seconded Lizzie, indicating a chair in
which he might seat himself.

"De Guere," said he. "Just came from a round of sparring
with him—practice, I mean, naturally. He's not bad." Lord
Halcot delivered this news with a grin, the happy smile of the
blissfully ignorant. Oh, for the gay, stupid selfishness of youth!
Poor Charlie was about to lose it forever, more's the pity, but
we must all put away childish things, I suppose.

"You idiot," hissed Lizzie all at once, unable to contain
herself. Perhaps if she had not been so glad to see him in the
first place, her disappointment now would have been less bitter. In any case she lashed out, "Your little friend has nearly
ruined our sister."

At the same moment as these words were delivered, Amy
Lewis sighed deeply and exclaimed, "Oh Charlie, if you
would only pay attention!" As mild a reproach as this was, it
was stronger stuff than she generally used with him, and I

think the nip from this gentle lamb hurt Lord Halcot more than the fangs of his sister.

The object of these animadversions dropped into a chair as if he had been shot and requested, with a dazed look, an explanation.

"Oh never mind," said Elizabeth, disgusted, while Isabella continued to bury her head in the flowers. Her face was hidden from view, and Lizzie wondered if she might be crying again.

"There was an unfortunate . . . contretemps last night," said Amy more helpfully. "Between your sister and de Guere. I don't think we need go into it again," she added, looking to Lizzie for confirmation, "except to ask you not to mention him to us—and certainly not to bring him here."

"You oughtn't to see him at all, Charlie," advised Elizabeth sharply. "Never mind why, Amy is right. The less said the better."

"Oh, I say, this is too much. Why are you abusing me so? It's a bit hard on a fellow, giving him half an explanation and a couple of orders in the same breath. Bella, you'll tell me, won't you?"

Isabella spoke directly into her flowers: "I had rather not discuss it."

"Come come, I haven't got all day. In fact I haven't got another five minutes," complained Halcot, jumping up as if to illustrate his point. At this moment he was interrupted by a knock at the door; answering it, Elizabeth found Bolton carrying a card on a tray.

"Miss Lucilla Partridge to see Lady Isabella," explained the butler.

"My sister gave orders she was not at home," Lizzie told him.

"Yes ma'am, indeed. And so I told Miss Partridge. But she was not to be turned away, I assure you. She seemed about to burst into tears, to say truth, ma'am. I told her I would do what I could."

"Oh, very well, for goodness' sake, send her up," said Lizzie impatiently, for behind her she could hear Charlie beginning to whine again about how little time he had and how much he was entitled to know, and she did not wish Bolton to be treated to the dialogue that seemed bound to ensue. She closed the door on his back and turned to the others. "Lucilla Partridge is here. She insists on talking to Bella."

"Oh Lord!" exclaimed her sister, while Halcot burst out, "Don't you understand, I must go at once! I have an auction to attend."

"An auction?"

"Yes. Collectibles. Er . . . ivory and—ah, porcelain and the like. At Phillip's sale-rooms. I mustn't be late."

"Oh no, that would be ghastly," agreed Lady Elizabeth. "Only fancy!"

"But perhaps we'd better tell him—" commenced Amy, suddenly concerned lest Halcot go to de Guere for an explanation.

"I can't. You do it," answered Lizzie.

"I know, come with me to Phillip's," said Charlie all at once. "You'll enjoy the auction I'm sure, and you can tell me what's up on the way."

Amy Lewis, always eager to accompany Charlie anywhere, nevertheless looked to the others for guidance. "Yes, go," Elizabeth finally told her. "You'll know what's best to say, and what is better left alone."

Lord Halcot began to protest at this, but he reconsidered and instead hurried Amy out of the room with him. "For Miss Partridge will be here in an instant," he explained, "and then we'll have the devil of a time saying good-bye." Miss Lewis gladly allowed herself to be swept off on his arm, and the two made their exit only seconds before Lucilla Partridge entered the room.

Miss Partridge was a diminutive creature, dark of complexion, hair, and eyes, with a sweet expression and a tendency to wear rather too much lace. She came into the room hesitantly, the tears which Bolton had mentioned still shining in her soft brown eyes. Isabella met their gaze only briefly before again turning her glance towards the flowers. "Miss Partridge," said Elizabeth civilly, with a bow. She offered the caller a chair.

"I hope I am not disturbing you—"

"No, no."

"But you see, it seemed absolutely urgent that I come . . ." The soft, husky voice trailed off into silence.

Elizabeth waited. Isabella (nose still in her bouquet) waited. Presently Miss Partridge said, "May I speak frankly?"

"Oh, please."

"Very well, then. I'll say it straight out, shall I?"

"Indeed. Please do."

Lucilla gulped. "It concerns—you won't be offended?"

"I shouldn't expect so!"

"Very well, then . . ." Another gulp. A sigh. Miss Partridge gripped her hands together and recommenced, "It concerns Sir Jeffery de Guere."

"Oh dear, I'm afraid—"

"Lady Isabella, I beg you will take note of my example and profit by it," Lucilla rushed on almost severely.

"But—"

"He is a wicked, wicked man! I know you will find this difficult to believe; so should I have once upon a time, but—"

"Dear Miss Partridge, I pray you will spare yourself—"

"You must positively not trust him. Positively! Believe me, I come to you as a friend. Perhaps you will think it is otherwise; perhaps you will even think—"

"Really, Miss—"

"That I am speaking out of pique, or spite, or . . . rivalry, but no! That is not the case," her words spilled out, "not at all, I assure you. I wish with all my heart I had never seen him. I saw him dancing with you last night and—forgive me—I saw the way you looked at him, and I even saw . . ."

No one interrupted her this time.

"I even saw you quit the room together, and I could not, no I *could* not, when you had been so kind as to invite me to your ball, let this go by without at least coming here, without advising—indeed, without *imploring* you to turn away from him at once!"

"Miss Partridge," Elizabeth at last broke in.

"Have I offended you? I am desperately sorry!"

"Miss Partridge, no, not at all. You are most kind to come and address my sister. But the fact is, she has seen just precisely the traits you mention in Sir Jeffery . . . I mean that he is wicked and untrustworthy, and—with all due thanks for your kindness in coming—in short, she has been spared your trials and yet learned her lesson already."

"She has?" This was delivered with a perfectly unfeigned amazement.

"She has."

"All on her own?"

"Just so."

"And without . . . without being pushed to the lengths which I . . ."

"Exactly."

Miss Partridge was silent for a moment. She looked bewildered. "I am sorry to seem so dubious, but I can hardly fathom one's becoming disenchanted with Sir Jeffery before he—that is, before—"

"Miss Partridge?"

"Oh me, perhaps I had better go now," said the poor girl, looking wildly uncomfortable. Knowing de Guere as she did, it seemed to her impossible that any woman should manage to elude him altogether. She had come all at once to the alternative solution, to wit, that Isabella had in fact been ruined by him last night, but had contrived to keep it from her family or from the monde in any case. The very idea of it embarrassed her. Looking closely at Isabella now, she could easily imagine it was so: the poor thing looked dreadful, and she hadn't said two words. If it were so this visit must be unwelcome in the extreme: indeed, it was but rubbing salt into a wound. Miss Partridge leapt to her feet. She looked so frail and distressed that Elizabeth imagined for a moment she would fall over at once; however, she did not. Sputtering apologies and thanks, she made her adieux and departed. Such was her awkwardness that she knocked over a mahogany candle-stand as she went. Elizabeth righted it as the sitting-room door closed behind her.

"What a very extraordinary visit," she remarked. "Isabella?"

But Lady Isabella would only stare at her bouquet, carefully stroking the stem of each flower in turn—as if counting them.

Amy Lewis was meanwhile busy putting Lord Halcot into possession of a set of facts he was not very happy to hear. Miss Lewis did not herself know all the details, and she edited what she did know so as to help Isabella appear in a better light, so it was but a milk-and-water version of the affair that reached Lord Halcot. Nevertheless, he heard quite sufficient to make him swear never to speak to Sir Jeffery de Guere again. "The cut direct, that's what I'll give him," he declared to Amy as, reins in hand, he directed his well-sprung perch-phaeton through the traffic in New Bond Street.

"Watch out for that coach, sir!" the tiger behind them dared to interject, just in the nick of time.

"I never was so deceived by a fellow in all my life. In fact, I'm not sure but what I oughtn't to call him out," went on our nonpareil. "What do you say? Shall I?"

"Oh no, Charlie, I pray you will not! The cut direct will be quite adequate, I am sure." Miss Lewis's sterling heart beat a little faster with alarm at the very thought of her Charlie in a duel.

"Well," said the buck reluctantly, "if you say so . . ."

"Hi there, to your right sir!" shouted the miserable groom, as a vast wagon lumbered out of an alley.

"Oh, I do say so," replied Miss Lewis fervently, not the least bit concerned for her own welfare when Charlie's was under discussion.

"You know, Amy, I've always had a great deal of respect for your judgement."

"Have you?" It was not a terribly feminine point on which to be admired, but it sufficed to bring a blush to Amy's cheeks.

"Yes. In fact—"

"Oh, sir, the curb, the curb!" shrieked Jack, the poor tiger, as the phaeton veered perilously near the pavement.

Lord Halcot corrected his reins but murmured to the lady, "The silly fellow is probably drunk, but I humour him, for he knows every trick about horseflesh."

"In fact *what* Charlie?" Amy could not prevent herself saying.

"I beg your pardon?"

"You were going to say something. You said, 'In fact—' and then the tiger interrupted."

"He did?"

"Yes."

"That's cheek!"

"Well, I think he was frightened . . ."

"Still," insisted Halcot.

"Yes. Well, in fact—what?"

"I beg your pardon?"

"What you were going to say."

"What I was . . . Oh! What was I going to say, you asked. Hmmm," he frowned, drawing the carriage up to the doors of Phillip's rooms, "I wonder what it could have been. What was I talking about?" He looked at Amy perplexedly, then jumped from the carriage and ran around to hand her down, leaving the ribbons for the tiger.

Poor Amy, who knew perfectly well what he had been talking about, nevertheless felt it was best to yield to circumstances. "I don't remember," she lied, accepting his assistance. Lord Halcot shrugged.

"I expect it was nothing of importance," said he, dismissing the subject. A moment later they entered the crowded auction room together.

"Lord Halcot!" cried the Honble. Middleford Lemon, spotting them and descending upon them at once. "What a relief you are here; I was afraid you might be late. They are putting up those Russian pieces first, of all things." Mr. Lemon delivered this news as if it were the most astonishing since the disappearance of M. de Lavalette.

Charlie mustered up a considerable show of enthusiasm in replying, then introduced Miss Lewis to Middleford.

"We have met, I think," said Amy, suddenly struck by the hideous possibility that Susannah Lemon might have accompanied her brother. In an instant this apprehension was confirmed, for both Augusta and Susannah drifted languidly up to join them.

Susannah's bow was decidedly cool, her sister's little less so. Amy, determined not to lose her temper this time, gave a civil nod in return and even forced herself to smile. "What a lovely costume you wore last night," she remarked to Augusta, requiring of herself ever greater displays of courage. "Wherever did you find those darling gloves? Was that *point d'Espagne* at the cuffs?"

Miss Lemon looked bored. "Oh la, *those* gloves? Did you like them? My father brought them home for me from the Continent simply ages ago. I was a little ashamed of wearing them, but they were the only ones I had that matched the particular blue in my shawl and slippers. What did you think of them, Susannah?"

"Oh, they were pretty enough in their day, I suppose," said that young lady carelessly. "One sees so much of *point d'Espagne* this season, however."

"Indeed?" said Amy, a little stunned by the nonchalant rudeness of this exchange, but steadfast in her resolution to be courteous herself. "In any case your gown suited you most wonderfully. I wish I could wear green, but it seems to take the colour from my cheeks."

Augusta Lemon only stared at her. "Charles," said Susannah suddenly, while Amy drew a sharp breath at the unexpected familiarity of the appelation, "have you really come to see these tiresome old porcelains? Or did you come to see me? Be honest; you can speak freely." She had been looking dead with boredom (for Halcot had been speaking to her brother), but she now roused herself to quite a pitch of animation, sparkling up into his face with all the considerable power of her long green eyes. Miss Lewis noticed the shimmer on her copper-coloured hair, and felt wretched.

Lord Halcot gave his ready smile but looked uncomfortable. "I can agree with you that the porcelains are old," he said, "but not that they are tiresome. Don't you find them beautiful?"

"Oh well . . . But which is the more beautiful, then," Susannah went on with a winning pout, "I or they? If you were shipwrecked on a desert isle, for example, which would you prefer to have with you?"

She delivered these words without removing her eyes from his face and spoke as if there were no one in the room but themselves. Amy Lewis was beginning to feel embarrassed for her, as well as distressed on her own account. Lord Halcot, his blue eyes as bright as Amy had ever seen them, suddenly gave her a sidelong glance as if to say, "Did you hear what this woman is asking me? How am I to answer her?" The secret message improved Amy's spirits a thousandfold. "I am sure Lord Halcot would not wish such a fate upon you," she volunteered on an impulse, "and would rather make shift alone with the porcelains than involve you in so tedious a situation."

Lord Halcot thought this an admirable answer and laughed aloud. Amy's spirits rose even higher. Miss Susannah, however, appeared rather nettled. "Charles can answer for himself, I am sure," she said in a low, unpleasant tone. "How do you answer, sir? Would you prefer a China doll or a breathing one?"

"Oh, I say, Susannah—" commenced Middleford Lemon, coming out of his private oblivion for a brief, rare appearance in the world. He had noticed at last how peculiarly his sister was behaving, and it discomfitted him. However, as he did not in fact say anything following this startled, "I say," his waking to consciousness carried but little consequence.

"Oh dear," said Charlie presently, "I suppose if I were ship-wrecked on a desert island . . . what I should like most was another fellow, to help me build a boat and get away from the blighted place. How's that?" he finished, with an uncomfortable grin and another look askance to Amy Lewis. She answered this look with a grateful smile and a kind of warm shining in her eyes that must surely have struck him as more lovely and more valuable than any glitter or sparkle Miss Susannah Lemon could summon.

In any case, Miss Susannah had given up trying to look charming—or, if she had not given up, she had certainly stopped succeeding. In sooth she looked positively grim as she replied, "Sir, I perceive I have asked you a question that is beyond your powers of answering—for you have failed to reply to it utterly. Next time I must choose a simpler one, that will not elude you. Try this—will you excuse me?"

"Why of course," returned Charlie, not so much disappointed as angry. The two Miss Lemons, without a bow or a glance at Amy, took their brother by both arms and drew him off to the central sale-room, where the bidding was just starting. Middleford Lemon threw a helpless, rather comical smile to his friend Halcot as they dragged him away, and managed a sketchy nod to Amy Lewis; it was clear he regretted their rudeness, but he seemed powerless to interrupt it. Miss Lewis and Halcot stood alone in the now emptying entrance hall. They were silent for a moment. Then, "Do you know, I find I am not much of a mind to look over these porcelains after all," said Charlie. "Would it be too awful of me to take you home again?"

The reader can imagine whether Amy Lewis objected.

"Let me send for Jack then; I hope the rascal hasn't ducked

into a tavern." Lord Halcot beckoned to a footman and gave him his instructions. "We should not be obliged to wait long," he went on to Amy.

She nodded. Her heart was so full of love for him in that instant that she dared not open her mouth lest her feelings spill out in words. Unless she mistook the signs very badly, Lord Halcot was coming to a new understanding of the Lemon girls in particular and women in general. He was looking at her in a new way. It was all she could do not to let out a whoop.

And, indeed, the slightly rusty but essentially competent wheels of his lordship's intelligence were beginning to run again in earnest. It came to him that Miss Susannah Lemon had been not only rude but also coarse and vulgar, in a way the lady now by his side could never dream of. It came to him that he had been insulted and laughed at by a woman to whom he had never done harm, and for whom on the contrary he had gone to a great deal of trouble. He was further aware, slowly, that he was utterly, perfectly angry, and that his anger was justified. Moreover, Miss Lewis had come to his aid: she had stood by him, and though he had been made to appear ridiculous, and though she herself had been treated with abominable incivility, she had rallied to his cause and rescued him. A dim awareness that she had, perhaps, done as much before—possibly often—though he had never noticed it commenced to take hold of him, and Charlie at last put a name to the emotion now awakening in him. Affection, was the word he chose. Within a few hours of their return to Haddon House he had renamed the sentiment love.

━━━━━━

Mr. Searle, who had the honour to be employed as butler at number 21 Cavendish Square, was growing just a wee bit tired of standing at the ready by the front door of that place. He had already opened it twice in the last five minutes, for he could have sworn he heard Lady Emilia's voice proclaiming her readiness to depart, but each time the lady had recalled some other errand or detail, it seemed, for though the gentlemen were hatted and cloaked (Searle knew, for he had seen them himself) the party did not leave. Again he heard her ladyship's voice floating down the stairs to the entrance hall, this time speaking to her maid: "Can you imagine, Mary, how that fan could have found its way to such a place? It passes all understanding. Truly, I sometimes believe objects pick themselves up and walk away to wherever they like, for if you or I ever put a fan in a hat-box I . . . well, I'd eat a fan if I thought that. Anyhow, I'm glad we found it, and doubly glad I remembered to look for it, for these private recitals can be so tedious, and if Lady Mufftow were to see me yawning . . . Oh Jemmy," she interrupted herself, and Searle knew she had again joined her brother and Lord Weld in the drawing-room, "are you quite out of patience with me? I know I have kept you waiting this age, but I simply could not have sat through an entire concert without something to hide behind. I don't know how you men do it. Jemmy, are you quite all right? You look rather grey, dear. Doesn't he look grey, Lord Weld?"

"He looks more . . . ivory to me, ma'am," said that gentleman.

"Oh, ivory, does he?" she answered vaguely. "Well, but how do you feel? How does he feel, that's the question."

"Perfectly fit," said Marchmont, as Searle had known he would. "Do you think you have everything now, my dear?"

"Oh yes," she said, distraction still in her voice, "I'm only concerned for you." Searle heard steps descending and opened the front door a third time, nodding as he did so to the waiting coachman. "You look so drawn, love. Doesn't he look drawn, Lord Weld? Surely you see that!"

"Perhaps . . . finely drawn," admitted Weld, with a little smile. "Nothing too dreadful in any case."

The party had now gained the entry hall, and Searle began

his farewell bow to them, thinking fondly as he did so of a certain beefsteak pie he happened to know was in the kitchen. Lady Emilia was looking lovely as ever, he noticed, as she swept past him, and also noticed that she was right about her brother. The man looked worn, or worried. So did his friend. The party had almost departed—Lady Emilia was just being handed into the carriage—when a messenger ran up on foot, waving a letter, out of breath.

"Here, boy," said Searle automatically, for the young messenger was hesitating, evidently unsure as to whether or not to hand the note directly to the Quality.

"Oh Lord, what's this?" Emilia exclaimed, stepping back from the carriage and looking at Marchmont. "Jemmy, is this political business, do you think? You're already tired enough—"

"I'll take that, boy," Marchmont interposed, without answering her. He gave Searle a nod of dismissal; at least Searle hoped it was dismissal, for that pie would not keep warm forever. Nevertheless, he lingered in the doorway—duty first.

Lord Marchmont had given the messenger a coin, and the boy wandered away; Emilia was glad to see this, for if the missive had been political in nature he would almost certainly have stayed for a reply. Her brother had broken the wafer on the letter and now held it under one of the two great lamps that flanked the front door of number 21. He read it, it appeared, with one sweep of the eyes, then crumpled it and thrust it into a pocket of his cloak. Lord Weld was looking at him attentively. "Well?" he asked finally, as Marchmont came away from the lamp.

The earl's expression was unmistakably severe. He said nothing, but his eyes locked with those of his friend and he gave a decisive nod. Lady Emilia saw their exchanged glance perfectly clearly, in spite of the dark night and dim lamplight, and wondered what on earth it betokened. However, it looked as if she was not to be informed, for though she asked and asked, when all three had at last entered the carriage and driven away, neither Weld nor her brother would reply to her. In fact, Lord Marchmont hinted it was a *billet-doux*, and further intimated that it was very rude of Emilia to pester him so about it. Having seen the look on his face when he read it, Emilia did not believe this for a moment; however, she was obliged in the end to desist. By the time they arrived at Lady Mufftow's door, the conversation had turned to old Lord Frane, who was said to be in a dreadful state of unhealth, and who, moreover, was expected to leave nearly all his holdings to his daughter Dorothea and her husband Mr. Stickney, instead of his own son Humphrey.

The reader will be relieved to know, by the by, that in spite of all delays and alarms, Mr. Searle's meat-pie was still steaming at the centre by the time he broke into it. A certain Rosellen, the second upstairs maid, had thought of him and kept it warm in the oven till he came—whether through sheer human kindness or for motives more particular and more interesting, it does not belong to our story to inquire.

I doubt if there is anyone even distantly acquainted with the activities of the London monde who is not already well aware of the excellence and refinement of Lady Mufftow's musical Evenings. Whether the reader has been so fortunate as to have attended one himself (in which case we may perhaps have met!), or if, as seems more likely, he has only heard of these delightful occasions at second-hand is really of no great moment: in either case, he will understand that Lord Marchmont and Lady Emilia, their friend Lord Weld, the Trevors and all their brood, Sir Arthur and Lady Maria Lemon and the fruit of their happy union, Sir John Firebrace, Miss Pye, and even Mrs. Stickney (Dorothea Frane that was, of course, who naturally continued a trifle distracted by her father's uncertain condition) all enjoyed the recital thoroughly. Mr. Braham sang very beautifully, indeed, and if I have listed only the names above as having appreciated him, it is not because there were no others whose ears were also well repaid for listening, but rather because there were so many others that their names would be tedious to record. I refer the reader to the *Times* for a complete inventory of guests, as well as an unedited account of Mr. Braham's repertoire, and pass on to other aspects of the evening more pertinent to our tale.

There were two events that night that concern us nearly. The first was a conversation that took place at the supper-table between Lord Marchmont and Lady Elizabeth. The former had made sure to take the latter in to supper, and I am sorry to say that neither made a very good companion to his other neighbours at the festive board, for they spoke only to each other. Here were the words they exchanged, I need not explain *à propos* of what:

"Is it arranged?" This from Lady Elizabeth.

"Is what arranged, dear ma'am?"

"Your—meeting." On second thoughts, and with alarm: "It cannot have taken place already!"

"Oh! No, indeed. But I think we agreed you would forget all about this little matter, did not we?"

"How can I forget it?" In a tone mixing equal parts unhappiness and pique: "Do you have such a low opinion of me as that? Surely you do not suppose I can think of anything else. Can you?"

Uncomfortably: "I can. I can think of you. It is altogether more pleasant. Do you mind it?"

With distraction: "I do not—oh, and yet it does concern me . . . My lord, there's a footman at your elbow, I think he wishes to pour you more wine. Yes—no, thank you, none for me. But, Lord Marchmont, is there nothing I can do to dissuade you from pursuing this . . . matter? My sister is somewhat moped—indeed, she stopped at home this evening, as you can see—but she is not harmed in any other way, I assure you. The thought that you may come to injury, or worse—" A shudder interrupting her, Lord Marchmont broke in.

"I told you, did I not, that the matter was closed. Lady Elizabeth, you are not to disturb yourself in this wise. I am in no danger."

"Am I to be put off by an assertion you will not even support with your work of honour?" Unhappily, Lady Elizabeth raised her goblet to her lips—only to discover it was empty. She set it down again. Presently, in a low mutter no one but Marchmont could possibly have heard, she gave him this warning, "I tell you to your head, sir, I will murder you if you allow yourself to be killed. Do you understand me? I should never forgive you."

The earl turned to look at her fully. A sweet, sad, unmistakably loving smile hovered about her mouth. It was all he could do not to kiss her. "Lady Elizabeth," he returned in an urgent whisper, "may I speak to your father? If I am not killed, I mean."

Her qualms and scruples struggled with her admiration of his lordship and her pleasure in his hopeful smile—and were subdued. "Yes," she answered, so shyly that he could not even hold her glance. She stared unseeing at the rim of one of Lady Mufftow's handsomest Sèvres plates and, blinking at it as if it were a sunburst or a blinding mist, repeated that small, important word: "Yes."

The second scene of note (for there were two, remember) that night at Lady Mufftow's concerned Lady Elizabeth's brother Charlie, and had more to do with "No" than its so-pleasant opposite. Miss Susannah Lemon, something fatigued by the hum of conversation in the drawing-room after supper and wishing (if truth be known) more than anything else to go home and loosen the bodice of her gown—which was cut very tight, and buried in which she could have sworn there was a pin of some kind, for it pricked her every time she turned round—Miss Susannah Lemon, I say, tired of throwing anguished and meaningful glances at her sociable parents, decided instead to go outside onto a balcony to refresh herself with a breath of midnight air. It so happened that Lord Halcot, who had been trying to win her attention all evening, observed her at this instant and decided in his turn to follow her out there, and it also happened, by a stroke of ill fortune, that Amy Lewis was deep in conversation with Sir John Firebrace at just this moment and had inevitably lost track of Charlie as a consequence. Young Charlie, having first won grudging permission from Miss Susannah to address her, began by making a few awkward remarks on the subject of the night, which was cool and pleasant. Miss Susannah agreed, though rather warily, for she sensed that something was up with Charlie. She was correct: after a few moments of insubstantial conversation he turned the discussion to their afternoon's meeting at Phillip's sale-rooms.

"I was left with a rather uncomfortable sensation," were his exact words on this head, and he added, "to be perfectly candid."

Miss Lemon remained unruffled. "I beg you will not be perfectly candid for my sake," she returned. "I am quite happy with conventional lies and half-truths from you."

"I trust you are joking," said Charlie uneasily.

"Not at all. There are situations which demand honesty and situations entirely better off without it. Between you and me, sir, I see no reason to impose any rigorous candour."

"Very well, then," said Halcot, with a growing awareness of how meanly she had trifled with him, "suppose I see such a reason. In fact, I do see such a reason, and I should like to address you, if I might, in a quite serious vein."

It was at this moment that Amy Lewis, having concluded her chat with John Firebrace and finding the drawing-room disagreeably close, drifted within earshot of the couple on the balcony. Lord Halcot had naturally left the door partly open behind him—for he wished to avoid any suggestion of impro-

priety—and Amy had very nearly stepped out onto the plat-
form for a breath herself when she caught his familiar voice
saying the last of those words recorded above. There will be
those among my readers I am sure who will opine (from the
comfort of their arm-chairs) that Miss Lewis ought to have
moved away at once, the moment she became aware that she
was, albeit inadvertently, eavesdropping; and perhaps those
readers will be right. Nevertheless, I must ask them to examine whether or not they themselves, in similar circumstances,
would have had the strength to act according to such excellent moral precepts. I know I should not have had such
strength—to be perfectly candid, as Charlie said.

In any case, Amy Lewis did not immediately move away
from the unique vantage point she had stumbled into; and if
she was wrong, she was more than adequately punished for
the act by what she overheard—or I should say, imagined she
overheard. For Miss Lemon's answer was (with a languid pout
Amy could not see), "You may address me, my lord, since you
ask so urgently."

"I thank you. I hope you will speak plainly, for I mean to do
so myself," he returned earnestly—and on the other side of the
door Miss Lewis's alarm (for she was already alarmed) increased.

Miss Susannah observed, "So you have warned."

"Yes. So I have warned."

"Pray, go on," she encouraged, when he was silent.

Oh heaven! thought Amy, during this lapse. He is going to
ask her to marry him! The poor girl naturally had such a
prospect on the brain, and so was in no position to note that
the tension in Charlie's voice was not that of nervous excitement but rather that of irritation, nor that Miss Susannah's
subdued tones betrayed more ennui than girlish pliability.

Charlie cleared his throat. "Very good. In that case . . . it
concerns your—the esteem in which you hold me, if I may call
it that."

Oh Lord, Amy thought, here it is! If she accepts him—and how can she not?—what shall I do? But I must—that is, I mustn't listen—

"You may, if you like. I beg you will speak your mind directly, sir," said Miss Susannah, "for it is a bit chilly out here—"

"Oh, are you cold? Shall I—?"

The gesture he made was toward the drawing-room and indicated his willingness to fetch her shawl, but of course Amy could not know that, and she naturally assumed her Charlie had moved toward Susannah.

"No, pray do not trouble yourself," said that young lady now, an odd response, in Amy's opinion.

But I really must not listen any longer, thought she miserably. I am no better than a spy if I do. I must . . . I shall . . . By dint of much silent exhortation, Miss Lewis succeeded in forcing her feet to move away from the half-open door. In a moment Lady Emilia had swooped down upon her with some trivial question, obliging her to turn her mind, though only momentarily, away from the imagined crisis on the balcony.

For imagined it was indeed. If Amy had listened a little longer, she would have heard her idol take Miss Susannah quite severely to task for the rudeness she showed that afternoon before the auction—not, as Charlie pointed out to her, so much for his sake as for Miss Lewis's. He explained, with as much civility as he could muster, but in no uncertain terms, that he could not sit idly by while the Misses Lemon employed their superior wit (he was diplomat enough to include this reference) to discomfit his sister Isabella's dearest friend. He further admitted, quite handsomely in fact, that he himself was not the cleverest fellow on earth, but he was sure he had never meant Susannah any harm, and he was sorry and sad the same was not true of her. In short, he spoke up for himself very finely indeed, and said no word which was not manly and precise.

Whether or not Miss Susannah would have taken this chastisement to heart, however—for she certainly did not demonstrate much chagrin at this juncture, or even much interest—is a moot point, for Susannah and Amy never met again. Susannah's father married her off to a rich West Indian planter before the year was out. She passed the balance of her life fanning herself on a long Jamaican verandah; whereas Miss Lewis . . . well, the reason for Miss Lewis's sudden withdrawal from the London scene will be known to the reader soon.

12

THERE IS rain, as the reader is doubtless aware; and then there is Rain.

Rain of the first order, which is to say, rain simple, is composed of small drops of water which fall from the sky and cause that upon which they fall to become damp or, at the worst, wet. Rain of this type is a normal aspect of climate; one cannot impute to it any particular designs or sentiments. One might say, "Dash this rain!" but one says it with a reasonable amount of good humour, by and large, often capping the exclamation with a grin, or possibly a shrug—some indication of cheerful, if mildly piqued, resignation. This is the rain to which Portia referred when she spoke of the quality of mercy. This is the rain which nourishes crops and flowers; it replenishes supplies of water; it is, in fine, a useful thing.

And then there is Rain, or as one may say, rain complex. This is an utterly different beast, and brings no good to any man. It is composed, one imagines, of condensed spite; it is hurled from the sky like handfuls of tenpenny nails; what it falls upon, it first stings, then soaks. It drops with malice aforethought. It lands upon one claws first, like a wildcat, then hunches imperturbably upon one's shoulders, be they covered with never so many cloaks and capes. There it clings till it gets its way, drenching greatcoat or pelisse, slyly persisting until it penetrates to the neck, spreading its steamy, clammy fingers till the mere idea of having ever been dry seems a dream or a joke to the hapless Rained-upon. This is the rain that lashed King Lear as he wandered the heath with his fool. This is the rain that fell, at five o'clock on a Saturday morning, on Lord Weld and the Earl of Marchmont.

They stood in that malignant storm on a far edge of Putney Heath, looking for Jeffery de Guere. An affair of honour is just that—no accident of weather can delay it. There was a coach, of course, in which they had driven to this place of rendezvous, but Marchmont had prudently sent it down the road some half a mile—the less conspicuous the duel the better. "What the deuce can be keeping him?" was what Lord Weld kept muttering, while the tiny, arrow-like drops of rain assaulted his cheeks and chin. "This is a devil of a place to keep a fellow waiting, by God!"

Lord Marchmont replied to these questions with shrugs and shudders. The chill of the dawn combined with this relentless downpour was such as to keep him jumping up and down for very warmth; he bitterly cursed every poet who had ever used May as a metaphor for mildness; and so far as what could be keeping Sir Jeffery went—well, he was quite painfully aware that his cousin might well have risen at four A.M., taken a glance out of his bedroom window, and hopped directly back into bed. He had warned Marchmont after all; he had told him straight out that refusing a duel meant nothing to him. Why should reneguing be any different? A man without a code could not be counted on. Jeffery's code was whatever suited him best at the moment.

Lord Marchmont presently said as much to Lord Weld. "But you forget the vehemence with which he answered your cartel," said that gentleman. "His answer specifically referred to his pleasure in having the opportunity—he did say 'opportunity,' remember—of meeting you on equal ground. Why would he say that, and then not come?"

"Why indeed?" muttered Marchmont, clapping his arms against his sides to keep warm. "By the time the villain arrives, I'll be too cold to pull the trigger." Lord Weld did not answer. "I'll probably sneeze at the crucial moment," he presently added, hopping up and down on the muddy ground in a most unheroic fashion.

"I'll lay wager this is his second's handiwork. A shabbier chap I never saw," said Weld, watching with interest a steady stream of water that dripped off the brim of his own hat. He sniffed deeply, then continued, "He calls himself a captain. I'll lay odds he's never even stood next to a captain, let alone been one himself. Curious company your cousin keeps, old boy."

"Rotten low beggars can't be choosers," answered the earl, whose temper grew shorter as the wait grew longer.

Weld looked a little surprised at this display. "No, I dare say not."

"Damme, it's practically full morning," Marchmont burst out a few minutes later. "If we stop here much longer, we'll be just in time to entertain the young couples coming to the Heath for a pic-nic. 'Oh look, Mary! A duel! Isn't it exciting?' And then says Johnny to Jack, 'What do you say, Jack? I'm betting on the fellow in the bottle-green coat. Two bob he's still standing when the shooting's over. What about you?' And then Mary squeals, 'Oh no, Johnny, you mustn't make a wager on a wicked thing like that! Why, suppose one of the gentlemen should be killed? You'd much better pray for them both, you know . . . But isn't it exciting?' "

"Marchmont, my lad," Lord Weld finally broke into this fantasy, "if any young couple should show up today with a pic-nic, let's you and I run like blazes, shall we? Because a couple mad enough to be out in a rain like this is sure to have broke out of Bedlam."

Lord Marchmont nodded curtly and was about to reply when the sound of a carriage approaching stopped him. It was only his own carriage, however, as he soon realized. The surgeon who was waiting within it in case of an injury had grown impatient and ordered the coachman to drive back up to where the gentlemen stood.

"Do you realize you could have scotched the whole thing?" Lord Marchmont demanded of him tensely, shouting across the rain into the carriage—for the good doctor had no intention of entering the downpour himself. "Suppose we'd been about to fire?"

"If you stand in all this wet much longer you'll soon be firing on each other, I dare swear," said Dr. Birchfield coolly. He had been over in Spain with Wellington; a little bad temper could not dismay him. "And hoping to be shot, I should think, too. Better to die under fire than drown in water, eh, my lord?"

Marchmont looked to Warrington Weld for assistance, but that gentleman only took a few steps toward him and spoke in a low tone. "I'm afraid he may be right, dear boy," he said. "It looks very much as if your man is not going to show."

But Marchmont was unwilling to yield. "What time is it?" he demanded of the physician.

Dr. Birchfield consulted his watch. "Five forty-five A.M.," he announced and added, "Perhaps the coward is hoping you'll catch your deaths of cold."

Lord Marchmont said nothing. "Well, James," Weld began briskly, after a moment, "shall we pay a call to your cousin at home, then?"

Marchmont regarded him gloomily.

"He's not going to come," said Lord Weld gently. "If you like, I'll stay a while myself, just to make sure. Oh, when I see that Captain What-do-you-call-him . . . won't I have a few choice words to say!"

Lord Weld's generous offer had the effect of bringing his friend to his senses at last. "No need for you to stay," said he, laying a cold hand on Weld's dripping shoulder. "Stupid of me to be so stubborn. You're right, of course. Let's leave." So saying he drew the other into the carriage. Dr. Birchfield sprang away from them to the opposite bench while the coachman shut the door.

"I say, you are wringing wet, the both of you. Why, you're making puddles on the floor!" exclaimed the man of medicine. "Mind you drink something hot the moment you get home—and don't wear those clothes an instant longer than you must."

Lord Marchmont thanked him for this brilliant prescription.

"Not at all, my lord. To say truth, I'm just as happy your fellow has failed to show. I never like attending a duel. Now the matter is settled, and no blood shed."

"I beg your pardon," said the earl, still shivering from the damp, "but the matter is not settled, not at all."

"But surely if the other party fails to show—"

"I think you had an excellent idea, Weld," his lordship went on, ignoring the doctor's protest. "We must certainly pay a call on de Guere."

"What? Is Sir Jeffery de Guere your defaulter?" Dr. Birchfield suddenly interposed.

"Does the name mean anything to you?"

"That name? I should say it does! Why the scoundrel owes me seventy pounds—not that I have much hope of recovering it. He's been in debt to me a year or longer now."

"What was it for, Birchfield?" asked Lord Marchmont, leaning forward. "Was Sir Jeffery ill?"

"No, no, it was—" Dr. Birchfield checked himself all at once and sat looking at the gentlemen as if confused. "Well, it was a favour I did for a . . . a lady friend of his. His wife, he said it was. But I didn't believe him, if you must know."

Lord Marchmont said nothing. He was feeling grateful not to have had to entrust his life to the kind of doctor who did such favours for ladies. Of course, Dr. Birchfield was not his own physician; one took whomever one could find for such a nasty business as a duel.

Dr. Birchfield was looking rather shamefaced. "I don't suppose he has a wife, come to that," he said tentatively.

Lord Weld confirmed this suspicion.

"Oh well, then, at least there was no one crying at home," said the physician philosophically. "But he's a bad lot, that man. I'm almost sorry you didn't meet him after all, my lord."

The earl saying nothing, it was left to Weld to answer, "But then your bill might never have been paid, Mr. Birchfield." This light rejoinder closed the discussion, and a few moments later the coachman pulled over in front of the doctor's house and the gentlemen bade him good-bye.

Lord Marchmont instructed the driver to continue to his cousin's house. As the butler was not yet downstairs (it was scarcely half past six), the housekeeper answered Lord Marchmont's knock. She opened to him, and he and Lord Weld strode straight into the entrance hall and began to mount the stairs. "But where are you going, my lords?" asked the housekeeper, alarmed.

"To see your master, my good woman," Weld told her grimly.

"But he's not at home."

"He's at home to me," said the earl over his shoulder.

"But he's not at home to anybody," she objected. "I don't mean he's not 'at home,' sir, I mean he isn't at home. He's out."

"Thanks very much, but I think I'll have a look just the same," Marchmont shouted down at her, for he had by now reached the top of the narrow stairway. The housekeeper, who recognized Marchmont for Sir Jeffery's cousin, decided to quit this debate and retired, with a shrug, to wait in the doorway. She had made a sensible decision, for a moment later the earl descended, demanding to know where de Guere was.

The housekeeper shrugged again. "I'm afraid he didn't say, sir. Sir Jeffery occasionally omits to take me into his confidence," she added with a trace of sarcasm.

Lord Weld demanded, "When did he leave?"

"This morning, at four thirty." The housekeeper yawned.

"Frankly, I've been hoping for a nap. I was just going to bed when you gentlemen—"

"Yes, we'll be out of your way in a minute," Marchmont interrupted her, then turned to his friend. "Do you suppose he really did set out to join us and met with some accident?"

Lord Weld admitted the possibility.

"Tell me, was he alone when he went out? He didn't have a Captain . . . er, what was his name?"

"He didn't have anybody with him, my lord," said the housekeeper, looking less interested every moment.

"Perhaps he was on his way to the Captain's house," suggested Weld quietly. "We ought to call on him, I guess, and see if de Guere ever reached him."

Lord Marchmont was displeased with the turn events had taken, but there was little he could do. His clothes and Weld's were still wet through and through, and it occurred to him they ought to return home and change before pressing forward, but his anger at Sir Jeffery was steadily mounting, and he did not like the idea of further delays. In a moment he had made his decision; he and Lord Weld thanked the housekeeper briefly, left no cards for de Guere (for it would have been an inappropriate gesture, Marchmont maintained, though perhaps a useful one), and set out for the lodgings of the Captain. Lord Weld had forgot the man's name, but he still recalled his direction, since he had met him there to plan the duel. As the coach bore them to the desired place, Lord Weld racked his brains for the missing name—and of course succeeded in recalling it the moment he despaired of ever doing so.

"It was Firbank!" he cried triumphantly. "The self-styled Captain Firbank."

But when they had arrived at the Captain's cramped quarters, they found the gentleman in question still abed, and still asleep. Questioned, he seemed to have forgot the duel altogether, and certainly he had not seen Sir Jeffery that morning. In fact, Lord Weld had a strong impression he had never really expected to attend a duel at all—an impression, he found when they had again reentered their coach, which was shared by Lord Marchmont.

"Something is up," the earl declared, "but I'm damned if I can say what. I suppose we might just as well go home and wait now . . ."

Weld agreed. "If it weren't for Firbank's confoundment, I'd say it must have been an accident de Guere met with on his way from home. But it's clear the man didn't expect him . . ." He went on musing as the carriage rattled towards Cavendish Square. "And yet, what else could wake a man up at four in the morning? Where else could he have gone to?"

Lord Marchmont, nonplussed, did not answer at first. When he did speak, it was only to sigh wearily and say how happy he would be to see his dressing-gown and slippers. "We might as well go back to sleep, I expect. Thank God, Emilia's not an early riser. She'll never suspect we were gone. I don't wish her to know anything about this, of course."

"Understood, old man," said the other.

"I'm not giving up, you know. I'll get a meeting out of that blackguard if it's the last thing I do."

"Let's hope it is not."

"I don't know how to thank you for standing by me through all this, Weld. I'm sure no man ever had a better friend."

Lord Weld's pale cheeks turned pink. "Don't be foolish, old chap," he said. "It's nothing you wouldn't do for me."

Marchmont looked at him gratefully. "I hope you will rely upon that," he said presently.

Weld acknowledged this with a nod and a smile. The carriage rolled on for a time in silence.

"I'm going to offer for Lady Elizabeth Stanbroke," Lord Marchmont then suddenly stated. "I mean to speak to her father today. What do you think?"

Lord Weld, tired and wet though he was, immediately saw through the nonchalance of this announcement and broke into a wide grin. He reached across the carriage and grasped his friend's hand, then, on an impulse, stood up so far as he could and threw his arms round the earl. The carriage jolted suddenly, and Lord Weld was thrown into Marchmont's lap. The two men disentangled themselvès, laughing at the mishap. "By Jupiter, old man, this is the best news I've had in months —in years," corrected Weld, pleasure evident in all his features. "Have you spoken to the lady? Is it certain with her? She's a splendid woman—I told you so!" he rushed on, before Marchmont could answer, then demanded additionally, "Does Lady Emilia know?"

"Yes, we have spoken, no, it is not certain, indeed, you did tell me, and no, she doesn't know."

"Well, won't she be braced!" answered Weld. "Let's wake her when we get home and tell her."

"My dear man, get hold of yourself. It isn't as if I've found the philosopher's stone. I'm just offering for a woman's hand."

" 'Just'! When Emilia hears it—"

"Anyhow we can't wake her without explaining what we ourselves are doing prowling round London at this hour."

"Oh. Yes, I suppose we have rather been prowling."

"We have practically been skulking," said Marchmont. "I assure you, Emilia takes a very dim view of my risking my life. I think you heard her on the subject of the Continental wars."

Weld admitted there was truth in this. "In any case, she'll be cheerful as a cat the next time you venture out to an uncertain fate. From now on she'll have a sister to keep her company when you're gone . . . and someone to inherit from you, instead of de Guere."

"Yes, I dareswear she won't care two figs if I survive or not."

"Oh no. Why should she?"

"But it isn't quite decided yet, don't forget. I've still got to ask the lady—and to say truth, she's been acting deuced strange about it lately. First she seems all for it; next she wants to think it over and worry, as if it were a desperate problem."

"Perhaps she doesn't wish to appear over-eager?"

Marchmont shook his head "No" as they drove into the carriage sweep at number 21. "That's not like Lady Elizabeth, not at all. If she hesitates, it's because she's hesitant—depend upon it."

"Well, if she refuses you, she'll have me to answer to," asserted the other. Safely arrived, they descended from the coach and in a very few minutes found their several ways to dry night-clothes and warm beds.

Noon discovered Lord Marchmont sitting at the dining-table, munching contemplatively on an apple puff, wondering how best to get at his errant cousin. Mr. Searle discovered him there, too, entering to hand him a sealed note, along with the information that it had just been delivered by a female messenger who insisted upon its utmost urgency. "She wanted to hand it to you herself, in fact, sir, but I dissuaded her," the butler added, a hint of triumphant satisfaction in his voice.

Marchmont dismissed him and tore into the missive, in hopes it was from his cousin and contained an explanation of his absence, but it was not. It was in a woman's hand, unfamiliar to him, and it read thus:

Dear Sir,

> *I write in haste and send this to you by my maid. My sister has disappeared. I fear the worst. Please if you can come at once and ask for me. Forgive this imperious summons.*

> *Yr. svt.*

> *E.S.*

I leave it to the reader to imagine the celerity with which our hero responded to this. Our hero had, after all, been itching for something heroic to do all day, and this looked to be right in that line. Sisters vanished! The worst feared! It was more than the average fellow dares to dream of. Lady Emilia having gone out about ten that morning, according to Searle, and not come home since, Marchmont left word for her of his destination and arrived at Lady Elizabeth's door some twenty-three minutes later.

Elizabeth received him alone. "The household is in such an uproar, nobody even thinks to chaperon me," she explained. "For which I am thankful, since I must show you something the others have not yet seen . . ."

"Which is?"

"This note from Isabella. Oh, thank goodness you have come!" she exclaimed involuntarily, producing a folded paper from within the sleeve of her gown. "When her maid went to wake her this morning—which was at nine-thirty—she was not there. I found this note in my riding boot. That was the place we used to leave messages for each other when we were children. Go on and read it, please," Elizabeth went on almost frantically. "I've no notion what to do next!"

Lord Marchmont scanned the letter, which contained the following mysterious sentences:

> Be happy for me, dear sister, for I shall soon have all my Heart desires. Pray assure the others I am well, but keep this Epistle to yourself; I am in the hands of One who will allow no harm to come to me. Tell them too I will return to them on my own. When I step from this dwelling-place today I pass from the shades of childishness into the sun of womanhood. Burn this missive.
> My love.
>
> Isabella.

The note read, Marchmont peered over it at Lizzie. She met his glance and held it for a moment, then made an impatient gesture. " 'The sun of womanhood!' " she hissed. "That's Bella all over. How such a ninnyhammer could be born to my own parents I do not know . . . Anyway," she went on, her tone changing to one of anxiety, "what must I do? I have only just found the letter an hour ago. No one else knows of it." She paused to smile gratefully. "You were good to come so quickly."

Marchmont spoke gravely and carefully. "What do you suppose the significance of this letter to be?"

She looked surprised. "Why, that she has gone off with de Guere, of course! That was all a sham, I suppose, in the breakfast-room that night. Look at the way she makes the O large when she mentions him. 'I am in the hands of One who will allow no harm to come to me,' she writes. She is simply too odious. In any other girl one would imagine she had gone off to a convent, but with Isabella . . . I'm afraid it's unmistakable. She's ruined herself." On these last words she abandoned the tone of vexation she had begun with and approached tears. In truth she was aghast at what her sister had done; she could hardly conceive of it. "When I think how she'll regret this day—!"

Elizabeth buried her face in her hands. For a moment Lord Marchmont hesitated; then he stepped to her and took her into his arms. She burst into tears, sobbing whole-heartedly into the blue superfine of his coat. "Please, you must help me think what to do," she brought out presently, her words muffled by their being delivered directly into his lordship's chest. "Must I tell my father what I know?"

The earl placed a kiss on the top of her soft blond hair, so lightly he was not sure if she felt it. "I'm afraid so. This is very serious, as you understand."

Elizabeth nodded brokenly.

"Shall we go see Lord Trevor together?" he asked.

She nodded again. "Oh, I am sorry to behave so stupidly," she said, still warbling a little from her crying spell. "Ordinarily, you know, I'm just as strong and as sensible as . . . But when I think she's gone and done it she'll never recover from it! What do you—what do you expect he'll do with her?"

But Lord Marchmont knew better than to honour such a question with an honest answer. "I think it will be best if we do one thing at a time," was all he said. "For the moment, let us seek out your father."

She replied quietly, "He's in his library. Come." Elizabeth held out her hand to him and led him to the room in question. "I'd better speak to him first," she said at the door, then vanished inside for a minute. When she came out to fetch him she appeared a little paler than before, but also a little calmer. "My father understands you are aware of our predicament," she told him. "He would like to speak to you."

Marchmont followed her into the little room. Behind a massive desk sat the Earl of Trevor, a tall, brittle-looking man with a habitually worried aspect. He now appeared even more worried than usual, of course, and even as he rose to shake Marchmont's hand broke into speech concerning the immediate crisis. "My daughter tells me you are prepared to act as our friend in this," he began. "I thank you."

The other man made a gesture to dismiss this gratitude.

"It seems my children have been keeping secrets from me. This is an heavy burden—" His voice cracked and he stopped.

"I thought it was all finished, Papa," Elizabeth explained miserably. "I thought I had dissuaded her . . ."

Trevor swallowed hard. "At all events, it would appear Isabella has gone off—has been abducted by this . . . what was his name?"

"Sir Jeffery de Guere," Elizabeth supplied.

"This de Guere, then." He paused, then burst out, "Lizzie says the fellow is your cousin. Would he really do such a horrible thing?"

Lord Marchmont sadly confirmed that he might.

"Then we have no choice but to ride out after her—after them, I mean to say—and see if we can't prevent even greater . . . that is, if we can't catch them before . . ." His voice faded.

"I agree with you entirely, sir," interposed Marchmont. "By all means, let us follow. I have a couple of excellent horses at my disposal—"

"But this is not your tragedy," objected Trevor. "It's too much to ask—"

"No one has asked," said Marchmont tersely. "I offer myself. Will you accept?"

"But, of course, it's only—"

"Excellent, then. Now I should also like to offer the help of my friend Lord Weld. You may rely utterly upon his discretion, and as he speaks French with uncommon fluency, and as he is but lately returned from the Continent, I suggest we send him across the Channel, in case they have fled in that direction. Perhaps Halcot will go with him. You and I, sir—I assume you will join me?" he interrupted himself.

"Yes, but—"

"You and I, sir, will travel north, towards Gretna Green. If we leave at once, we may save ourselves much effort, so I suggest—"

"Elizabeth, where is Halcot?" Trevor broke in, standing up suddenly.

"I don't know, sir. With my mother, I think, in her sitting-room."

"Very well then, go and fetch him. We'll send him to France with your friend Weld, shall we?" asked the old earl.

Elizabeth hesitated, looking from Marchmont to Trevor and back again.

"Well, don't stand there gawking, my girl," snapped her father. "Go and fetch Charlie!"

So ordered, Lizzie paused no longer but turned at once and hastened to find her brother. The two men continued their conference, discussing horses and routes and the desirability of bringing others into the search. They decided against this latter course, however, as it seemed imperative above all to maintain as much secrecy as possible. "I'm sure we'll catch up with them, sir," said Marchmont, with a confidence he did not feel.

"Why should my daughters have kept this from me?" Trevor wondered aloud. "I have never given them reason to hide from me. I have always encouraged them to be frank.

Why did Isabella not come to me and speak her mind? I can't make it out."

They were waiting for Charlie, who seemed to be an age in coming. "I'm afraid de Guere is such a bad bit of business," Marchmont explained tentatively, "that Lady Isabella was afraid of your displeasure if she had asked."

"It would be nothing compared to this!"

"Of course not . . . but I suppose she is young yet, and not as sensible as she might be—"

"No, she's always been hot-headed. Nothing like Elizabeth, although I must say I'm disappointed in her as well. If Bella did not come forward, at least Elizabeth might have done."

"I believe she felt it a point of honour not to break her sister's confidences. She did tell me, however."

"She did?"

"And I thought I had taken the matter in hand," continued the younger man. "I should have known something was up when the wretch failed to show this morning—"

"I beg your pardon?"

Lord Marchmont looked embarrassed. "A little affair of . . . er, honour, sir. I felt the need of, ah, responding to an insult to Lady Isabella . . ."

"Indeed?"

"Yes, I am afraid so. And the villain did not appear this morning, even though he had sworn to—"

"Am I to understand you had challenged your cousin to a duel?"

Feeling strangely sheepish, Marchmont confessed this was so.

"May I ask, sir, what particular interest you have in the sanctity of Lady Isabella's name? You do not consider yourself a—suitor for her hand?"

"Lord, no!" was surprised out of Marchmont rather bluntly.

"Then—"

"It is . . . well, I've been meaning to speak to your lordship of this very matter. The fact is, it's your daughter Eliz—"

At this moment the door reopened, and Lord Halcot burst in, accompanied by Elizabeth. Lord Marchmont stopped in midsentence, naturally, but not before the intelligent Trevor had had time to guess at the tenor of his aborted disclosure. There was far too much to think about, what with getting the search underway, for him to consider this new bit of information until much later, however. In the meanwhile, Lord Weld was sent for and advised of the situation; a system of communications was worked out between the two embarking parties; and it was arranged that Amy Lewis and the ladies of the family would retire at once from the London scene to their quieter home in Warwickshire. "We'll have to give out that my wife is ill, I suppose," said Lord Trevor. "Either way there's bound to be talk, but at least no one will know Isabella is missing."

Lord Marchmont spoke up. "I think my sister Emilia might like to accompany them, if you would be so kind as to invite her. I should not like to leave her alone in London, in any case—"

"But, of course. I shall call on her at once," said Lady Elizabeth. There were many other details to be arranged, but the gentlemen worked well together, and by five o'clock that day the ladies of Haddon House were packing for their retreat. They were to depart for the country the following morning; whereas the gentlemen, having first made a fruitless tour of the London inns in hopes of finding their quarry's point of departure, had already ridden out north and south, onto the open road.

13

LADY LEWIS hurried down to the drawing-room of the Nest-ling, a small, handsome house in which her husband's family has resided for generations. She had been reading to Amy, who lay, looking markedly pale, on a day-bed in an upstairs parlour; but a servant had advised her that Lady Elizabeth was in the drawing-room, and she wished to have a few words with Lizzie before she came up to her daughter. "Is there news?" she asked before she had even said hello. Her plump face betrayed an entirely unwonted anxiousness, and even after she had rushed into the drawing-room she continued to wander nervously from table to window to chair.

"Good morning, ma'am," said Elizabeth, with a slight bow. She carried a basket covered with a napkin and looked so completely the country gentlewoman one would scarcely have believed that four days before she had been rubbing shoulders with the cream of the London monde.

"Oh yes, good morning. The post—? Was there news?"

Elizabeth was sorry to have to disappoint her—almost as sorry as she herself had been when the letters from her father and her brother had been read. "We have heard from them both again," she told Lady Lewis gently, "but they have neither of them found much to speak of. My father and Lord Marchmont" (she could hardly pronounce this name without a conscious blush), "did hear of a young couple called the Jeffrey's, in York, but the innkeeper recalled him as having been fair and her as being dark, instead of the other way round. In any case, they are pressing ahead. Charlie and Lord Weld wrote just before they left England. They hadn't heard anything at all. Lord Weld was out making inquiries of the packet-boat captains on the channel, however."

"Oh dear me, oh me, it's a bad bad affair all the way round," sighed Lady Lewis. "How is your poor mother?"

"She keeps her spirits up remarkably," Lizzie answered; and indeed she marvelled at the strength and fortitude with which her mother had met this catastrophe. "Lady Emilia is a great help to her—and to me. Naturally we shall none of us sleep well till Isabella is home again."

"No, naturally not."

"And how is Amy?"

Lady Lewis looked, if it were possible, even more fretful than before. "The poor thing is wretched, simply wretched. I have never seen her this way, Lizzie; I tell you, she has me positively frantic. Mr. Aikens" (naming the local apothecary) "came to see her again this morning, and he insists it is nerves . . . he left her some powders to take, but they do not seem to help at all. A nervous decline, he calls it, brought on by her distress over Isabella. Well, and so it may be . . . but I can't help feeling—oh, it just isn't like Amy to meet disaster with a collapse. Is it at all possible—Lizzie, do try to think back—is there any chance she was already weak before you left London?"

Elizabeth did her best to consider. Amy had in fact been

very quiet in the carriage on the way back from Lady Muff-tow's recital, but Lizzie had attributed this to the fact that Bella had not been with them. Ordinarily the two girls chattered between themselves after an evening in society; so it was natural that in Isabella's absence Amy would have little to say. Anyhow, she might have been fatigued. Certainly she had shown no signs of ill health earlier that day, when Charlie had invited her to the auction. Elizabeth conveyed these impressions to Lady Lewis, who still paced the room, wringing her hands.

"Well then . . . I suppose little Bella's sudden—er, disappearance is sufficient to have caused . . . and yet—" She stopped on this note of doubt, then went on, "So, my dear, suppose you go up to her now. What have you in that basket?"

"Some muffins Lady Emilia and I have been baking, that's all." The two women mounted the steps to Amy's parlour, chatting in desultory fashion of neighbourhood concerns. Elizabeth was dismayed, on reaching Miss Lewis at last, to observe that she appeared several degrees less healthy than she had on the previous day—both paler and weaker. She approached her with an involuntary cry of distress, bending to kiss her forehead. "My dear Amy, what is the meaning of this?" she asked, without intending to. "Surely you cannot hope to help matters by losing your looks and your vigour!"

Amy was apologetic. "I know I am only making more trouble for everyone," she said, in a low, quite piteous tone. "I should like very much not to do so."

"Oh, I did not mean to blame you, of course," amended Lizzie, "but for you to feel this so very deeply . . ." Her voice trailed off.

Miss Lewis looked oddly disturbed by these words, though the look came and went fleetingly. "I think I will leave you two alone," said Lady Lewis gently, withdrawing from the parlour with a nod to Elizabeth. Lizzie was glad she had taken this moment to depart, for the expression on Amy's waxen countenance had not escaped her.

"My dear," she said, "I know you and I have not been nearly so close as you and Bella, but—I hope you will speak frankly to me anyhow. I assure you, there is nothing you can say that will unnerve me, and I should so like to be of assistance. Is there any other thing that concerns you besides Isabella's disappearance?"

Amy's glance glided away from hers towards an empty corner of the room, giving her rather a furtive appearance. She was silent for some moments, then, in a whisper, she brought out, "Elizabeth, will you think me very rude if I decline to speak of it?"

"Then there is something else!"

"Please, it is not the sort of subject that bears discussion," said Amy. "Indeed, the less said of it the better. And in any case, I'm afraid my anxiety for Bella would have unsettled me considerably."

"No one doubts that," Lizzie answered gently, for she guessed how painful it was for Amy to appear selfish. "I am sure you love her very much; as do we all. But if there is some other matter—might not you feel better if you shared it with someone? I don't mean to pry; it need not be me, of course . . . but your mother is beside herself with worry for you . . . Oh dear, now I've made you feel worse."

Amy shook her head no. "Perhaps you are right. If only Bella were here, I might unburden myself to her . . . but I'm afraid I'm simply being absurd. I had no right to hope for—what I was hoping for; and now that it's gone from me, I am certain it's only a question of time . . . I mean to say, surely I will feel better soon, and stop behaving so preposterously." She essayed a little laugh at herself, which did not at all succeed.

Elizabeth had not been born with intelligence for nothing. She needed to hear no more than these words—needed to hear only the tone of Amy's voice, in fact—to know that the root of the matter here was Halcot. Moving forward to the girl so that she could take her hand, she said quietly, "Is it Charlie again, then? But I thought you and he were beginning to understand one another!"

Amy's cheeks were instantly flooded with tears. The silly thing had no notion how transparent she was, and what she imagined was Elizabeth's extraordinary sensitivity and insight moved her profoundly. She spoke, choking a little to repress a sob. "Yes, oh dear, it is! You will think me a perfect fool—and so I am—but did you know he is going to marry—" She swallowed hard as her voice failed her and resumed, "He is going to marry that Lemon girl, and I'm afraid he'll be so dreadfully unhappy!"

"Going to marry—?"

"Susannah, that cold, hard . . . but I'm sure if Charlie loves her she must have some redeeming qualities. Oh Lizzie," she wailed suddenly, "haven't I any redeeming qualities? I'm so miserable!"

"My poor girl, what is all this talk of Charlie's marriage? I am sure—mustn't I have heard if such a thing were so? I promise you, he has said not a word to any of us."

"He hasn't had time to, I should think," Amy explained in a kind of mumble. "He only asked her at Lady Mufftow's, that last night."

"Do you mean you heard him?"

"Well—I tried not to hear . . ."

"He asked her?" demanded Elizabeth, astonished.

"I did not exactly hear that—but he was about to."

Still holding Amy's hand Elizabeth drew up an ottoman and sat down. This unexpected information had the effect of making her feel dizzy. For a few moments she was silent. "Do you suppose she accepted him?" she finally asked.

"Could she refuse?" inquired the loyal, lovesick Miss Lewis.

Lizzie considered this briefly. "I think she could very easily. My idea of Miss Lemon is that she does what her parents tell her. Now if they had not advised her to accept my brother, I am sure she would not have done."

"And if they had?"

"But how could they have known such a thing was coming? I assure you I for one had no idea of it."

"Perhaps he has asked her father for permission," suggested Amy tearfully. "He may have, you know."

"But what about my father? Charlie would certainly have consulted him before taking such a step."

"Perhaps he did," was delivered on a broken sob.

"Well, I shall ask him at once—Oh Lord, what am I thinking of? My father must be in Scotland by now. And Charlie's in France."

Amy so far forgot her own miseries for an instant as to ask if there had been any news from either of the search parties. Lizzie repeated the information she had given Lady Lewis, then reverted to Amy's earlier remarks. "In any case," she said energetically, "the very idea of comparing you and that idiotish fashion-plate is ridiculous. You're worth six hundred of her, and if Charlie has in fact failed to notice that, it's only because he's such a mutton-head. Now you wouldn't wish to be married to a mutton-head, would you?"

Amy looked extremely dubious. "I suppose not," she whimpered.

"Of course not. There must be a dozen eligible men back in London just frantic to know where you've gone. I'm sure any one of them would suit you better than my shatter-headed Lord Halcot. Haven't you a fancy to any of them? What about Sir John Firebrace?"

But Amy, though she endeavoured to be brave and careless, could only shake her head "No" and burst into tears again. Lady Elizabeth, though truly sorry for her, could think of nothing comforting to say. Still she did finally point out that Amy did not know for certain, in the end, that any offer had been made, or that (if made) it had been accepted. "So you will try to be cheerful, won't you, and not dwell on it till Charlie has come home and we learn for sure?" she concluded.

Amy said she would. "Elizabeth," she then added softly, "please do not tell my mother what I've confided to you. I fear she'd be awfully ashamed of me if she knew."

"I don't think your mother could be ashamed of you if her life depended on it," answered Lizzie sensibly, "but since you have spoke in confidence, I shall certainly respect it." With these words she rose and made ready to quit the parlour.

"Lady Emilia and I made these muffins," she said, profering the neglected basket.

Miss Lewis accepted it with thanks. "My compliments to her, and to your mother, of course," she murmured. "Oh, and Lizzie—"

"Yes?" prompted the older girl.

"You won't think I'm utterly and entirely selfish, will you? You know I am dreadfully concerned for Isabella."

Elizabeth smiled a bit sadly. "Of course, you are, my love. We are all of us very concerned. I know your heart is much the truest and best of any of ours; I only wish you knew the same."

But Amy could not receive this honest assessment easily. She denied it and, thanking Elizabeth again and again for her kindness and sympathy, finally allowed the other girl to leave.

Poor Amy! How much distress might have been spared her if only she had been able to overhear a conversation taking place that very hour in Paris! Why is it that, eavesdropping inadvertently or by intention, we so often hear that which hurts us, and so seldom that which comforts? Is it because so many more things are said that are cruel than kind? It is a philosophical point deserving of inquiry; I should like to read an essay upon it. I should not like to write one, however; and so I desist.

The pertinent fact is, that at the very time Miss Lewis was unburdening herself to Lady Elizabeth, young Halcot was confiding in Warrington Weld an emotion that had been growing inside him nearly a week now. He had got round to the subject only after much hemming and hawing, much stammering, much orotund observation regarding the nature of women in general, and Englishwomen in particular—but he had, after all, got to it. He did not at first use the lady's name, but rather referred to the affair in this wise: that there was a lady he knew, with whom he had been acquainted indeed all her life, whose extraordinary worth and perfection had escaped him all those years till just last Friday; wasn't that remarkable?

Lord Weld, who was attempting to procure from the cook at the inn some breakfast composed of foods not entirely unfamiliar to his palate, agreed without hearing him that it certainly was. *"Du jambon, je dis,"* he then repeated to the waiting servant, *"et quelques pommes de terre—mais pas frites, je te pris!—et du café naturellement, et peut-être quelques fruits, si tu en trouves. C'est compris?"* He looked hopefully into the whey-coloured, moon-shaped countenance of the servant, whose slack mouth hanging perpetually open only increased the impression that he understood neither milord's French nor anyone else's—nor any other language either. He did rouse himself after half a minute, however, and ducking his head in a manner apparently intended to reassure repeated Lord Weld's final words. He then shambled out of the coffee-room, leaving Weld to shake his head in bemused frustration. "He'll bring us those damned pastries again, you watch," he prophesied to Charlie. "And the ham—if he remembers it—will have a dashed raspberry sauce all over it, or some such frippery. At least when I was last in France we had an English cook. You might get your stomach shot through in the afternoon, but at least you'd have put a pudding in it that morning." Having delivered himself of these observations, and receiving only a distracted "Hmmm" for acknowledgement from Charlie, Lord Weld and his stomach resigned themselves to the inevitable and turned their still sleepy attention to the younger man's next remarks.

"How do you suppose I can have been such a widgeon?" Charlie now demanded, as if stymied. "In all the time I've known her, never to see what a woman she's grown up to be! I can't understand it. And now when I think of how many other women I've paraded round with in front of her—not that there were all that many, you understand, but still—I don't suppose she'll ever forgive me. I wonder if she could, though," he immediately went on. "What do you think, old chap? Think she could ever consider me as a—well, you know, as a suitor?"

Lord Weld perceived he would be obliged to capitulate altogether and make a real effort to communicate with Halcot. This visit to France had not been an easy one for him, poor man, for the company of young tulips such as Charles was not what he was naturally drawn to. Indeed, he found the necessity of following the future earl's sudden enthusiasms and convoluted notions a severe trial to his nerves and his intelligence, not to mention his good humour. He was beginning to hope they found Isabella as much for his own sake as for hers; and he had a few choice words to say to Marchmont regarding his having paired himself off with the boy's sensible and distinguished father, while Weld was left to chaperon the apparently less fortunate son. Now he rallied himself for perhaps the hundredth time, however, and endeavoured mightily to understand what on earth Halcot was talking about. "My dear boy," he began, after a small yawn, "of whom are you speaking?"

Lord Halcot's colour rose at once, and his blue eyes looked down to the table. "I don't know if I should say, Weld. What do you think? Would it be ungentlemanly?"

"Beg your pardon?"

"I say, would it be wrong of me to tell you her name?"

"This is a woman you love?" asked Weld.

"Er, yes."

"And she is free?"

"Free?"

"I mean, she is unmarried. Not promised to anyone. Can you offer for her? Do you mean to offer for her?"

"Oh! Well, yes, I expect I do."

"Don't seem to have put much thought into it."

"Well, the trouble is, as I say, I've been overlooking her such an age, I don't imagine she'll have anything to do with me any longer. Know what I mean?"

Lord Weld struggled with exasperation. "I suppose you'll have to ask her if you want to find out," he suggested.

"Oh. Good idea," said Charlie vaguely.

"Fine," said Weld, hoping this would dismiss the topic.

"But you asked if she were free. She is. Shall I tell you her name, then?"

"Oh good heavens, if you wish to, yes!"

"Well, it's—Amy Lewis. Miss Lewis. You've met her, I'm sure."

"Dear me, yes, a very sweet girl indeed," said Weld, who indeed was a disinterested admirer of this cheerful little soul.

"Very," agreed Charles whole-heartedly. "And do you know what?"

There was a silence. "What?" Lord Weld at last replied.

"There was a time—don't think I'm being too swell-headed, will you—but there was one time when my sisters hinted she might be thinking of me. In that way, you know. At least, I'm pretty sure that's what they meant. Oh, but that was ages ago, it seems! Since then I've—good Lord, I dragged her off to see Susannah Lemon, and God knows what else! Oh no, I'm a fool to imagine she'd ever consider me again. She's too good for me by half in any case." He shook his blond head rather tragically. "I'd better put it out of my head. I'll go to my grave a bachelor, I suppose. Won't my father be disappointed, though! But what can I do?"

At this point Lord Weld succeeded in interrupting this doleful soliloquy—chiefly by banging a fork down forcibly in Halcot's field of vision. "Just a minute, for heaven's sake. Are you wondering if Miss Lewis returns your regard?" he demanded.

Charlie looked up, interested. "But yes, exactly."

"Well then, wonder no longer. I have it on excellent authority she does. You have only to go home and ask her for her hand and all happiness will be yours for ever and ever," said Weld, hoping against hope that Charlie would decide to abandon the search for his sister and post home on this errand directly.

"What's this?"

"I say, I know she loves you. Everybody knows she loves you. If you really want her, for God's sake, go and offer for her."

"But this is too wonderful to believe!"

"Don't argue with me, man, I tell you there's no question about it. Unless her sentiments have altered altogether, the lady's heart is yours."

Lord Halcot took this in. "But my dear Weld, who told you this? Are you quite certain?"

"Quite."

"You won't mind telling me who it was who said so—and when?" he persisted.

"Oh dear, must I? Can't you take it on faith? Where is that damned servant; I swear I could eat a ham with a radish sauce at this point."

"Please, tell me who it was," pleaded Charles. "I must know."

"For goodness' sake, then, it was Lady Emilia Barborough. Marchmont's sister, don't you know," he added, as Charlie continued to look blank.

"Of course, I know," he said after a moment, "but I'm afraid . . . Dash it, she's hardly an impartial judge. Why, she's had this notion for ages; I remember perfectly well, though it was weeks or months ago. She took me aside and—oh, without going into details" (here he blushed at the memory of what he fancied had been Emilia's infatuation with him), "she made it pretty clear she thought Amy had set her cap at me. But that was only a silly idea of her own, believe me." He sighed deeply as disappointment and hopelessness once more took hold of him. "It's nothing to do with Miss Lewis."

Weld looked annoyed. "My good man, what possible reason could Lady Emilia have for supposing Miss Lewis's feelings are other than what they are?" he asked. "If ever there were an unprejudiced well-wisher in a scenario, that well-wisher is Lady Emilia. You ought to thank her for taking an interest, come to that, for she had no reason to. Why, come to think of it, I believe she told me she'd brought the question up to you quite directly."

"I certainly don't recall it."

"One morning at your parents' home, it was, I think. She and Marchmont went calling on you—remember it, because they purposely discouraged me from joining them. Something about leaving Marchmont alone with your sister . . . Excuse me, old chap, I suppose you've seen the wind blowing in that direction, in any case?"

"The wind blowing—?"

"I mean, you've doubtless realized Lord Marchmont is deeply—well, that he admires your sister very much?"

"What, Elizabeth? Or Bella?"

"Oh, my God!"

"What do you mean, Lord Weld?"

But his lordship put his head in his hands and prayed silently for coffee. When he did answer, he only said, "Never mind, dear boy, pretend I never said it."

"Said what?"

"Perfect, ideal. Thank you. Now about you and Miss Lewis—"

"Look, if you don't mind my sharing a little confidence with you—" Charlie burst out.

"Not at all, why should I?" lied Weld.

"Then the fact is, Lady Emilia herself took a fancy to me once upon a time, and that was when she conceived of Miss Lewis as a rival. It was nothing to do with Amy herself, I'm sure. It was only the kind of thing a woman in love—well, a woman infatuated, at all events—does tend to imagine. So that's why I cannot take her testimony seriously; you understand, don't you?"

But Lord Weld had begun to be a little angry. "Lady Emilia take a fancy to you?" he cried, on the point of leaping to his feet. "I never heard of anything so ludicrous. Whatever gave you such a thought, sir?"

"Ludicrous?" echoed Charlie hotly. "I'll thank you to choose your words more carefully, my lord. And what gave me the thought was her coming to me and suggesting that we sometimes overlook what's right under our noses . . . something about speaking out and taking risks and declarations and—"

He stopped. "And?" prompted Weld, suspiciously.

"And . . . er, timid ladies." Charlie was silent again. Lord Weld almost fancied he might be thinking, from the furious, unfamiliar expression on his face. "Well now that we're talking of it," he finally brought out, "I wonder if she wasn't speaking about Amy all along after all."

Weld flung his hands heavenward, as if in a gesture of thanksgiving. "My dear boy, I shouldn't be the least bit surprised. Do you see now? She was trying to tell you even then that Amy loved you. You have only to dash back to Warwickshire and gather her up. In fact, why don't you go now? The sooner the better, after all. He who hesitates is lost. A stitch in time saves—"

But Charlie broke in on this stream of wisdom. "Go now?" he demanded, outraged. "What a shabby suggestion! When my sister is still in danger? A very pretty idea you must have of me, my lord. I wonder who you think—"

"Yes, very well, all right then," soothed poor Weld, his white hands patting the air as if to calm this storm. "You're quite right, I was a beast to suggest it. I don't know what came over me, I assure you. Now here, at last, is our breakfast—or at least, if it is not exactly ours, it is to be pawned off as such, and we are destined to eat it I perceive.

So let us break bread, and keep peace with one another, shall we?" And with these mollifying words, and with a sinking sensation caused by the sight of a greenish glaze on the long-awaited ham, Lord Weld restored amity and order to his little search party.

———

The author is not as common mortals! Miles of water, leagues, forsooth, of terrain, boundaries both political and natural melt under the author's scrutiny—fly away and are made nothing by the turning of a manuscript page. What would not the ordinary being give to own this power? To peer one moment through a keyhole in Tangiers, the next into the eyes of a Chinese monarch; to listen on page forty-three to the words of a filthy assassin, and on page forty-four hear the first remarks of a lisping babe. Even the weeks and years fall away beneath the pen: who was young and laughing in Chapter Two is old and bent in Ten. By Chapter Twenty he's mouldered away in his grave: he counts himself fortunate if he is so much as a good taste in the mouth of a worm.

Take note, for example, of the ease with which our scene now shifts from Paris to Penrith; for it was in that tiny Cumbrian town that two earls of our acquaintance, namely Trevor and Marchmont, found themselves on the morning in question. Darkness had overtaken them there on the previous night, stopping them a mere forty miles from the Scottish border. They had heard on the previous afternoon—with emotions most conveniently described as mixed—of a young couple fitting perfectly the descriptions of Bella and de Guere, who were travelling together northwards under the name of Amor. This awkward name, which of course signifies *love* in Latin, was so obviously the handiwork of Isabella that neither gentleman could doubt that Mr. and Mrs. Amor were in fact none other than the couple in question. Their being obliged to stop so near to their goal was consequently all the more vexing, and they rose from their beds before dawn to be on the road again—on horseback, for the distance was not forbidding, and it was much the fastest way—in time to see the day break. Naturally they could not gallop all the way: they paced themselves at a brisk, steady trot, but not so hurried as to prevent conversation. So it was that when they had been riding along an hour in silence Lord Marchmont, weary of the monotony, drew up alongside of Trevor and proceeded to speak as follows:

"I wish there were some way for Emilia to communicate with me. I am sure she is very happy, of course, with your family, but since I am all she has in the world, I do not like to be out of her reach."

"Of course, she could send a courier to us, if it were necessary," observed the older man, "and there is sure to be a letter from Haddon Abbey" (naming his family home) "awaiting us at Gretna Green."

"Indeed," agreed Marchmont, but with a sigh—for he was wishing to be able to hear from Elizabeth as well as from his sister. "I am certain she is perfectly fine, in any case, for Lady Elizabeth has always been extremely kind and amiable to her," he went on, thinking to speak of her, at least, since he could not speak to her.

Perhaps Lord Trevor guessed at some of this, for his next words were, "Indeed, it appears your sister and Lizzie have become fast friends. I am glad, for Lizzie has had enough of solitude. Bella and Amy Lewis were always too young for her, and Charlie too old, I'm afraid. The neighbourhood of Haddon Abbey is so sparsely supplied with gentlewomen, I'm afraid Elizabeth grew up very much alone."

"Her character does not seem to have suffered by it," observed Marchmont. "Perhaps, on the contrary, she is the stronger for it."

Lord Trevor assented to this possibility, and for a few minutes the gentlemen rode on in silence. Then the older man spoke again. "You've grown fond of Lizzie yourself, have you not?" he suggested lightly.

"I have," said Marchmont, but with a gasp in his voice, as if he were nearly choking. The oddly strained note did not escape Lord Trevor, and it rather made him smile to hear it. He was remembering his own keen discomfort when, many years before, it had been necessary for him to ask permission to offer for Lady Trevor, who was then the Honble. Miss Georgiana Blessingdon. Old Sir Ralph, her father, had been a terrible tartar; he had seemed almost intentionally to make it difficult for the young man in any way he could. Poor Trevor had attempted twice and failed twice to bring up the question to the old grouch before he at last succeeded, and even then Sir Ralph had grilled him as if he might be intending to carry Miss Blessingdon off to a life of exquisite squalor and pain. Lord Trevor, fortunately for Marchmont, was not one of those men who say, "I had it hard; let him suffer through it as I did." Quite the contrary, it was his habit to learn by his experience, remember its aches and difficulties, and then to try to spare others as much as possible the hurts he had had to endure. He was, it will be perceived, a man of mercy as well as a man of justice, and accordingly he now took pity on the squirming young man beside him, and brought up the ticklish subject himself.

"If I understood you aright, in fact, you were about to bring up her name in London, just before we left. I rather fancied—" he went on, then stopped.

"Yes?" said Marchmont, when the silence had become too much.

"I rather fancied you wished to ask for her hand, sir. Could that have been the case?"

Marchmont exhaled a sigh of pure relief. The morning seemed suddenly six times brighter than it had done. If they had not both been on horseback he might very well have embraced the other man. "That is exactly the case, Lord Trevor. I should give her everything . . . that is, I should love her as my life—no, better. And Emilia loves her, too, and as far as property, she will be provided for in any extremity, and as for dowry, I require none; in fact, I should be glad of an opportunity to do something for you . . . and, of course, she would be Lady Marchmont, a not inconsiderable title," he rushed ahead. "But perhaps you see it differently? Do you object? Do you consent? Oh for God's sake, sir, as you are a Christian, put me out of this ridiculous misery!"

Lord Trevor laughed and looked at the other with a wide, frank smile. "I could not wish for a better son-in-law than you, I am sure," he asserted, "and as for a dowry, Lizzie will have her portion whether you want her to have it or not."

The day was now simply dazzling; Lord Marchmont felt tears in his eyes. "I thank you sir," he said, not once but five times running. "I hope you can excuse my selfishness in asking in the midst of this—calamity. I had meant to wait, only when you mentioned—"

"I opened the topic myself," Trevor assured him. "You need feel no embarrassment. But tell me, how does my daughter encourage you? Has she accepted you already?"

"Lord no, sir," said Marchmont, almost shocked. "I haven't even offered. I was waiting to speak to you first, naturally. Anyway, I have it from Lady Elizabeth" (merely to speak the name made him smile) "herself that she will not accept any suitor unless you have told her to do so."

Lord Trevor felt this quite deeply and was visibly affected— for after all, Isabella's astonishing and ruinous flight had wounded him cruelly—and he murmured to himself, "She is a good girl, a good woman."

Regretting that his words had occasioned this saddening parallel Lord Marchmont quickly continued, "I am not without hope, however. She has encouraged me sometimes, though sometimes she has almost seemed to dislike the idea. And then again . . . well, she does seem to look on me with a particular, kindly—" He floundered, well out of his depth.

In a gentle but cautionary tone Lord Trevor broke in, "If she is not ready to answer you, you must not rush her, my boy.

No good can come of forcing a decision she is not prepared to make."

Lord Marchmont agreed, feeling strangely young and humble.

"A marriage lasts a lifetime, you know. You will wait until she is certain, won't you? Say you will, my friend, for I fear much for the happiness of my younger daughter. To see the elder make a false move too would be more than I could bear, I think."

Lord Marchmont found himself much moved by these simple words and perceived anew what an awesome enterprise a marriage was. For a moment the responsibility of it seemed too much for him, but then he remembered Elizabeth's eyes and felt at once he could no more easily live without than with her. Accordingly he nodded to Trevor in a sober but joyful silence. After a few more miles he reached quite suddenly for the other man's hand, and held it with his own as a brief, tender salute.

14

WHEN LADY Isabella caught the bouquet of flowers tossed to her by her unthinking brother—the reader remembers these flowers, I hope: they were few in number, but pretty and fresh, and tied with a velvet riband?—she counted them, found there were five, and knew that Sir Jeffery de Guere would arrive to collect her at five the next morning. It was the signal agreed upon between them; and never, Bella felt, had she managed so excellent a performance as she had that day in the girls' sitting-room, when even the observant Lizzie had believed her crushed and repentant. It had again cost her a pang or two to be obliged to deceive not only her sister but also her brother and her dearest bosom bow; but if the course of true love ran smooth there would be no songs or stories about it, and Bella could not then have known how to carry out her elopement. As it was she had read about it dozens of times, and was quite as prepared (she thought) for its hardships and sorrows as for its joys.

She was resolved that her elopement should be the finest ever contrived; and when she had achieved it she meant to write a three-volume novel recording its origins and its perfections. Its consequences she worried about very little, for she reasoned they must come when they would, and be what they were, and as they could not be planned there was no need of dwelling upon them. Perhaps she was right; certainly she was not the only young lady who ever dismissed love's consequences as the least interesting of its various aspects. She had still some misgivings; she did not quite see why she oughtn't at least to *try* to enlist her father's support for a marriage to de Guere, but Jeffery had been adamant. Isabella put the thought out of her head.

In keeping with her intention of carrying out her adventure in the most correct fashion possible, she kept herself up all through the night before her departure by reading Sir Walter Scott, writing interminable, passionate epistles to her beloved (which she later presented to him, and which he managed somehow to forget in the coffee-room of the Old George in Aylesbury), and praying to St. Agnes, the patron saint of young maidens, in whose power she did not entirely believe, but who might (one never knew) be able to do her a good turn anyhow. When the violent storm began about three o'clock—the Rain of which we have heard so much already—Isabella welcomed it: at least the furious pounding of the water made it easier to keep awake. Then, too, it was good to have a violent storm as backdrop for her adventure; it made a nice touch, she felt. And lest any reader suspect her of hypocrisy, be it known that, even when she found herself, at a quarter till five, huddled on the pavement in front of Haddon House all but drowning in this ghastly deluge—even then, I say, she did not revile the downpour nor wish it one drop less than it was.

Sir Jeffery did at last arrive, in a carriage owned (if Bella had only known it) by the obliging Mrs. Butler, and driven by Mrs. Butler's coachman, too. They would accomplish the first leg of their journey in this, then travel by post-chaise. Sir Jeffery, who did not keep a carriage himself and certainly had no funds with which to buy one for this occasion, had nevertheless wished to avoid hiring one—for that would have made it a simple matter to trace his direction and then his whereabouts, and he did not wish to be found quite so easily. No, it suited his purposes best to let a little time go by before he and his prey (as he supposed her) were discovered. That way there could be no question but that she had been compromised. She would clearly have been ruined; Lord Marchmont would drop the family; all would be well. So, he went to Mrs. Butler with a pretty honest account of his plans and, finding her disposed (for a little money) to assist him, borrowed of her her carriage and coachman—which he passed off to Bella as belonging to an unidentified friend.

To say truth, Isabella could not be troubled to consider this detail carefully. She was, when Sir Jeffery drew up before her, not only waterlogged, but in a state of over-excitement superior to any even she had known heretofore. She was practically in a fever. She was not so perfectly obtuse and dim-witted as not to be thoroughly scared by the fact that she was now leaving behind her every kind of safety and security she had ever known; nor did it escape her that she was entrusting her innocence and virtue to a man she had never even heard of last Christmas; but her courage (as she styled it) did not fail her, even though she trembled while she reached for his arms—and she left Haddon House behind her without a whimper. Heroines do not whimper. Isabella was a heroine first, last, and always.

Pity Sir Jeffery, dear reader: this was a fact he had reckoned without. Yes, I say pity him, villain though he is—for the poor man never dreamed, when he laid his vicious plans, of being led such a dance as now awaited him. De Guere, doomed devil, was but a pasteboard scoundrel—a peasant, a peon, in the world of machinations. True, he could seduce a countess in seven days, start to finish; true, he had tasted the charms of many a schoolroom miss; but in Isabella he had come up against a veritable queen of romantic calculation—and the foolish fellow never even noticed. Silly man, he was just not well-read enough in romantic novels. If he had been, Isabella could never have tripped him so easily. What he had in mind—simple, innocent rogue—was a quiet, classic abduction. Find the girl, remove her from her home, carry her off to an inn or some such, keep her there a day or two, let oneself be found by the proper authorities . . . and voilà, without further strain or effort on your part, the girl is ruined, the dirty work done. Neat. Painless. Effective. Sort of thing one hears about over port, after dinner. Family wishes to hush it up, avoids to that end prosecution of the abductor—but can't after all prevent its being an open secret in good society, which likes nothing so much as marking the occasional fall from grace of one of its members. To Sir Jeffery it seemed without flaw, mere child's play: it even had the advantage of affording him some pretty pleasant companionship, and the promise of some interesting nights.

How interesting he had not guessed. The very first evening, when darkness had compelled the fleeing couple to find shelter for the night, Lady Isabella leapt from the carriage and rushed through the gathering gloom into the inn. By the time Sir Jeffery, who had been obliged to give orders to the ostlers regarding Mrs. Butler's coach, regained her side, Bella had already found the wife of the innkeeper and was deep in conversation with her. "The poor girl," she was saying, having suddenly taken on a strange garrulity, it appeared to de Guere, "was simply desperately ill. At first I thought, well, what can I do? After all, she is—oh, there you are my dear," she interrupted herself to acknowledge Jeffery. "Mrs. Hatha-way, this is my husband. So as I was saying, at first I thought, what can I do, I must have a maid after all, I can't very well dispense with her! But then she was . . . ah, violently ill, you understand, and it was really more than I could bear to watch her in such evident distress. We thought she might recover— didn't we, Jeffery, my dear?—but no such thing, alas. She seemed to grow even whiter, and though I think she was shy of complaining, I had the distinct impression she quite wished herself dead. She was very courageous about it, mind you, but she confessed after a time that she had never in her life been in a closed carriage before, and rarely in an open one, and of course with the rain we could not let her sit outside—well, and then she admitted all that story about having been sent down from Sussex by her mother, to earn her keep on her own in London, was an out-and-out lie; the fact was she was London born and bred, the family very low, I gather, and the father a terrible scoundrel . . . anyhow, you can see we've had quite a day of it! So at last we left her, at a little inn about ten miles back—what was the name of that place, Jeffery?—with money and instructions to take an open carriage or a wagon or whatever, for heaven's sake, tomorrow, and join us at Lady Vaultenoy's then. And naturally I thought we'd be sleeping at Lady Vaultenoy's tonight ourself, and that Amelia—her lady-ship, I mean—could lend me a maid or some such, but you see we've been so much slowed down by this unfortunate business with this girl, this Dulcie, that we're obliged to stop with you instead. At all events, the reason I bring this up is to ask you if you haven't a maid I could use, perhaps your daughter, or—"

"I have a daugher, ma'am," the innkeeper's wife interjected swiftly.

"Oh, that is ideal!" squealed this peculiar, loquacious Isabella. "Naturally I shall pay her well for her services. Very well, it is settled then—it is settled, is it not, Jeffery?—we shall be needing two rooms . . . oh, and please to tell your daughter she must sleep with me, for I feel a dreadful sick-headache coming on after all this untoward adventure, and when I get the headache I am always sure to have nightmares. Will that be agreeable, Mrs. Hathaway? I should appreciate it so much."

Mrs. Hathaway found this more than agreeable, since she was ambitious for her daughters (she had four), and she saw in this an opportunity for the eldest to gain some experience as a lady's maid. Perhaps, she even dared to suggest to Mr. Hathaway later that evening, as they sat in the kitchen drinking chocolate together, perhaps Dorothy might even be permanently engaged by the lady who employed her tonight. It was not impossible; one heard of such things. And though Dorothy was only a rude country girl, at least she had a stomach of iron. Of what use to a fine lady was a maid who could not travel? And then Dorothy was good-natured, and biddable, and not so ugly as to be unsightly, nor so handsome as to attract Mr. Amor's attention . . . all in all it seemed to her at least worth suggesting to Mrs. Amor in the morning, provided of course Dorothy had no objections. Had Mr. Hathaway?

He had not. He had seen the colour of Sir Jeffery's gold, and it looked a rich yellow hue to him; besides, he'd taken the opportunity of visiting the stables that night to have a look at Amor's carriage, and the fineness of it had much impressed him. It was a little odd, he owned, that Mr. Amor had given orders that it should be returned to the city, while he and his wife would travel by post-chaise for tomorrow's journey—but who understood the ways of the Quality, after all? So long as Dorothy liked the plan, he was all for it. She was a grown girl now, in any case, and not likely to come to harm. One daughter less at the family board, to say truth, suited Mr. Hathaway very well.

So it was that Dorothy, as soon as an errand given her by Isabella took her to the kitchen, was intercepted by her parents and made a party to their plans. She was not long in agreeing to them, for she herself had long dreamed of escape from this everlasting inn, and in consequence she worked twice as hard as she might have to provide Mrs. Amor with satisfactory service. She even attempted to keep awake all night so that, when Mrs. Amor woke from her expected nightmares, she would be roused and ready to aid her.

She need not have troubled herself, for Isabella, after her previous all-night's vigil, slept a perfectly sound and dreamless sleep, secure in the knowledge that Sir Jeffery would not intrude upon her—could not, indeed, since she had taken the precaution of bolting the door. For love him though she did, when it came right down to the bare bones of the matter, Lady Isabella knew she was gravely in danger of de Guere's advances, and she had no intention whatever of succumbing to him till they were well and thoroughly wed. Not that she doubted his honour, of course! But now was no time to take chances. The reader may be surprised to see Isabella behaving, apparently for the first time, sensibly. By way of explanation I can only offer Isabella's own candid surmise in her diary that night: "I suppose I was never obliged to be sensible before," she wrote briefly, aching with fatigue, "but there are things about which one absolutely must!"

A second reason why Dorothy need not have tried to keep awake all night was that, had she been the very worst maid in the world, Lady Isabella would nevertheless have engaged her with a joyful heart. Indeed, it was much better than she dared to hope: she had expected to be obliged to invent some story, and find some chaperon, at every inn they visited. Now she was assured of an escort both in the carriage and during the nights, and without any of the trouble of securing one again. When, at breakfast in the coffee-room, Mrs. Hathaway dared to broach the topic and offer her daughter's services to the Amors, Isabella accepted with a smooth alacrity that left Sir Jeffery speechless at first.

Then, "But my dear, what will you do with, er, was it Darcy?" he objected, while Mrs. Hathaway hung on their every word.

"You mean Dulcie, my darling. But Mrs. Hathaway is right, I must have a maid who can travel with me. You know we have promised to be at Milcourt Tuesday week. How shall we go there unless I have a maid? And I shall not travel again with Dulcie, no truly I shall not," she insisted with vehemence. "It's too much to ask of me. Dorothy must come. We'll simply send Dulcie back to London and find some other employment for her. I did not like the way she lied, in any case, regarding her upbringing. Who knows if she might not steal as well? She's only been with us a week or two now," Isabella paused to explain to Mrs. Hathaway. "We're well rid of her, in my opinion."

"But what could Dorothy know of being a lady's maid?" Sir Jeffery parried weakly. "With all due respect to her worthy parents, she is after all a country girl. She was not brought up into this service; she can know nothing of your needs, my dear. And you know you are rather delicate; I should think you would wait and engage someone skilled and experienced, since you are determined to do without Dulcie." Recovering some of his wits, and feeling more than a little enraged by Lady Isabella (for he had been as much astonished by her behaviour on the previous evening as if, having taken a China doll into his hands, he had suddenly been bitten) he went on, "Remember how very unhappy you were with Maryanne, wasn't that her name? At first you said she was simple and unspoiled, and you *would* have her, but less than a se'ennight later you were utterly out of patience with her incompetence and her slowness. It isn't fair, really, my darling, to do the same to Mrs. Hathaway's daughter—"

But Isabella had begun to pout, and she now broke in with a petulant whimper, "You never let me have what I want, Jeffery! I tell you, Dorothy suits me wonderfully; she was terribly sweet and dear last night—and she doesn't snore, which is more than I can say for Dulcie. Indeed, it was the first time in ages I've had a good night's rest . . ." She went on ever more plaintively, now producing a gush of tears into the bargain, "I wish you wouldn't be so unkind to me; it makes me simply miserable, you know. It isn't as if I ask for much. I told you you could send those silly diamond ear-drops back to Love and Wirgman, since you didn't care for them, but now that I've found something I truly must have, you deny it me! It's wrong, it's wrong," she cried, feeling pleased as she did so to have succeeded in bringing in this reference to diamond ear-drops, which must surely interest Mrs. Hathaway more than any domestic squabble. "I am just wretched, Mr. Amor, and how you can treat me so after—after—" Her lip trembled, and she buried her head in her arms, as if she could not bring herself to say another word. Through the sound of her own sobbing, she could hear Sir Jeffery's voice. She smiled secretly at the table, still under cover of her arms.

"Very well, my dear, Dorothy comes!" he pronounced, on a note of real exasperation. He gave Mrs. Hathaway an embarrassed, distracted smile and instructed her, "Go and fetch your daughter, my good woman. And I suppose your husband as well, for we must arrange something suitable regarding her keep."

Mrs. Hathaway hurried out at once on this errand, hearing as she quitted the room Lady Isabella's voice call out, "Oh yes, Mrs. Hathaway, and pray send them both quickly, for we must be leaving soon." For Isabella well knew her safety was best protected by keeping others always about her; there would be time enough for her to be alone with her (now furious) beloved when the bonds of matrimony solidly conjoined them.

"By God, woman," hissed Sir Jeffery at his companion the moment Mrs. Hathaway had gone, "I'll wring your neck! What's got into you? Have you gone mad?"

Isabella, calmly drying the tears from her face with a corner of her napkin, smiled sweetly at her beloved. "Well, I should like to have a maid," she said softly, dimpling at him.

"But now we'll never be alone! It beats everything," he went on, betrayed by his anger into an involuntary bluntness. "I almost think you are trying to spoil our plans. Suppose your father were to find us now—for they must surely be looking for us. He would take you home nice as you please—don't you understand, my dear," he went on, striving to strike a conciliating tone, "we must make it plain you are—ah, mine forever, or they will never allow us to marry!"

Lady Isabella gave a tiny, genteel shrug. "If my father discovers us before we reach Gretna Green," she said, "I shall run away again with you as soon as ever I'm able. I'll run away ten times if I must. Does that satisfy you, my darling?" She gave him a smile of melting gentleness and patted his hand. To her relief, Mrs. Hathaway returned at that moment, her husband and daughter in tow. Vaulting ambition was writ large on Mrs. Hathaway's face; her husband wore a look of proprietary pride. Dorothy, the cause and object of their various emotions, beamed with pleasurable anticipation. The reader will be relieved to hear, since her keeping awake the previous night would have served no purpose, that she had not succeeded in doing so in spite of her best efforts and had instead enjoyed a very pleasant, restful repose. She now cast Isabella a joyful, grateful look, and vowed in silence even as she stood there to learn to perform her duties with all the finesse of the best London lady's maid ever.

And indeed, in the event, she did more than that, for she had a good heart as well as a quick wit, and Isabella stood in need of a great deal of comfort and support. Her elopement with de Guere was a dream come true, of course, but Isabella would have been a very odd girl indeed if she had not suffered keenly from this first separation from family and home. The strangeness of the rooms in which she slept, the rigours of the road, the desirability of keeping, at all moments, some neutral person or persons between herself and de Guere to act as a buffer, the attentions sometimes pressed upon her in spite of her efforts by this same adored hero—all these difficulties and more weighed heavily on Isabella and made her very glad for a friendly, female hand to hold. Though Dorothy could not be told, naturally, the exact cause of Mrs. Amor's sighs, she was a sympathetic enough soul to offer solace whatever the reason, and this Isabella appreciated and needed far more than any professional expertise her Dorothy might be lacking.

The great *coup* of Isabella's campaign took place at Gretna Green itself, for she had very rightly foreseen that it would be to her advantage to make the arrangements for her marriage to Sir Jeffery on her own. They had crossed the border towards evening and had of necessity passed one last unwed night in a Gretna inn called The Black Horse. Before she retired, and bidding her straitly to keep it a secret from Mr. Amor, Isabella had sent her faithful Dorothy on an errand into the neighbouring streets, with a letter and strict instructions to guide her. Meanwhile, she did not fail to notice that Sir Jeffery entertained a late-night visitor, a shabby-looking fellow he explained to Isabella as being the steward of a friend's estates nearby. "I thought we might put up there for a bit," he went on after the man had been dismissed, and Isabella permitted to come into the coffee-room (for Sir Jeffery had politely excluded her before, claiming she looked fatigued and ought to go bathe her eyes), "and cool our heels before returning to England, but it seems the place is closed up for the moment. We should hardly be comfortable there. So, my dear, where shall we go when we are married?"

"Then we are to be married at last," she breathed, taking his hand in hers. "I can scarcely believe it."

De Guere answered smoothly, "But of course; did you ever doubt it?"

"Oh, no! It is only . . . it has seemed such a long time in coming. But here we are! May we do it tomorrow? I should so like to."

"Naturally, my darling," said he, touching her hair. "I never thought otherwise. In fact, I have spoke to the innkeeper about a church to go to, and a minister to see, and he says he will arrange it for us for tomorrow, at noon. Is that too early, my pet?"

"Nothing could be too early," she said, glowing inwardly at the knowledge that she had exactly anticipated his choice of hour.

"Will you not entrust yourself to me tonight, Isabella?" Sir Jeffery now asked her, drawing her closer and kissing the top of her head lightly. The poor man had counted on being found by Lord Trevor days before this; he couldn't imagine where on earth the fellow was. Wasn't he looking for his daughter at all? Fortunately, at all events, de Guere had been faced with the necessity of enacting a false marriage at Gretna Green before. He knew just how it was done. If the earl did not show up tonight (but how could he fail? Sir Jeffery asked himself every ten minutes), he would simply avail himself again of the shabby fellow's services—for this particular shabby fellow was an actor, an acquaintance of Jeffery's from army days, and an adept in the matter of disguise—and meet him at Covenant Church round the corner on the morrow at noon, where he and Isabella would be mumbled over while the pastor ate his dinner. In the meanwhile—just in case Trevor did appear tonight—this might be his last opportunity of tasting the particular treasures to be yielded up by the young blond beauty before him. Those treasures he coveted all the more for having been denied them so long—he was only human— and so he held her even more tightly, and murmured ever more passionate flattery into her delicate ears.

But she held fast to her purpose and withdrew alone to her chamber. Truth to tell, she was trembling with desire herself and would not at all have minded giving in (for she did adore him, all her calculations notwithstanding), but it was quite out of the question. Tomorrow would be soon enough, and afterwards they would have all the time in the world.

For she had sent Dorothy to find a real minister and to arrange for a real wedding. Perhaps the shabby man Jeffery spoke to in the coffee-room was *not* summoned to help him contrive a false wedding, perhaps he really *was* a friend's steward, and all Isabella's fears were in vain. But it was hardly, as she told herself, worth taking chances. If she herself contrived the ceremony, then she could be sure of its being legitimate—and only then. Convinced that her logic was sound, and in loving hopes that her precautions had not been necessary, she slept peacefully that night, after having inscribed in her diary (of course) twelve pages describing the joy with which her maiden's heart burst on this, her last evening of singlehood.

In the morning she greeted her darling serenely and ventured out with him and Dorothy, who might after all prove useful, she said, and could anyhow be sent back later. Sir Jeffery *would* turn north, but Dorothy signalled to Isabella to head south, and so she cried out with great enthusiasm, "Oh, my dearest, I feel so dreadfully excited! Could we not walk about for a moment? We shall not be late. We are in plenty of time."

Sir Jeffery, in no hurry to undergo a wedding ceremony, either real or false, resisted her only a moment.

"What a lovely town," crowed Bella. "What a lovely day!" She kept a careful eye on Dorothy, who motioned her round the block. "Oh come, my sweet," Isabella cried, turning as she was directed. With relief she saw a church at once. A nod from Dorothy confirmed it was the correct one, and Lady Isabella (with a vigour not really suitable in a quivering bride) grabbed her beloved by the arm and dragged him bodily towards its steps. "My dear, just look at this quaint old church! Oh I must have a look. Can't we?"

Since she was already dragging him through the door, it would hardly have done for de Guere to refuse. With an exasperated glance skywards he followed her in. The church was empty; then a man appeared near the altar.

"Oh look," Isabella gave a soft squeal, "here is someone to marry us. Oh, can't we be married here, my dear? Father—do you call them father?" she wondered aloud, even as she addressed the clerical gentleman, "May I speak with you a moment?"

The worthy gentleman looked a little amused: this was not the first time a handsome young lady had sailed into his church with a shuffling young gentleman behind her. "Reverend," he told her gently. "Would you be—"

"I am Mrs. Amor," she interrupted him. Then, with a shamefaced glance at Dorothy, who only now understood the whole truth of the matter, she corrected, "I mean, I am Lady Isabella Stanbroke." Dorothy gave a little gasp, as her young employer continued, "And this is Sir Jeffery de Guere. We should like to be married."

But de Guere was not going to stand still for this. "My dear, I have already arranged for a minister, as I told you," he whispered furiously. "In fact, I think we must hurry down there at once, for he will not wait—"

"Oh no, but Reverend—I'm sorry, I don't know your name, sir."

"Oates," he supplied.

"Reverend Oates looks such a kind man. You will marry us, won't you, sir?"

"As I said last night," began the gentleman, with a nod at Dorothy, "I should be perfectly—"

"Yes, you see he will do it," broke in Bella. "Oh please, my darling, I like him so much, and here we are . . ." She looked anxiously at Sir Jeffery, who had begun to see the trap he was in. Dorothy (who, in addition to her own good qualities, was a broad, strapping, big-boned girl) stood squarely in the aisle behind him, looking none too docile. Before him waited the minister, book in hand; and to his arm clung the tenacious Isabella, a mist of tears already rising in her eyes. Surrounded though he was, he might have escaped even now, had Isabella not written so well the letter she addressed to the Reverend (then unknown to her) when she sent Dorothy out on the previous evening. The letter explained that her honour was at stake and that the cleric was on no account to allow the man she brought in with her the following day to leave before the ceremony was performed. She appealed to his sense of justice, as well as his kindness as a Christian, and in fact had penned such a tender and affecting account of her plight (mostly fabricated, naturally, but not the less moving for that) that the Reverend Oates had very nearly fallen in love with the writer himself. He would sooner have died than allow this so-called gentleman to desert his misguided lady in her desperate hour; so that when he observed de Guere's increasing discomfiture he spoke up forcefully and at once. He was a vigorous, youthful man himself (Isabella had instructed Dorothy to seek out just such a man), and his voice and bearing both suggested a strength not solely spiritual.

"I should be very happy to unite you in the bonds of matrimony," said he. "I'm sure my colleague—whoever it was you've engaged, sir—will understand how it was."

"Of course he will," put in Isabella. "We'll have the inn-keeper pay him just the same. Say you don't mind, my darling," she prompted, tugging at Jeffery's arm.

De Guere had broke out in a sweat. Fingering his cravat uneasily with his free hand, he looked all round the church, before and behind him, as if imagining divine intervention might come to his aid. But divinity had allied itself squarely with Bella: Sir Jeffery was brought to bay. If only Miss Partridge could have seen him, she and a dozen other young women! He made a pretty picture, ringed round by three righteous, expectant faces, a dew of perspiration on his handsome brow.

He did not know to what extent Isabella had played him false. There was no one thing he could point to as conclusively proving she mistrusted him, or had anticipated his duplicity—and yet he had the sense she had outwitted and outplayed him: the fox turning upon the hounds. Inadvertently or by design she had cornered him quite. "Very well," he finally gasped, his voice faltering and cracking with emotion. "What can I say, my dear, since you are adamant? Though if you would please your husband—"

"You are not quite my husband yet, love. Grant me this one last indulgence, will you not?" begged Isabella prettily, permitting a tear or two to spill over onto her cheek.

Sir Jeffery looked again into the stern eyes of Reverend Oates and decided, again, he must cede. Behind him he could feel Dorothy's gaze boring into his back. He gave a nod, and in that moment experienced a sensation he had thought was reserved for drowning men, or for those about to be swallowed up by quicksand. The feeling was so vivid that he coughed for a minute, as if fighting for his breath; then he recovered and faced the Reverend squarely. There is always annulment, he thought, clutching at straws as desperate men will do; there is always divorce. But he knew in his heart he was finished: the glorious days of Sir Jeffery de Guere's bachelorhood were ended. I shall not look, he thought with an inward sigh as he heard the Reverend clear his throat to begin the service, upon their like again.

15

LADY ELIZABETH gave a whoop. "They've found them!" she shouted, leaping up from her perch on the sofa-arm and waving her father's letter under Lady Emilia's nose. "They've found them," she repeated joyfully, flinging the paper high in the air and throwing her arms round her friend. "Oh Emmy, Isabella's safe with my father . . . I didn't even know how frightened I was till just this moment." Tears sprang to her eyes as she released the smiling Emilia and went to retrieve her father's note. "Thank God, she is found," she said in a husky voice, and did in her thoughts thank God.

"But where are they? Is she—did Jeffery—oh for the love of heaven, Lizzie, what does your father say?"

Elizabeth hastily scanned the page. "They are all on their way home—your brother, too—and she's . . . Oh my Lord, she's married de Guere." She sat down abruptly, as if this information had been a rough hand that knocked her down. "She's married him, Emmy. Well, I suppose," she went on, striving for a smile, "I suppose we'll just have to make the best of it."

"I'm so sorry, my dear—" Emilia began, feeling dreadfully at a loss for words.

"Perhaps it's for the best, who can say?" Elizabeth answered dubiously.

"Your father does not mention an . . . an annulment?"

Lizzie looked again at the letter. "No, it would seem they are wed and will stay so . . . Marchmont sends you his best love," she added, colouring a little, as she always did when saying his name. "They've already sent word to Charlie and Lord Weld, though there's no saying if it's been received . . . I think I'd best go wake my mother, don't you?" she added, for Lady Trevor had taken to lying abed nearly till noon of late, and she had not yet been seen downstairs that day. "She'll certainly wish to know at once."

"Remember it will be a shock," Emilia advised her as she left, then went on aloud, though to herself, "It certainly would shock me to hear *my* daughter had married Sir Jeffery de Guere. The poor woman! Oh, the poor girl!"

Lady Elizabeth stayed closeted with her mother more than an hour, leaving Emilia plenty of time to shake her head over Isabella's fate. Then she and Lizzie went over to the Nestling to break the news to Miss Lewis. They found her as Elizabeth had last seen her, on a day-bed in her sitting-room, still pale though apparently a trifle more cheerful. Elizabeth burst out at once with the information, then sent a servant for Lady Lewis and repeated it to her. As had been the case with Emilia, the relief both ladies felt was followed at once by consternation: marriage to Sir Jeffery did not seem a happy fate. Still, after all their anxious conjecture, it was wonderful to know Isabella was whole and safe, and the four ladies drank a celebratory glass of wine together before Emilia and Lizzie returned to Haddon Abbey.

Also before they departed, Amy Lewis dared to ask Elizabeth if her brother had been heard from as well. On being told he and Weld had been advised to come home, the girl first turned pink, then white—the first from natural joy at the thought of seeing her Charlie again, the second from re-collecting the voice of Susannah Lemon out on the balcony that terrible night in London. The poor girl had not been at all comforted by Elizabeth's attempts to reassure her during the past few days; instead she had been spending all her time of late bravely endeavouring to reconcile herself to the idea of a Lady Halcot other than herself, without, however, much success. The moment she was alone again she indulged in a good cry—not, as she scathingly reminded herself, for joy at Isabella's safety, nor even for sorrow at the consequences of her rash elopement, but from her purely selfish misery at the realization that Charlie would now be reunited with his fa-ther, and so would have an opportunity to discuss with him his marriage to Miss Lemon. Amy tried, in the days that ensued, to pull herself together. That evening she came down to sup-per for the first time since she had been home, but she did not eat anything. The following morning she appeared at the breakfast table, too, but she looked more like a ghost than anything human. By the afternoon of the succeeding day, when the party headed by the Earl of Trevor at last reached Haddon Abbey, Amy had managed to exhaust herself utterly in these heroic attempts and was hardly even vigorous enough to climb into the carriage and visit her newly married friend. Lady Lewis thought it best that she wait a day in any case. The good woman could only imagine the kind of confusion and high feeling that must be rampant at the Abbey, and she thought it extremely probable that a visit even from so close a friend as Amy would be more intrusive than welcome until a little time had passed. And so Miss Lewis waited yet another day, listless and pale and trying to sound more cheerful than she felt.

When at last she did arrive at the Abbey, things had already settled down a great deal. Lady Trevor looked somewhat worn by her ordeal, but tranquil enough; Elizabeth and

Marchmont were not in evidence. Lady Emilia told her they had walked out together in the village. "But I'm sure you have called to see Isabella," she went on. "Let me go and fetch her for you."

"Thank you. Is she—"

"She is astonishingly well, as you will see," Emilia filled in. "De Guere's having another long talk with Lord Trevor this morning, I think. I know Isabella will be anxious to see you." With this she departed, leaving Amy to muse doubtfully on the changes marriage might already have wrought in her old friend. She was Lady Isabella de Guere now. How curious! Amy tried the name out aloud to hear how it sounded. She was trying it for the third time, still slowly and questioningly, when its new owner entered the room and threw her arms round her.

"Oh my darling!" exclaimed Bella at once, apparently quite as full of warmth and enthusiasm as she had ever been. Amy asked herself what she had been expecting. For some reason she had thought Bella would be more sober, or more wise, than when they had last met. But here she was, glowing with good health and pleasure at seeing Miss Lewis, drawing back from her for a moment to survey her better, then embracing her vigorously again. "How are you? I am so sorry I could not tell you that I was leaving when I went off with—ah, with my husband," she ended on a choked giggle, releasing Amy and drawing her to sit on a sofa by her side. "Does it not sound odd to hear me say that? But he is my husband, after all. Have you seen him? Where is he?"

"Lady Emilia says he is closeted with your father," Amy told her. "But how are you, Bella? Are you happy? Has he . . . do you regret—"

"No, I do not regret it one bit," said Bella. "I would do it all over again just the same way, if it needed to be done. It was splendid, simply the most splendid adventure—you have no idea! Of course there were parts of it that were just the tiniest bit trying," she added, thinking in particular of the second night out of London, when she had sobbed for an hour straight while Dorothy held her hand. "But I found the sweetest maid to keep me company," she went on, "and you should see how jealous Margaret is" (naming the maid who had served her since she was fourteen). "She nearly had a fit thinking she'd been replaced. But of course I shall keep them both on, for I shall need a dresser as well as a maid since I am to be quite a grand lady, and live in London half the year round."

Amy, listening, was reminded of a child who ransacks her mother's wardrobe and joyfully dons her shawls and slippers, then smugly parades up and down before a glass with the silks trailing and the huge shoes clacking on the floor. She tried to put the image out of her head as she answered, "Is it all decided then? You will live in London and—where else?"

"Oh, you don't think I am deserting you, my love, do you? We are to have Sturton Cottage all to ourselves during the other six months, so we shall only be a stone's throw away from you. In fact, I believe the Cottage is rather closer to the Nestling than the Abbey, don't you think? How lovely that will be, Amy, only think. You will come and dine with us every day if you like—just you and me and Jeffery. What cosy evenings by the fire . . . I shall be a matron, you know, so I can invite anybody you fancy as well. Doesn't it sound delicious?"

In point of fact it sounded rather ghastly than otherwise, but of course Amy could not say so. She was realizing for the first time that her Isabella was hers no longer, and it was beginning to make her want to cry. For a moment she thought Bella rather cruel for not recognising that, while the three-some might sound ideal to her, it only felt to Amy as if she were losing the intimacy she had always shared with Bella; but she soon reminded herself that this was after all the inevitable and natural order of things. One did not dwell forever in the bosom of girlhood friendships: one married and became a wife, and then a mother, and friendships subsisted as they might. Amy's conviction that she herself was fated not to marry (for if she could not have Charlie she did not want anybody) made this home-truth even less welcome than it might have been, but her lifetime habit of struggling against selfish and useless thoughts came to her rescue now and enabled her to smile at Isabella with something like genuine goodwill.

"I am so happy you are looking forward to it," she brought out quietly, patting Isabella's hand. "Naturally I must get better acquainted with Sir Jeffery now. Do you know, I don't think we have exchanged two words!"

"Of course, you are right—but once you do know him better, you will like him very much, I am sure. He really is the—ah, he is . . ." She stared off into space for a moment in silence, as if looking for words written on the air. "He has excellent qualities," she finally said, with a little catch in her voice that went immediately to Amy's heart.

"My dear, has he been unkind to you?" she demanded, horrified, before considering what she was about to say. "You do love him, don't you Bella?"

It was clear at once that her friend was struggling to hold back tears. Her brave, reckless air had vanished. She carefully avoided looking into Amy's soft eyes (for it could only have made her cry more, she knew, to see their tenderness) and answered, "Well, I must confess he is not . . . to say truth, Amy, he's been a little disturbed since the wedding. You see, I'm not sure he gave—well I can't be certain he gave enough thought to what it would be like to be married," she went on, stressing the word enough, "for he's been in quite an evil temper . . ." At this a tear did escape her; she brushed it away hastily. "One or two times he's even . . . in any case, I think he will soon be accustomed to it, and we are sure to have a very . . . happy . . . life . . . together." These last words were delivered so haltingly as to be painful, and at their conclusion Isabella buried her head in her hands and sobbed outright. Amy flung her arms round the weeping girl.

"My darling, don't live with him until he's calmer," she burst out, again without knowing what she was going to say.

"You mustn't allow him to be unkind to you. I won't have it!"

"I do love him," Isabella asserted in muffled tones. "It's just—he hasn't at all seemed himself since . . . Oh, Amy, I must confess it to you, even if I never do to anyone else—I don't think he really meant to marry me at all. In fact," she went on, sitting up again, her face very white, "I sort of knew that before I went off with him. Of course *I* always meant to get married," she clarified, "but I do not believe he did. Amy, I feel such an idiot!"

With these words she crumpled again, and cried for nearly half an hour, while Amy held her and comforted her. Miss Lewis reminded her again and again that she was not obliged to live with de Guere, even if he was her husband, and begged her not to do so until he was behaving to her much more kindly. She assured her he would do so in time (though she had no way of knowing this) and repeatedly recommended to Bella that she stay in her father's protection till then.

"That's another thing," Isabella broke in, sitting up again and dabbing at her face with a lace handkerchief. "My father has been absolutely the most angelic . . . it makes me feel twice as bad, you can't imagine."

"But of course he has. He only wants you to be happy," Amy told her reasonably. "How do he and Sir Jeffery get on?"

"Well, naturally there is a great deal of . . . tension between them," said Bella, sniffing loudly. She sighed. "But I think they will deal together tolerably well in the end. My father is trying to find some kind of—occupation for Jeffery, to keep him from what he calls his idleness and frivolity. He's right, of course. Jeffery ought to do something with himself. And then he's given us Sturton Cottage, as I said, and he's going to help us sell Jeffery's bachelor quarters in London so we can take something more suitable together nearer Haddon House. Oh, it's just mortifying how good he is being! How could I have been so stupid as not to have confided in him in the first place?"

Miss Lewis did not know what to say, so she made little sounds instead.

"Even Lizzie has been decent," Bella went on, as if this were the most astonishing of all. "And then my mother—! She has never once said a harsh word to me, not once since we've been back. I tell you," she concluded, essaying a little laugh, "if my family were any better to me, I'd simply die of embarrassment. It's all too much."

Amy stroked her hand and smiled at her. She felt so sad for Isabella, she quite forgot about Charlie for a minute. In fact, she was meditating on how very lucky she herself was to be surrounded by parents and friends who loved her, and to have her whole life still ahead of her. When she did remember Charlie, it was like a little stab of hardship in the midst of prodigious good fortune, and she went home to the Nestling in much better spirits than she had been able to muster for quite some time. Isabella, collecting herself after Miss Lewis's departure, felt somewhat comforted too: she had forgotten hitherto what solace Amy's friendship could bring her. She resolved to regulate her mind a little better from now on, and especially to be sensible and civil towards de Guere. She would try to take the long view of things, she told herself; and though she had forgotten this three times before nightfall, she nevertheless succeeded in remembering it better the next day, and even better on the one after that; so that before the week was out, she was pretty much in the habit of approaching the mending of her splintery marriage with good sense and forthrightness. Heaven knows it did not come easily to her, but her hard work soon began to be rewarded. Sir Jeffery, at first too enraged at having been trapped by this insignificant chit to bother to get to know her any better, gradually calmed down and started looking about him in earnest.

Lord Marchmont had come down pretty hard on him, as had Isabella's father. It had been evident from the first he was not to be permitted to waltz out of this bind as planned. Between the two of them they seemed determined to make a good husband of him, as well as a useful member of society. There was talk of his taking a seat in Parliament. He was obliged to write to Mrs. Butler, explicitly severing his connection with her. He was made to take an oath to give up gambling. His comfortable bachelor lodgings were to be got rid of, his housekeeper turned off. Lady Trevor made small-talk with him. Lady Elizabeth began to establish an astringent, bantering tone in her conversations with him—the start of a lifelong relationship. And Isabella herself no longer fluttered her eyelashes at him, looking soft and silly; on the contrary, she spoke her mind clearly and mildly, addressing him with a modest kind of shyness but no trace any more of coquetry. She still kept to her own room at night—until, as she put it, they understood one another better. The honeymoon, it seemed, was over before it had begun. De Guere was beaten.

But he could have bolted, if he had wanted to. He might have fled to the Continent, simply vanished, leaving Bella in the lurch (and she deserved it, turning tables on him as she had! he reflected) and his cousin Marchmont to make over his estates to whomever he liked. It had become clear to him in any case that Lord Marchmont was going to pursue Lady Elizabeth in spite of her sister's foolish elopement; half the sting of the scandal had been taken out of it anyhow by the fact of her having returned a married woman, rather than a ruined girl. He could have bolted—as he reminded himself dozens of times—but he did not.

The fact was, he rather liked Isabella, now that he began to see what she was made of. He liked Isabella, and he rather liked her father, who for all his righteousness was a tough old bird, not given to scoldings or rantings but rather determined to look to the future and make of it what he could. Indeed, Sir Jeffery found a certain pleasure in being "made over." He was almost as curious as anyone else to see if they would succeed in reforming him. It was a game, for the moment, and certainly one that had the charm of novelty. At the very least, he told himself, he would play out his hand till he had had the benefit of his conjugal rights—for Lord Trevor had been waiting for the happy couple at the Black Horse Inn when they came back from the wedding, and it had not seemed quite right to initiate their conjugal relationship while being hauled back in disgrace by Marchmont and the old man. In fact, de Guere rather doubted Lord Trevor would have permitted it, marriage or no marriage. And since their arrival at Haddon Abbey he had fared no better in his attempts to get close to his bride: she eluded him nightly, asserting (he could hardly deny it) that in spite of their legal relationship they did not know one another very well. But he was coming to know her, and she him. Thus far it was rather an interesting adventure for Jeffery, who was never one to let circumstances get the better of him in any case. Besides, he liked seeing Marchmont obliged to deal with him as family again. In that connection de Guere was hard to swallow, and he knew it. Lady Emilia fairly squirmed when she found herself seated next to him, or alone with him in the breakfast-room, and Jeffery enjoyed watching her. No, he was not of a mind to turn tail just yet.

Besides all the considerations above, he was now in the interesting position of being married to an extremely well-dowered young lady. Ought he to take to his heels before discovering just how well-dowered? Sir Jeffery rather thought not.

Such, approximately, was the state of affairs Lord Halcot found when he returned to his home with Lord Weld in tow. We left his young lordship, if the reader will recall, in a state of extreme excitement regarding Amy Lewis. Only the most rigorous self-discipline had prevented Charlie from giving up the search for Bella altogether and posting home at once to speak to Amy. Rarely had he been so happy as on the day when word came from England informing them Isabella had been found. Rarely, for that matter, had Lord Weld been so happy, for Charlie's company, he had found, was not a privilege his enjoyment of which grew as time went on but rather quite—quite—the contrary. This, added to their mutual relief at knowing Bella to be safe, made their return to England a swift and agreeable one. Lord Weld would have stopped in London and stayed there, but Halcot insisted on extending his parents' hospitality to the man who had done so much for his sister and dragged him up to Warwickshire with him. Anyhow, as he pointed out, Marchmont and Lady Emilia would almost certainly be there, too, from what his father had said, and surely Lord Weld wanted to see them?

Lord Weld admitted he did and reluctantly finished out the journey with Lord Halcot. He was indeed glad, on reaching Haddon Abbey, to be reunited with his excellent friends. His second inquiry (after making sure of the welfare of Isabella, and Emilia, and Marchmont himself) was whether or not Lord Marchmont had offered for Elizabeth as yet. "Done what?" demanded Emilia, gasping. The three of them stood alone in the Abbey's vast Green drawing-room.

"Lady Elizabeth," repeated Weld mildly. "I thought surely you must have had time to offer by now, old man."

"Have you decided to—" Emilia began.

"Dear God, Weld, you've not been in this house ten minutes and look what you've done already!" broke in Marchmont. "Not only haven't I asked Lady Elizabeth, I also was waiting to tell Emilia till I had. What's happened to your manners, old man? You've been hanging about with our friend Charles too long, that's what it is, very bad form—"

"Oh, and I should like to have a word with you about that, my friend," Weld interrupted indignantly; indeed, all three of them were speaking nearly at once. "What did you mean by sending me off with that young . . . er, cub, while you went off yourself with Lord Trev—"

"Jemmy, answer me before I throttle you!" Emilia demanded. "Are you meaning to offer for Lizzie or are you not? Why haven't you told me? What are you waiting—"

"One question at a time," laughed Marchmont. "It's a fact I had decided to ask Lady Elizabeth—"

"You had! Oh Jemmy, how could you know that and not tell me?"

"But now that I've spoken to Trevor and got his approval and all—"

"Oh, you have! Beastly, beastly! Jemmy, when will you learn to take me into your confidence the moment, the very moment you—"

"But now that I've done all the preliminary work, I'm not so certain I ought to ask her just yet. When we are alone together—"

"Yes?" Emmy prompted breathlessly, as he hesitated.

"Well, she seems nervous, as if she's always looking for something to say. As if she'd rather I didn't ask. I'm certain she knows it's on my mind—though I don't know if Trevor's mentioned it to her. I rather think so, though with all the excitement over Lady Isabella . . ."

"Do you mean you aren't sure if she'll accept you?" asked Emilia.

"Well, yes, to put it bluntly."

"I don't believe my ears," Lord Weld now interposed. "Do you mean to tell me you two have been in this house together four days now and never yet discussed this matter until *I* brought it up? I say, you positively *need* me! I don't know how you managed before I came along."

"Don't blame me," Lady Emilia defended herself. "I'm perfectly receptive—now don't say I'm not, Jemmy—but this man simply refuses to entrust me with anything more exciting than his opinion of the weather. A dozen times I've tried to bring up the subject—"

"You have?" exclaimed her brother.

"I certainly have, the subject of Lady Elizabeth exactly—and all to let you know how obvious it's become to me the girl is head over ears in love with you—"

"She has a funny way of showing it, if that's the case," countered Marchmont, "for this very morning, when I caught up with her in the East Garden, she talked to me without drawing breath—for thirty minutes straight. About poultry, if you will! Poultry! How to raise it, how to cook it, how to serve it . . . frankly I felt very queasy before she was finished, and certainly not at all of a mind to introduce the topic of love."

"I am sorry, my dear," said Lady Emilia primly, "but I can only assure you there is not the slightest doubt in my mind of her feelings towards you. For reasons which are fast becoming entirely mysterious to me, this girl has taken it into her head to believe you the most charming and admirable man she has ever met, and the very idea of her refusing you—"

"I'd like to hear her do it," interjected Warrington Weld fiercely.

"—is preposterous," finished Emilia. "So no more foot-dragging, my boy, the next time you're alone with her, out with it and no nonsense, is that understood? And if she brings up poultry or shellfish or topsoils, well so much the better. You just tell her topsoils always make you amorous and carry on from there, do you hear me?"

Lord Marchmont had heard her—and so, very nearly, did Lizzie, who came into the drawing-room to welcome Lord Weld the moment she had finished saying hello to her brother. Lady Emilia and Lord Weld (two minds with but a single thought) instantly attempted to quit this room together, leaving Marchmont alone with Lizzie; but they were foiled in this scheme by Lizzie's determination to make sure Lord Weld was comfortable in the chamber assigned him. She insisted on accompanying him up the stairs herself, and would on no account allow Emilia to fulfill this hostess's duty herself. "For my whole family owes Lord Weld a debt of gratitude, and we feel it very keenly . . . quite as much as if it were he who had found my sister. I am sure you would have," she told him as she drew him from the room, "if they had gone to the Continent instead of to Scotland." She put her arm through his in a friendly, confidential way and added *sotto voce*, "For the sheer heroism of passing a week alone with Charlie you ought to receive a medal at least. No, do not deny it, dear sir. I know how it must have been. You will be wanting a bath after your labours, and perhaps a week or two of conversation with the nation's greatest savants, till you've recovered somewhat, I daresay. Does that sound appealing?" With these words she led him off, leaving Emilia to scold her brother on the subject of Keeping Secrets.

Lord Halcot for his part had not been home two hours before he again set out. He was on his way to the Nestling, of course, having first taken a minute of his father's time to discuss what he planned to undertake there. The idea that his son might someday marry Amy Lewis had naturally often occurred to Lord Trevor. It was not so overwhelmingly attractive an idea as to make him inclined to push for it, but on the other hand, it had distinct advantages, and did not at all seem to him a bad thought. Its chief appeal was that it would unite the lands surrounding the Abbey with those owned by his lifelong neighbour, Lord Lewis. The two properties being adjacent, this could not fail to increase their worth. And then he rather liked the thought that Halcot would be allied with a family he knew and could trust implicitly. Coming on the heels of Isabella's mad alliance, this aspect was doubly comforting. Lord Trevor's only concern, then, was for Charlie to make certain this marriage was really what he desired. He advised his son to wait at least another se'ennight before speaking to Miss Lewis; but since Halcot would not hear even of so short a delay as this, Lord Trevor merely gave his consent and his good wishes and sent the young man on his way.

Poor Charlie suffered a severe attack of nerves while he waited for Amy in the drawing-room at the Nestling. He kept looking and looking at his reflection in the pier-glass, combing his butter-yellow hair with his fingers, and starting furtively from the glass each time he thought he heard a sound in the hall. By the time Miss Lewis actually entered he was as close to fainting as she—and she was very close indeed, for she had made up her mind to say something to him, and it was not going to be pleasant for her. In fact, when she caught her first glimpse of him, she very nearly gave up all thought of carry-ing through her resolve, for he was so handsome, she thought, so lean and tall and graceful! His liquid blue eyes smiled meltingly upon her even through his nervousness. Must she really relinquish him after all? Could she bear it? But she straightened her shoulders (and went a shade paler—Charlie thought her very beautiful, but quite a good deal more pallid than he had recalled) and made up her mind to it again.

Then (after the formal courtesies had been exchanged, and Miss Lewis explained both her parents were occupied—going over household accounts with the steward, as it chanced) Lord Halcot cleared his throat with a painful, cracking harrumph and began, "Miss Lewis, will you permit me to speak of a matter of some significance to me? I understand from my mother you have not been quite well, but—"

"Please be easy on that head," she interrupted, going a shade whiter. "I feel perfectly recovered. In fact, I had been meaning to speak to you on such a matter—"

"If you don't mind, I think I'd best bring this up first—"

"But it may be the same thing; in fact I think it must be. I want you to be perfectly comfortable with me, sir, and never fear that I can be otherwise than—" She stumbled trying to get the words out, then forced herself to clarity, "—otherwise than happy if I know that you are happy. So if it is a question of marriage—"

"How did you know?"

She looked away. "I heard . . . on the balcony . . . well, if you please, I had rather not discuss it—" Tears came to her eyes. "I guessed it, that's all, and I—I wish you very happy!" With this she turned away altogether, and took a few halting steps towards the door.

"But how can you wish me very happy when it is you—" He stopped, puzzled. "Miss Lewis, won't you let me speak as I had planned? I've been thinking how to put this since France!"

"Oh, I beg you will not call me Miss Lewis," she cried

frantically. "It simply makes me miserable! Just because you are taking a wife does not mean we can no longer be friends, I hope."

"Well, under the circumstances, I should hope you are right!" said he with a kind of laugh. "But do you mean to say—do you accept me, then?"

"I beg your pardon?"

"I say, have you accepted me? Am I to understand . . . since you speak of my being married, does that mean—? Oh, I *wish* you had let me deliver the proposal as I'd prepared it! Now I've made an awful botch of it!"

But Amy was staring at him with her mouth open. "You don't mean—" she commenced, and stopped.

"I don't? But I do!"

"You haven't come—" In a whisper, she resumed, "You haven't come to offer for *me*, have you?"

He hesitated only an instant, but it seemed an eternity to her. "But naturally I have," he answered at last, very mildly. "What else?"

"What else? Oh, my—my dear!" she exclaimed, confusion and joy so overcoming her that she sank down upon a settee. "What else? Never mind what else—I shall tell you sometime when we are very, very old. I thought—but never mind. Oh Charlie, give me your hand, I beg you! You have made me very, very happy."

Lord Halcot seated himself beside her and gladly took the proffered hand. In the half-hour that ensued he repeated not once but twice the entire text of the proposal he had prepared; and she accepted not twice but thrice. Then they went off together to confront Lord Lewis with news they had every good reason to believe would please him, and later that afternoon Amy returned with Halcot to the Abbey to be present when he announced his happiness to the family there.

That evening, after supper, Lord Marchmont and his sister encountered one another by chance in the large, dim library of the Abbey. "I was hoping for something by Mrs. Radcliffe," said Emilia, "or perhaps Walpole. All this matrimony is having a decidedly depressing effect on my spirits. I believe a little terror might pick me up."

"You ought to get married yourself," commenced Marchmont. "Then you wouldn't find—"

"No, thank you," she said crisply. "But while we're on the subject, why are you here looking at books and not elsewhere looking at Lizzie? I thought you'd made up your mind to speak to her at last."

"Dear God, Emmy, don't you think there have been enough betrothals announced for one day?" he asked. "There is such a thing as timing, you know."

"Oh, pooh," she said. "Do you mean Halcot and little Amy? That's only one. I should think a healthy family ought to be able to absorb—oh, seven or eight betrothals in a day, at the least. Why don't you try them? Go and find Elizabeth."

"It's after ten."

"My goodness, aren't we rustic? In London after ten would mean time to go out and begin the evening. Surely Elizabeth hasn't gone to bed!"

"No, but my dear Emilia, don't you think we would be stealing Charlie's thunder if we were—if she were to accept me, and we wanted to let the others know?"

"You can't still imagine she is going to refuse you!"

"It isn't impossible, believe me. I appreciate your kindness in pretending to find the notion absurd, but the last time I broached the topic with her she turned three different shades of ivory and looked as if she were about to swoon. When she gave me permission to address her father on the topic she wouldn't even look at me. Kept staring at her plate. Went all crimson."

"She gave you permission to speak to Lord Trevor? Well for heaven's sake, what do you suppose she meant by that except—"

"Emmy, it isn't as simple as you think! I tell you she looked wretched the last time I—"

"When was that?"

Marchmont looked a trifle shamefaced. "In London."

"London! So you haven't spoken to her since then? The poor girl must be frantic, wondering what happened—"

"Well, she doesn't seem very frantic to me!"

Lady Emilia remembered the value of reasonableness and strove mightily to calm herself a bit. After a few deep breaths she turned to her brother, took his hands quietly in her own, and said, "Jemmy, you know you are the dearest thing in life to me, don't you?"

Lord Marchmont owned that he did.

"And you know that I would never suggest to you any course of action I expected would bring you pain. Don't you?"

He admitted this was so.

"And you know, most of all, that I have just spent ten days solid with Elizabeth, watching her and listening to her—and especially, watching her when she talked about you. Granted?"

Marchmont granted it.

"Well then, my dear," Lady Emilia concluded, giving his hands a shake, "kindly take my advice and seek out this girl at once. Ask her for her hand in marriage and do it cleanly, quickly, and mercifully. The poor thing probably thinks you've changed your mind. It's really too unkind of you."

"But she—"

"No, there are no buts. Goodnight, my dear, and may I be the very first to congratulate you. You could not have chosen a more splendid woman." She kissed him on the cheek, dropped his hands, and started to walk away.

"But Emilia—"

She sighed. "Yes?"

"Mightn't I wait till tomorrow morning? After all, she's bound to be thinking about Halcot, and . . ."

"Oh, for the love of heaven, all right. But first thing in the morning, you understand? If you don't I won't speak to you, ever again."

"First thing," he repeated. "I promise."

Lord Marchmont thus cleverly afforded himself the opportunity of passing an entire night in wakeful agony, tossing and turning on his feather-bed, as he imagined every possible disastrous reply Lady Elizabeth could make to him. When he was not amusing himself in this wise, he reminded himself of Charlotte Beaudry and how she had hurt him. At about five o'clock, having decided for the twentieth time that Lizzie would doubtless laugh in his face, he finally dropped off to sleep, only to wake from a nightmare at seven. The nightmare presented to him an Elizabeth who was secretly suffering from some dreadful, lethal malady. He was so anxious, on waking, to be assured it was only a dream that he rose and dressed at once in order to be ready to speak to her the moment she came downstairs. All thoughts of Charlotte Beaudry (good and bad) finally forgotten, he accosted his beloved as she entered the breakfast-room about two hours later, and could not prevent himself from checking her delicate countenance for signs of a ravaging disease. There were none, he saw joyfully, pouring her a cup of coffee and praying he would think of some pretext with which to lure her out into the gardens after her breakfast. He cursed every mouthful she ate, as delaying the moment when he could at last unburden himself, and nearly refused when she innocently asked him to pour her a second cup of coffee. "Doesn't it make you nervous?" he asked, to cover his response.

She looked at him blankly. "Not particularly."

"Oh. It does me," he replied with an edgy laugh.

"So I see. How much have you drunk this morning, my lord?"

"Oh, only a cup or two."

"Indeed? I should have guessed potfuls."

Lord Marchmont gave another nervous laugh. "Fine day, I think," he observed, glancing through the long windows.

"Yes, indeed. Finer than the last time you remarked upon it, do you think, or less fine?" she inquired, rather amused by his apparent discomfiture. She ate another mouthful of muffin and decided, finally, to take pity on him. "Lord Marchmont, is there anything troubling you?"

He nearly jumped out of his chair. "Hardly! Scarcely! What should be? Fine day, I think, don't you?"

She continued mildly, "I have the distinct impression you are ill at ease somehow. If you are, I beg you will feel free to—" She hesitated, looking for words.

Lord Marchmont burst out suddenly, "Lady Elizabeth, there is something—if you don't mind, I—"

But he had no sooner commenced this sentence than Lord Weld walked in—a piece of bad timing, in Marchmont's private opinion, previously unparalleled in the history of the civilized world. He nodded at Weld irritably, then resumed his address to Lizzie with these words: "Dear ma'am, haven't you finished your breakfast yet? In the name of mercy, pray let it be and walk out with me in the gardens, won't you? It's a frightful fine day—"

Elizabeth laughed, though she hadn't meant to, and looked with some embarrassment at Lord Weld. He nodded affably at her and she rose, dusting crumbs from her skirt, to move round the table to Marchmont. "You are right," she said charitably. "It is a terrifyingly fine day. Suppose we take some air, shall we?"

"Good idea," exclaimed the earl. "You don't mind, old chap," he added, nodding at Weld. "Probably rather take your breakfast alone anyhow, wouldn't you?"

"Oh, absolutely," Weld murmured, adding in a private aside to his eggs, "Happy to see the back of you." Lord Marchmont and Lizzie quitted the room.

"Fine day," Marchmont remarked a few minutes later, when they had reached a quiet path in the East Garden.

"Oh, fabulously. A little tedious, but fine," said Lizzie, beginning to feel nervous herself. It was clear she was about to be confronted with something—doubtless the very thing she had been careful to avoid in the past few days. Her father had told her days before that Marchmont had spoken to him and that he approved the suit provided Lizzie herself desired it. Again and again she had been obliged to confess to herself she did not know what was best to do. She had certainly been keeping him at arm's length, mostly by talking like an idiot—an extremely garrulous idiot—whenever they were alone together: he had been right about that. She knew he had been trying to sound her out, and she had indeed been giving him mixed signals back. But this morning, it appeared, she had found the limit of his patience. Tense and uncomfortable as he was, he had obviously resolved to press his question home today. Elizabeth braced herself mentally.

"Dear ma'am," he commenced abruptly.

"Sir?"

"If you will permit me, I should like to address you on a subject I gave you some reason to believe was of interest to me—that is," he recommenced, finding he had got himself hopelessly tangled in his own polite phrases, "I hope I may take up a topic about which I think you know I . . . er, it can't be a surprise to you, after what I asked you in London, to know that— Oh dash, this is coming out absolutely all wrong." He reached out to a hedge as they passed it and angrily tore off a sprig. As they walked on he fretted at the little spray, bending the small leaves and breaking them off one by one.

"Sir?" Lizzie finally prompted, as he marched on in silence.

"Devil take it, Elizabeth, you know perfectly well what I'm struggling with. Why don't you help me? The fact is" (he had been increasing his pace gradually, and now he sped up even more, so that she fairly had to trot to keep up with him), "the fact is I love you very much, and I wish to marry you very much, and if you'll have me that's exactly what I'll do, so for God's sake, say you'll take me and I'll do what I can to make you a happy pleasant life. There! I've said it. That's all. Now go ahead and laugh at me; I had a feeling you were going to. Elizabeth, are you all right?" he suddenly interrupted himself, stopping in his tracks and turning to face her, for she was so out of breath from struggling to keep up with him that her cheeks had gone red and she was audibly gasping for air.

"Yes," she said, panting. "Quite."

"You're not ill, are you?" The horror of his nightmare returned to him suddenly, and he demanded, "You haven't got an illness, have you? Oh please, say you haven't!"

"Lord, no," came the reply, now almost in her normal voice. "You've just been walking so quickly, I've hardly been able to keep even with you."

"Have I?" said he, surprised. "I am so sorry! But—did you hear me? Will you . . . am I—?"

"My dear Lord Marchmont," she began, feeling that same ghastly dizziness she had felt in the library of Haddon House, when the earl had first asked her if he might approach her father. "My dear sir—" But the vertigo was so marked that she felt the need of sitting down. "May we—please, there is a bench a little further on. I should like to sit."

She took his arm this time and leaned on it until they reached the bench. Then, bidding herself breathe deeply, she resumed her answer. She did not know what she was going to say until she heard herself say it. In fact, she listened with as much interest as Marchmont himself.

"Lord Marchmont, there is no one on earth whom I should like to marry except yourself. You are brave, and honest, and handsome, and kind, and intelligent, and—oh, I don't know what else, but in any case, everything that is admirable and pleasing to me. I am very fond of you indeed. I am—" she faltered suddenly. "But here is my great fear!"

"Your fear?"

"I think I may have—forgive me, but you know, ever since childhood I have known how to get what I want. And the first night, the very first night I ever saw you, I told my sister and Amy Lewis—ask them if I did not—I told them I meant to marry you." Her cheeks flamed crimson as she made this admission, but she forced herself to go on. "I do not know why I did so. I think I meant it for a joke or some such—and yet I did mean it too . . . anyhow, it was so cold-blooded, and so calculating, that . . . My point is, I'm afraid I somehow—ah, snared you . . ." She put her head down into her hands and felt herself beginning to weep. "I don't think I'm worthy of you," she finally brought out, through quiet sobs. "I'm afraid I made—made you love me!"

Lord Marchmont's nervousness had vanished as soon as he saw Lady Elizabeth's distress. The hands he now placed on her shaking back were warm and calm and reassuring. "My dear girl," he said quietly, leaning over so that his mouth was very near her ear, "my dear girl, do you think I have gone through all I have gone through in life only to be hoodwinked by a naughty, scheming girl? My poor, dear love, is that what has been tormenting you? I beg you will give it up," he went on gently, daring to place one hand on her shining blond hair and stroking a curl by her cheek. "I promise you, my regard for you has come to me quite on its own, without prompting from either you or me. It is perfectly genuine. It is yours, if you will take it. Now, will you take it?"

Lady Elizabeth at last uncovered her face. She looked up at him through damp lashes, with pink eyes and a shiny nose. She could hear her own heart beating, it seemed to her it would burst. She sniffed deeply, brushing away a tear with the back of her hand, then, looking squarely into his grey eyes, she smiled at him and answered, "Yes."

Epilogue

"But LIZZIE you can't be!" exclaimed Isabella, her hand flying to her open mouth in an involuntary gesture of disbelief. "It's only six months since you gave birth to Jimmy." She gave a nod to the infant as she referred to him, then continued, "How can you bear it? Aren't you beside yourself?"

Lady Elizabeth Marchmont laughed. "I bear it very well, my dear! Remember, I don't get sick the way you did, poor thing. And not only can *I* be," she pursued, while Isabella pulled various faces at her and the baby, "but I've had a letter this morning from Haddon Abbey, and Mother says—"

"Oh! Amy is expecting," Bella interrupted with a smile. "I've known about that for weeks, only she asked me not to say anything."

"Well, you little minx! I never knew you could keep a secret," Elizabeth replied, quite astonished. "You certainly never keep mine."

"Oh fiddlesticks, you never have any worth keeping," accused her sister, watching with interest as Jimmy spat a thin, milky dribble onto his mother. "I can't think how you got to be so patient, Lizzie," she observed, while Elizabeth calmly wiped the mess from the front of her pretty lawn gown. This interesting scene was taking place in a cosy sitting-room on the third story of Six Stones, the Earl and Countess of Marchmont's enormous manor in Sussex. Outside a steady snow had been falling since dawn, nearly eight hours straight now—while inside a bright fire burned in the hearth, casting a warm glow through the wintry light in the room.

The Countess of Marchmont shrugged. "Oh well," she said, "I expect it's something nature provides."

"It certainly hasn't provided it for me," remarked Isabella, who had had a most dismal confinement, and who had cheerfully handed over her first born, a daughter, to the wet nurse at the first possible moment. Elizabeth on the other hand had taken to motherhood with a facility and a zeal no one had ever expected. In fact, Isabella occasionally opined, it was developing into a positive mania. But that was nothing next to the quite outrageous delight her own husband took in fatherhood. Indeed, it sometimes seemed to Isabella quite a nasty trick that the dashing, dangerous man she had run off with only two years before should now have become such a safe, solid, *domestic* gentleman. What had she done to deserve this? Sir Jeffery did not even belong to a club. It was really too vexing; but even she could not reflect on this without smiling a little at her own good fortune.

Lady Emilia appeared in the doorway. "Oh, here you are," she said, rubbing her arms for warmth as she moved towards the fire. "Lord, this house gets cold in the winter! Isabella, Lord Weld and I have decided to rescue you from all this domesticity. There's a skating party being got up—Lord Weld and myself, to be precise—and you are invited. Will you come?"

"Will I!" Isabella jumped up at once, then murmured

apologetically, "You don't mind, do you Lizzie? After all, I'll be here for weeks."

Elizabeth smiled the serene smile that had come to her at about the same time Jimmy had been born. "Of course not, Bella. Have Nurse send little Amy in to me, if you like. She and Jimmy like to lie about and watch each other."

Lady Isabella stood up and gathered her shawl about her. "If I live to be a hundred," she said, shaking her head, "I shall never understand what you and Jeffery see in infants. Children I can understand; at least they talk . . . but babies!"

But Lizzie only laughed at her. "Send Marchmont up to me, too, if you don't mind. Where is he, anyhow?"

Emilia raised her eyebrows. "He and Jeffery had gone out to look at the kennels, if you please. They are probably shouting at each other this very moment about what the dogs should be fed and when, and how much, and by whom, and—heaven knows how they find things to quarrel over whenever Jeffery visits, but they certainly do."

"Oh well," Isabella put in, "if you want my opinion, Jeffery enjoys it. Whenever we're here he's always complaining about how nobody listens to him at Six Stones—but then when we've been away a month he's frantic to come visiting again." She gave another shrug and asked humorously, "Who can understand the ways of men?"

The other ladies laughed, but Lord Marchmont had heard her, and his voice could be heard coming from the corridor, "Sit down, young lady, and I shall explain them to you in five minutes." He entered the sitting-room, which was rapidly becoming crowded, and kissed his wife on the top of her head. "They are much, much easier to comprehend, I assure you, than the ways of women."

But Isabella declined to hear this explanation and instead danced away in Emilia's wake. "Tell Jeffery I've gone skating," she tossed over her shoulder at Elizabeth. "Tell him he can come too if he likes."

But Lord Marchmont told her, "Oh no, I'm afraid not. Your

husband and I are scheduled to have a long argument on the subject of horses this afternoon. I'm thinking of purchasing another Arab, and he is going to demonstrate to me why only an imbecile would think of such a thing. I expect we'll be tied up till dinner."

But Isabella had vanished before he even ended this sentence, leaving his lordship alone with his wife and son. "And another one on the way," he said contentedly, placing his hand on Elizabeth's belly. He smiled.

"You are turning me into a Mrs. Charles Stickney," Elizabeth charged, but without much conviction. "Remember what motherhood did to her?"

Marchmont remembered perfectly well that first quarrel they had had that long-ago evening, but the idea of comparing his rosy, glowing wife to poor Dorothea Stickney was so ludicrous as to make him laugh. He did laugh, and Elizabeth joined him. Then he kissed Jimmy on the top of his curly blond head; and then, with a surge of love equally divided now between affection and passion, the earl kissed his beautiful lady.